"I am your lord's wife," Endredi whispered, looking up into Adelar's piercing dark eyes.

"Yes."

"Then there is no more to be said between us."

"No." He regarded her steadily, his expression inscrutable.

"I will not betray him." She felt the brush of the fur against her skin.

"Nor will I."

His breath stroked her cheek. She glimpsed the flesh of his chest where he had not laced his tunic. He placed his strong hands on her shoulders. "I must go," she whispered.

"Yes," he replied quietly, pulling her into his embrace. Her hands pressed against him as if she would push him away even while she lifted her face for him to kiss.

She thrust herself back. "This is wrong! Do not touch me, Adelar!" She ran to the door and grabbed the handle, then bent her head and whispered, "Please, for both our sakes, do not *ever* touch me!"

Dear Reader,

This month, popular author Margaret Moore returns to Europe with *The Saxon*, the sequel to her award-winning book, *The Viking*. In this exciting tale, the brooding Adelar comes face-to-face with the woman who has haunted him since their youthful encounter years before, but now she is married to the man to whom he owes allegiance. We hope you enjoy it. And keep a look out for *The Welshman*, in December, the sequel to *A Warrior's Way*, which earned the author a 5* rating from *Affaire de Coeur*.

Our other titles this month include *Redwood Empire*, a Western saga by A. E. Maxwell. This reissue by the talented writing team of Ann and Evan Maxwell is the powerful story of a woman torn between a strong-willed businessman and his renegade son.

Highland Heaven by Ruth Langan, another tale in the series that includes *The Highlander* and *Highland Barbarian*, and contemporary author Susan Mallery's first historical for Harlequin, *Justin's Bride*, complete this month's list of titles.

We hope you'll keep an eye out for all four titles, wherever Harlequin Historicals are sold.

Sincerely,

Tracy Farrell
Senior Editor

Please address questions and book requests to:
Harlequin Reader Service
U.S.: 3010 Walden Ave., P.O. Box 1325, Buffalo, NY 14269
Canadian: P.O. Box 609, Fort Erie, Ont. L2A 5X3

MARGARET MOORE

The Saxon

Harlequin Books

TORONTO • NEW YORK • LONDON
AMSTERDAM • PARIS • SYDNEY • HAMBURG
STOCKHOLM • ATHENS • TOKYO • MILAN
MADRID • WARSAW • BUDAPEST • AUCKLAND

ISBN 0-373-28868-9

THE SAXON

Books by Margaret Moore

MARGARET MOORE

confesses that her first "crush" was Errol Flynn. The second was "Mr. Spock." She thinks that it explains why her heroes tend to be either charming rogues or lean, inscrutable tough guys.

Margaret lives in Scarborough, Ontario, with her husband, two children and two cats. She used to sew and read for reasons other than research.

To Mom, Deb and Bill.
Thanks for listening.

Chapter One

Wessex—902 A.D.

"Leave me in peace," Adelar muttered drowsily, one arm draped over the naked woman beside him. The serving wench sighed and burrowed deeper under the warm blankets laid upon the fleeces in the storage hut.

"My lord Bayard summons you," Godwin repeated, a wry grin on his round, perpetually pleasant face.

"Bayard sends his gleeman to give his orders?" Adelar growled skeptically, barely opening one eye to squint at the minstrel. "I expect you to sing them, then."

"Alas, oh my bold lover, your game must now be o'er. My lord calls you to the hall and you must away ere break of day," Godwin warbled, his fine voice filling the hut as he took hold of the Saxon warrior's exposed bare leg and tugged.

Realizing Godwin had no intention of leaving him alone, Adelar rose from the makeshift bed. "You do not rhyme well and the noon repast finished long ago," he noted sarcastically while he drew on his breeches.

The wench sat up, displaying a pair of enormous breasts and a pretty, pouting countenance. "You must go, my lord?" She twisted a strand of her tangled dark hair around her finger.

Gleda was her name, Adelar recalled. She was relatively clean, had breasts like small mountains and a most enthusiastic manner, but her high-pitched voice was enough to drive him mad. Not that he had to listen to her much, of course.

"Indeed he must," Godwin said mischievously. "But not I, my dear, my own!" He threw himself down beside her and wiggled his eyebrows comically.

"You had best be telling me no falsehood, Godwin," Adelar muttered.

The minstrel clasped his hands over his heart in mock dismay. "I, my lord? I, who am but a humble gleeman in the hall of the *burhware* of Oakenbrook? Of course I speak the truth, for I am honored to act as messenger to Bayard. Indeed, I am honored to breathe the same air, eat the same food—"

"—Talk too much and rouse men from their well-deserved rest," Adelar finished.

"Aye, you need the rest, after what you've been doin'...and doin' and doin'," Gleda said with a giggle and a lustful look in her eye as she gazed at Adelar's muscular body.

Adelar bent down to pick up his tunic. "What is so important that Bayard summons me?"

"He wants you to help him bargain with the Danes."

"I have no desire to be among Vikings, or Danes, or whatever you wish to call them," Adelar replied harshly. He was happy to be of use to Bayard, but the only time he wanted to be close to the Danes was in battle. He reached for his *scramasax* and tucked the short sword into his belt.

"Then you never should have let anyone know that you speak their language," Godwin retorted, his hand straying toward Gleda's naked breasts.

Gleda studied Adelar warily while neatly intercepting Godwin's caress. "You can talk to those animals?"

"I understand them."

"A most fascinating tale, my buttercup," Godwin began. "He was kidnapped by a vicious band of Vikings when he was a child and—" He stopped when he saw the warning look in Adelar's eyes. "I shall tell you some other time."

"What kind of bargain does Bayard seek to make with those thieves?" Adelar demanded.

"I am not in Bayard's council," Godwin answered lightly. "Nor am I his cousin. I only do what I am told to do and since Bayard was in no mood for my amusements, I think his request must be somewhat urgent."

"You should have said that before," Adelar snapped. He slung his sword belt over his right shoulder and across his chest, his broad sword brushing his left thigh.

"Will you be coming back soon?" Gleda asked.

"Perhaps I will," Adelar said when he saw that she was waiting for an answer. "It will depend upon what my lord decides. Or how long the bargaining takes." He tugged on his boots. "Dagfinn probably wants to increase the Danegeld. We already pay those dogs enough money to keep them from our land."

"And Alfred never should have allowed the Vikings to have the Danelaw," Godwin added somewhat wearily, as if he had heard these words many times before. "It was that, or fight forever."

"Then we should have fought forever. There is no honor in buying off our enemies."

"I am no warrior, but it strikes that me that there is no honor being dead, either," Godwin replied.

Adelar marched from the shed, not bothering to wait for Godwin, who might very well decide to stay with Gleda, which troubled Adelar not at all.

As he hurried to the hall, Adelar surveyed the newly completed walls of the *burh,* which had been built on a rise at the junction of two rivers. Nearby, a forest of oak, beech and hazel trees was beginning to show the first signs of early spring.

Although it was not the Saxon way to live in villages, the invasions of the Vikings and Danes had forced the Saxons to construct fortresses, an idea the recently deceased king, Alfred, had championed. Cynath, Bayard's overlord, had been one of the first to see the wisdom and the necessity of such structures, for his lands bordered the Danelaw, a large portion of land Alfred had given the Vikings as a way to ensure peace.

Cynath, in turn, had ordered Bayard to oversee the building of this *burh* and named him the commander, or *burhware*.

Bayard had more than obeyed his overlord's orders. The fortress's walls were of thick timbers, with a gate at the main road. Inside, the other buildings were all nearly finished. The hall, where Bayard's people ate, slept and spent their time when not working or, in the case of the warriors, practicing for the warfare that would inevitably come, was the finest Adelar had ever seen.

Around the hall the more important and richer thanes had built bowers, smaller buildings that doubled as personal halls and sleeping quarters. Bayard, too, had a bower, the largest, of course, and his was closest to the hall.

Adelar hoped he would never see this *burh* aflame, destroyed by marauding Vikings. Indeed, he would fight to death to prevent it.

When he had arrived here months ago, he had made no claim of kinship on his cousin, yet Bayard had accepted him into his household at once. Bayard's nephew Ranulf had protested, citing the tales of Adelar's father's traitorous and criminal acts. Bayard had discarded them all, although Adelar had revealed to him privately that everything Ranulf had said was true. His father, Kendric, *had* led the Viking raiders to their village. He *had* paid them to kill his wife, and when that plot failed, Adelar had no doubt that his mother's death had been no accident, as Kendric had claimed. Because of all this, Adelar had disowned his father, and his father had disowned his son.

Bayard had listened to everything, then he rose and said simply, "Welcome to my hall, cousin." For that, and the trust that Bayard had demonstrated thereafter, Adelar would be forever in Bayard's debt.

Adelar entered the hall and divested himself of his weapons. Low, guttural voices and an outburst of raucous laughter told him where the Danes stood.

Filled with the anger that always rose in him when he saw Vikings, Adelar strode down the hall beside the long central hearth.

Bayard, high-born, well-respected, handsome and proud, sat in a chair at the far end of the hall. To the right of him, seated on benches and stools, were the Danes, including Dagfinn, the leader of the band that lived closest to Bayard's land. Ranulf and several of the Saxon warriors sat to Bayard's left. Father Derrick, Bayard's priest, stood behind him in the shadows.

The Saxons' faces were carefully blank and their sword belts obviously empty. Nor were their visitors armed, for no weapons were to be worn in the hall. Nonetheless, several Saxon swords, bows, axes and spears were hung about the hall, a silent reminder that the Danes had best think again before provoking a fight.

Bayard did not immediately acknowledge Adelar's presence, despite the Danes' glances in his direction, and Adelar knew his cousin was not pleased with his tardiness.

"Ale, Dagfinn?" Bayard offered.

"Ya." The huge, fair-haired fellow held out his goblet for a young female slave to fill. He gave her a long, lustful look, making the girl flush deep red as she moved quickly away.

As he watched them, Adelar realized that Bayard could be held somewhat accountable for these maggots waiting to have a part of his flesh. Even now he wore his finest brooch on his shoulder, with the Danes sitting close enough to count the jewels in it. His tunic was of wool dyed with the most costly of blue dyes, his sword's hilt was of silver, the belt of soft worked leather. If he were the *burhware,* Adelar thought, he would take care not to be so ostentatious...but that would never happen. The only *burh* he stood a chance of commanding would be that of his father, and he would take nothing from him.

"Adelar, here at last," Bayard finally said with a slight smile on his lips and displeasure in his eyes.

"Aye, my lord." Adelar stepped forward, aware of the Danes' scrutiny.

"Ah, you bring this fellow to our counsels again," Dagfinn said, his Saxon words slow and halting. Although his tone was jovial, Adelar knew the Dane was not happy to see him, either.

"Since this meeting must be important to bring you onto my land, I wish to ensure that I understand correctly," Bayard said smoothly. While Bayard did not like the provision for the Danes that Alfred had made, he thought it was too late to make them leave the

country entirely. Bayard favored allowing the Danes to
remain in England as long as they agreed to abide by
Saxon law and to acknowledge Edward as the rightful
king. He wanted peace above all things.

Adelar translated Bayard's words into the Danes'
tongue. He did not agree that peace was acceptable by
any means, but he had no right to interfere if Bayard
wished otherwise. He was simply one of Bayard's warriors, although kin. "I gather you wish to propose
some kind of alliance?"

"Ya. A marriage alliance."

Adelar stared at Dagfinn in stunned silence.

"What did he say?" Bayard asked. When Adelar
spoke, Ranulf and some of the others shifted and began to mumble. Even Father Derrick moved a little as
Adelar repeated the words. Bayard's expression betrayed only slight surprise. "Tell him that I have no
wish to take a wife again," he remarked calmly.

"Why not?" Dagfinn demanded rudely. "You do
not have a wife, or any sons. I have the perfect woman
for you. And—" he paused a moment "—I might be
persuaded to lower the Danegeld if our families were
united in marriage."

"I do agree that the Danegeld is much too high and
welcome the possibility of altering it," Bayard replied,
"but I am not convinced a marriage alliance would be
a wise solution."

Adelar looked quickly at his cousin. Not only had he
not scoffed outright at the Dane's suggestion, he
sounded as if he was actually considering the pro-

posal. Yet such a thing was truly impossible. What would Cynath think of this marriage, let alone the king?

Dagfinn belched and shrugged. "If you do not agree, the Danegeld will remain as it is. Of course, you do not have to pay it. Then my men will attack your village, kill your warriors, burn the buildings to the ground and take your people as slaves."

"Or perhaps my warriors will kill your warriors and you will get nothing. Then King Edward will make such war on you that your people will be driven back across the seas."

"Or maybe Aethelwold will be acknowledged king."

"The Witan has chosen Edward," Bayard responded. "He is a proven leader in battle and Alfred's eldest son. Although Aethelwold might believe he has some legal claim to the throne, no member of the Witan wants him for a king. He is a traitor and completely without honor."

"In his will, Alfred did not say who was to succeed him," Dagfinn countered.

Adelar masked his surprise as best he could, but how did this foreigner come to have such a clear understanding of the problem of succession?

"The Danes have acknowledged Aethelwold," Dagfinn insisted stubbornly, as if what they did should influence the Saxons. "He already commands Essex."

"So why do you wish to make an alliance?" Bayard asked.

Why indeed, Adelar thought, unless Dagfinn had little confidence in Aethelwold's ability to rule or the Danes to control him. Adelar ran his gaze over Dagfinn's men. Dagfinn was old and fat, and his men were not in good fighting trim. Only one of them, a red-haired fellow who watched Adelar constantly, looked to be capable of beating any of the Saxon warriors.

Was it battle Dagfinn feared? Did the Danes have as little wish to fight as Bayard? It didn't seem likely, until one considered how long this band had been settled in the Danelaw. Years, with few true armed conflicts. And perhaps Bayard was not the only leader in the hall who sensed that Edward was going to be a more aggressive commander than his father.

"This squabbling need not touch us," Dagfinn said in a slightly wheedling voice. "We are neighbors. And no one can profit during such times."

That made sense, for the Vikings Adelar had known were more concerned with gain than the business of state and the succession of kings.

Unexpectedly, Bayard smiled and said, "Tell me of this woman you wish me to wed."

Adelar wondered what kind of tactic this was. A marriage alliance with the Danes was completely unacceptable, given the situation between Edward and Aethelwold, and suspicious for the Danes to suggest.

"The woman is young and beautiful," Dagfinn said with a leer, and not a little relief.

"I want to know if she is healthy," Bayard asked.

"Very. And she knows much of healing. My people will be sorry to lose her, but the alliance is more important."

"Is she strong-willed?"

"She is no simpering girl," Dagfinn replied carefully.

Adelar fought to keep a satisfied expression from his face. Bayard had never liked strong-willed women. He liked his women placid, or at least filled with awe at his looks, his status or his wealth. And most women were. Even if Bayard was considering this marriage alliance, Dagfinn's answer would put an end to it.

"Nor is Endredi a scold," Dagfinn continued.

Adelar could not breathe. He couldn't think. Surely his heart had stopped beating, the sun no longer moved across the sky, the fire had died. He saw nothing except sea green eyes regarding him steadily, containing neither condemnation nor pity, but understanding and complete acceptance, because Adelar had not meant to bring harm to Betha, only to get back home to his village. As they fled, his sister had fallen ill, and when they were taken back to the Viking settlement, she had died. Endredi had said little, but her eyes . . . her eyes had said everything. How much her silent comfort had meant to his lonely heart!

And then his father had come with his warriors. He had destroyed the Viking village when the men were away trading, taken the women and children captive and slaughtered the rest. His father had even dragged

Endredi to his hall, intending to rape the girl barely on the brink of womanhood.

The remembered sights and feelings rose in Adelar's mind, strong and terrible, for Adelar had followed them there, prepared to do what he must to save Endredi. She had escaped his father on her own, but he had killed a guard who would have sounded the alarm.

His father was worse than a traitor. Vicious, cruel, lustful...and ever since that night, Adelar had been tortured by the notion that he might someday grow to be like his sire. So he had left his home and traveled here to Bayard's *burh*.

He pushed away the memory and told himself that this woman could not be the Endredi he had known. It was merely a coincidence. Two women with the same name.

"Ask him if the woman is a virgin," Bayard said.

Adelar managed to get the words out.

"No. She is my brother's widow."

Endredi lived in the northern land of the Vikings across the sea, not in the Danelaw. Adelar took another deep breath as some of the tension fled from his body.

"Does she have children?"

"No."

Bayard's eyes narrowed suspiciously. "Is she barren?"

"She was married for less than a month before Fenris died. In bed."

No wonder Dagfinn wanted to be rid of this widow, Adelar thought. Viking men wanted to die in battle, with a sword in their hands. Otherwise they could not enter Valhalla to spend eternity feasting with Odin. The widow was probably regarded as a woman who would bring misfortune.

Bayard rose and drew Adelar away from the others.

"Tell me honestly," he said quietly. "Do you trust Dagfinn? Will he abide by this agreement?"

At once an almost overpowering temptation to urge Bayard to refuse filled Adelar. He didn't trust any Danes. He didn't want his cousin to have a Viking wife.

But more importantly, he didn't want to find out that this woman was the Endredi of his youth, the Endredi he had been too ashamed to seek again. The Endredi he was constantly trying to forget.

He regarded Bayard steadily, looking into his cousin's eyes. He did not doubt that Bayard had already made his decision, for it was not Bayard's way to rely on any man's advice. This was likely a delaying tactic, or meant to annoy Ranulf, something Bayard seemed to delight in. Nonetheless, Adelar answered Bayard with his true opinion. "Dagfinn wants this marriage, or he would never agree to reduce the Danegeld." He hesitated for a brief moment, then went on firmly. "I do not trust any of them, as you know, so of course I would refuse. However, it would be wise to delay your decision. If Dagfinn speaks sincerely, he will wait. And what of Cynath? He has great faith and trust in you. I would not want *him* to question your loyalty."

"I know you say what is truly in your heart, Adelar," his cousin replied. "So I will tell you what is in mine. I think this is a sign from God. I am going to take the woman for my wife."

Adelar nodded. Bayard was wise and respected. If he saw nothing wrong with this marriage and he honestly believed it was a sign to make peace, then Adelar could not question it. And yet…and yet Adelar had seen that love could change a man or a woman. Had not his nursemaid married the Viking who had taken her captive and remained there when Adelar had gone home? Perhaps this woman would be able to sway Bayard and weaken his resolve to regard the Danes with suspicion.

It was already too late. Bayard had decided. As he returned to his place, Adelar silently vowed that he would watch this woman and protect his cousin to the best of his ability.

Bayard sat in his chair. "Adelar, tell Dagfinn of my decision, provided the woman is truly comely. I will not let him give me an old hag, even if it means peace."

The Saxons looked at each other with undisguised surprise as Adelar did as he was told. Ranulf tried to appear both distressed and certain that Bayard was acting wisely. That way, Adelar knew, he could later say he agreed with both those who welcomed the alliance and those who were against it. As for Father Derrick, he was like a marble effigy, expressionless except for his disapproving eyes.

"She is as lovely as Freya, as wise as Baldur, and Endredi speaks the Saxon tongue," Dagfinn said eagerly.

Again Adelar had to struggle to keep his face expressionless. Surely, surely there were other Viking women who had learned the Saxon tongue and who were wise in healing arts.

"What did he say?" Bayard demanded.

"He says the woman is wise, beautiful and speaks our language."

Suddenly Father Derrick stepped forward. "Is she Christian?" he asked sternly.

"She has had the ceremony of the water," Dagfinn answered.

His Endredi was not a Christian, and she had never been baptised. But years had passed and everything could have changed.

Father Derrick, apparently satisfied, returned to his place in the shadows.

The men haggled for a short time over the bride price, and again over the gifts to Endredi, but all knew it was only because it was expected. The true goal had already been achieved when Bayard had agreed to the marriage.

"We are finished, then," Dagfinn said, heaving himself to his feet when they decided on the sums. "We will bring her in a fortnight when the roads are clear."

Bayard rose, too. "I will have the wedding feast prepared."

The Dane nodded as Adelar finished speaking. Then he turned and strode to the entrance of the hall, followed by his men. The Saxons watched silently while the Danes collected their weapons and left.

"You are making a mistake, Uncle," Ranulf declared immediately. "Cynath will not be pleased."

Not for the first time, Adelar was disgusted by Ranulf's lack of discernment. He had been one of Bayard's men for longer than Adelar, yet he could not seem to comprehend that there was no point to question one of Bayard's decisions after it had already been made.

Bayard faced his nephew. "Unless I have lost my wits," he said with deceptive calm, "it was you who first suggested making an alliance, Ranulf. There is no cause for second thoughts now. Cynath knows that he has my complete loyalty, and so does the king."

"By king you mean Edward?"

Bayard's expression was hard as flint. "He is the *Britwalda,* King of the Britons, and anyone who says otherwise has no place in my hall."

"Of course, my lord," Ranulf replied hastily. "I meant nothing else. But what of the woman's loyalty?"

Adelar darted a condemning look at Ranulf's lean, anxious face. "Are you saying you doubt that Bayard can control his own wife? That he will be influenced by a bright eye or soft cheek?" he asked, inwardly hoping it would not be so, and that perhaps Bayard would hear his words as a warning.

"Not at all," Ranulf answered, reddening under the scrutiny of the two men whose haughty, stern eyes were so alike. "Naturally I wish that this marriage may be a happy one."

"Women are evil creatures, full of sin and temptation," Father Derrick said, his stern, deep voice commanding silence. "Men should beware their traps and snares."

"Yes, Father," Bayard replied peaceably. "I regret that I cannot be as strong as you in denying the desires of the flesh, but I shall be very careful. And this is merely a marriage of necessity."

"That is good, my son."

"Now you must all join me in a pledge of loyalty to any future children this marriage will bring."

Ranulf struggled to look pleased. "Yes, my lord. To your children."

Bayard lifted his goblet. "To my heir." For only a moment, Adelar thought he saw a look of pain in Bayard's eyes, but it passed before he could be sure it was pain and not mere annoyance with Ranulf. "This alliance should ensure that my land will be safe for *someone* to inherit when I am dead. The woman's dowry will also enrich my estate."

"My lord, surely you know I hope you will live a long and happy life and leave many sons to follow you," Ranulf said.

"I know precisely what you hope, Ranulf," Bayard replied.

"Beware the yearning for earthly wealth," Father Derrick intoned. "A camel can pass through the eye of a needle sooner than a rich man enter the Kingdom of Heaven."

"Thank you, Father, for your timely reminder," Bayard responded with his usual good humor. "Someone find Godwin. We need music—oh, there you are, Godwin. No time for hanging about in the shadows, gleeman. Sing something suitable for the occasion. Adelar, where is your ale? Are you not going to drink to my impending marriage and my future bride? What was her name?"

"Endredi," Adelar replied, looking about for that timid female slave. "Ale!" he shouted impatiently. He wanted to get very drunk very quickly.

But not for celebration. He wanted to forget.

Ranulf's wife shoved his wandering hand away. "I'm talking to you about serious matters, dolt!" Ordella said sharply, her pale blue eyes seeming to glow in the dim building.

Ranulf, lying beside her in bed, gave her a peevish look. "And I'm acting like a husband."

"Speak quietly, you lustful beast. A *husband* would have his family's interest in mind, and that is what I am trying to discuss."

"Oh, very well." Ranulf shifted to a sitting position in his bed. In the other part of the building, which was only half the size of Bayard's hall, slaves and servants slumbered. His wife, however, had the amazing ability to sound as if she was almost shouting without waking anyone. "What is it?"

"I want to know what you are going to do about this marriage."

"Do about it? Nothing. An agreement has been made."

"Because of your stupidity."

"Mine? I am not marrying some Viking widow. And you yourself said we should make peace with the Vikings. If the betrothal is broken now, who knows what those savages might do?"

"I didn't mean a marriage alliance."

"And I tell you again, *I* did not suggest it. Dagfinn did, and Bayard agreed."

"Yes—and for that reason alone you should have stopped it."

"I should have stepped into the middle of the discussion and ordered Bayard to refuse?" Ranulf asked scornfully. "He would have had me tossed from the hall."

"If you had been witless about it, of course he would," she snapped. "You merely needed to find a way to delay the negotiations. Then you could have dissuaded him."

"I did protest his decision, after the Danes had gone."

Ordella fought the urge to scream. "*After* was much too late. You should know that about Bayard by now. The time was already past to influence him! He will never alter his course now—never!"

"How was I to even guess he would consider a marriage?" Ranulf whined. "All I knew was that he was prepared to argue over the amount of the Danegeld. It's taken me many days to convince him to go *that* far. Nor has he ever so much as hinted at a marriage."

"Bertilde has been dead these three years," Ordella reminded him, all the while wishing she had waited a little longer before agreeing to marry Ranulf. Then she might have had a chance for Bayard, rather than this clod.

"So I thought he had no interest in marriage."

"That is the stupidest thing you have said yet. He is a wealthy thane with no children. You should *never* have dismissed a possible marriage."

"As you have just pointed out, Ordella, it is done. I cannot undo it."

"But now he might have children, too."

"He hasn't yet, and he's had many women."

"That is no guarantee. He so rarely stays in one place for long, it could be that he is gone before a woman knows. Or perhaps he has never acknowledged any children, if they were born out of wedlock. If you had the sense of a donkey, you would have considered these possibilities."

Ordella was almost weeping with frustration. Her only reason for marrying Ranulf had been to become part of Bayard's wealthy, important family. Unfortunately, she had come to realize she had chosen the least promising member of the clan. "She is young, too. She could give him many children."

"Or maybe he will hate her and never go near her. This is a political match, Ordella. Don't forget that."

"I hope for your sake it is so. Or you can forget any hope of inheriting anything from him."

"You said the same thing when Adelar arrived."

"That was before I knew the kind of man Adelar is—and for that you should thank God. If he was more ambitious, he could have you living in some hovel at the edge of the wood. It is clear Bayard favors him, and their mothers were sisters."

"You are forgetting the stories about his father."

"That old tale? No one believed that Viking. Imagine trying to imply that a Saxon thane would betray his own people."

"Yet Kendric has never tried to be in the Witan, and any other man of his stature would have."

"The main thing to consider now is how to increase your importance to Bayard."

"I am his nephew. What more reason should Bayard need to listen to me?"

"If that's the only cause he has to suffer your presence, he can easily discard you, fool!"

Ranulf started to climb out of the bed. Ordella grabbed his arm and held on. "Forgive me," she said in wheedling voice. "I am upset to think that Bayard did not take you into his confidence. After all, you deserve to be. You *are* his closest relative. Adelar is but a cousin."

Ranulf relaxed a little. She crawled closer and encircled him with her thin arms. "I simply fear you may not get what is your due, Ranulf, and then I get angry. Forgive me for taking out my indignation on you." He sighed softly as she caressed him. "You do forgive my harsh words, don't you?"

"Yes." He twisted and his mouth swooped feverishly over hers. His hands groped her breasts.

Ordella made all the appropriate noises. But her mind was not on Ranulf, or his clumsy attempts at lovemaking. She was wondering how to proceed when Bayard's bride arrived.

"The hour grows late, and I think I have done enough celebrating," Bayard proclaimed as he rose clumsily to his feet. Around him, his men raised their drinking horns in yet another salute.

Except for Adelar. He had left the hall some time ago, his arm draped over a serving wench with a high-pitched voice and a constant giggle.

Bayard made his way past his men and past the servants who were already asleep. Once outside, he walked casually around the outer wall of the hall and into the shadows.

Then, with a muffled groan, he suddenly doubled over.

His malady was worsening. There could be no doubt of it. The pains were coming more frequently and growing in intensity.

When the spasm passed, Bayard straightened slowly, certain of two things. His plan had to work, and he had little time left to implement it.

Chapter Two

A fortnight later, a Danish maidservant fussed about Endredi as they stood in Bayard's bower. They had been told to wait there until the marriage ceremony, while Dagfinn and the others had gone immediately to the hall.

Thick, colorful tapestries hung over the wattle and daub walls. The chest of the bride's goods stood in a corner. Other, larger wooden boxes were placed throughout the room, a testament to the groom's wealth. There were also two intricately carved stools beside a delicate round table upon which sat a jug and two silver chalices. Light came from a many-branched iron rod bearing several tallow candles. A large bed, ornately carved and hung with heavy curtains, dominated one end of the building.

The older woman brushed off Endredi's gown, straightened her belt and tidied a stray wisp of her mistress's thick, red-gold hair.

"Will you please stop?" Endredi asked, trying to keep annoyance from her voice and reminding herself it was simply Helmi's way to be always hovering about like an insect.

"Dagfinn said you had to look—"

"Beautiful?" Endredi looked at Helmi skeptically. "I look presentable—beautiful will be for Bayard to decide."

"Unless the man is stupid and blind, he can't help but think so. Still, he is a Saxon, so who can say how his mind might work? Everyone knows they are all vicious, horrible barbarians—"

"You have done your best," Endredi said, interrupting the woman before she began another tirade against the Saxons. Endredi knew that there could be good Saxons as well as bad, just as there were good and bad Danes.

"I don't know what that oaf Dagfinn is trying to do, marrying off his brother's widow to some Saxon."

"Dagfinn seeks peace."

"Huh! I think I am not the only old woman among the Danes here! When I was young, a man was glad to fight. *Wanted* to fight. Dagfinn is a coward."

Endredi put her finger to her lips. "Take care, Helmi, lest he hear your insult."

Helmi straightened her slim shoulders. "Well, he and his men could not win a battle if Odin himself was on their side."

Endredi could not argue with her servant's observation. Indeed, Dagfinn's thoughts were all too obvious, despite his attempts at subtlety. Nevertheless, she felt duty bound by her respect for her dead husband to say,

"Dagfinn may be acting with more wisdom than you think. After all, who among his people would marry a woman of my ill luck? Besides," she finished, "Dagfinn is the chieftain, so I must obey."

"I do not believe Dagfinn thinks of anything but his silver and his belly. And where would he be if he didn't have Bera to oversee everything?"

"I shall miss her."

"I will not. A harder mistress never breathed, I can tell you."

"She was always kind to me," Endredi answered truthfully, although now she knew why Helmi had offered to go with her to the Saxon village. Obviously Helmi considered even the Saxons less threatening than Bera.

As for Endredi, she would miss Bera, but she had always been alone. Even as a child, she had had few friends. The sins of her mother had made her an object of curiosity and scorn, and she had soon learned that sometimes it was better to be alone than to be questioned, or worse, pitied.

"I almost forgot!" Helmi cried, hurrying to Endredi's small chest. "Dagfinn said to be sure you wore this." She took out a jeweled crucifix.

Endredi stood motionless while Helmi put it over her head. She had heard that Bayard's priest had asked if his future wife was a Christian.

She put her hand to the crucifix. Thanks to her stepmother, she understood the Christians' beliefs and indeed found it no hardship to believe them, too. When a priest had traveled to their village, she had been baptized. Nonetheless, she wore an amulet of Freya beneath her gown. Surely the Christian god would understand that it was hard to ignore the old beliefs.

"I have never seen such an enormous building as that hall," Helmi said. "I wonder what it is like inside. Why, I wouldn't be surprised if the tapestries are full of gold thread."

When Endredi didn't respond, Helmi went on. "It is also a good thing you speak that Saxon language, although I must say it has a most horrible sound to it."

"My mother was a Saxon."

"Oh, yes, well then, have you heard anything about Bayard? His looks, I mean."

Helmi's eyes gleamed eagerly, and Endredi knew she would hear what Helmi had learned whether she wanted to or not; however, Bayard's appearance mattered less to her than the way he would treat a foreign wife. "Dagfinn said he is not old," Endredi said slowly.

"A mature man and no foolish youth, thank the gods. Handsome, too, I hear."

"He is a respected leader."

"He wears fine clothes and much jewelry, Erik said."

"If he were not just and good, surely he would not have so many men under his command."

"He washes regularly and trims his beard."

"I hope he will be patient."

"He has no children."

Helmi's last announcement caught Endredi's attention. "No children?"

She shook her head. "And he's been married at least two times."

"Oh?"

"Still, I hear he is quite virile. Rumors abound that he has bedded dozens of women."

"And yet no children?"

"Not one."

"How could anyone you know come by that knowledge?" Endredi asked, her immediate surprise replaced by suspicion.

"I heard some of the men talking about it."

"Why would any Danes know about Bayard's children?"

That seemed to shake Helmi's confidence in her sources. Which was quite as it should be. Surely Helmi could have no valid information concerning Bayard's wives or women or children. Nonetheless, Helmi's gossip had disturbed her. Endredi had agreed to this marriage because she had few alternatives, but also because she dearly wanted children.

It could very well be that Bayard did have illegitimate children. He was a Christian, and if they were born out of holy wedlock, he might seek to keep their parentage secret. Or it might be that Bayard's other wives had simply been unable to bear children, although that would be a rare misfortune.

"If he doesn't give you children, you could always divorce him," Helmi noted optimistically.

"No, I could not. Christians are not allowed to divorce for any reason. Besides, where would I go?"

"You could go home to your father."

"My father has other children and other responsibilities. When I married Fenris, I became his family's concern. Because of his death, I must do as Dagfinn wishes, since he is the head of the family as well as the chieftain, and he desires this alliance."

Endredi sighed as she moved away and sat down on a stool. Her father had married a Saxon woman, and their union was a joy to both. Perhaps, just perhaps, she might find it so with Bayard.

She fingered her crucifix, trying to calm her growing dismay and bury her memories of the boy she had once cared for but who had left her to her fate, never trying to find out what had become of her. Despite what he had done—or not done—she had hoped, dreamed . . . until years had passed, and she had grown into a woman. Adelar had never returned. So Endredi had put him from her heart and from her hopes, and wed another.

Although Fenris was kind, he had inspired no passion within her, and she feared there was no passion left to inspire. When Dagfinn had told her what he planned for her, she had thought not of her own seemingly impossible happiness. This marriage might bring a measure of peace between Saxon and Dane, so she had agreed.

Helmi paused for a moment in her bustling near the large curtained bed, an object Endredi had been doing her best not to notice. "I think someone's coming!" she cried. "Stand up, stand up!"

Endredi obeyed and despite her resolve to face this marriage resolutely, she had to clasp her hands together to keep them from trembling.

Dagfinn entered the bower and surveyed her slowly. "Good," he muttered. He nodded toward the door. "Come to the hall."

Endredi followed the big man out of the bower. In the yard before the hall several women and children were standing at a respectful distance and staring at her. They looked well-dressed and well-fed, a sign that Bayard took care of his people.

Some were curious, others openly hostile as they stood silently. Endredi raised her chin. She was the daughter of Einar Svendson, and no hint of fear or doubt must show on her face.

She continued to walk proudly as she entered the huge wooden building, which was as richly decorated as Helmi had guessed.

There was another crowd of Danes and Saxon men inside. Here, Endredi lowered her eyes as a woman should in such company, lest she be thought immodest, but she glanced up when they paused before proceeding. Standing at the front of a group of Saxons was a tall, bearded, finely dressed man who moved with the natural arrogance of a nobleman. He had to be Bayard.

There was another, younger man at his elbow, with light brown hair, a cruel mouth and thin lips. He looked at her with an impertinent curiosity that annoyed her, despite her anxiety. A woman stood beside him, thin, too, and motionless, her face placid but her gaze darting everywhere.

On the other side of Bayard was a man who had to be a priest. He wore a huge wooden crucifix and a strange black tunic that reached all the way to the ground.

Dagfinn walked ahead of her. "Bayard, here is your bride," he proclaimed.

Helmi moved behind her and gave her a gentle shove. "Go forward! Go forward!"

Endredi went toward her betrothed slowly, looking at Bayard steadily. He was handsome, dark and well-built. His tunic was a brilliant red, his belt studded with gold, his boots made of fine soft leather, and he wore a beautiful silver brooch with many jewels.

But there was an expression in his eyes.... Suspicion? Reluctance? Then it was gone, masked by a charming smile.

"You spoke the truth, Dagfinn," Bayard said when she was close to him. "She is beautiful."

Another man spoke, this time in the Danes' tongue, obviously translating Bayard's words. She recognized the voice instantly and quickly scanned the crowd, her heart beating as rapidly as the wings of a bird trapped in a net.

Adelar! Here! She knew him at once, although it had been years. The color of his hair, the shape of his features—even the way he stood was as familiar as her own body. Her mouth went dry, and for a moment she thought she was going to faint.

She had tried to forget Adelar and had convinced herself that she had, but she knew now it was a lie.

For a moment she saw recognition in Adelar's eyes and something that thrilled her beyond words, something that made all the long years disappear. She could not marry Bayard now. She would refuse, no matter what Dagfinn said or did.

Then Adelar's demeanor changed, as if a flame had been blown out, replaced by something hard and cold as iron. He looked away.

Oh, Freya! Was he his father's son, after all? Kendric had been a base traitor, a man outwardly handsome, but inwardly as corrupt as a man could be. Had Adelar grown that way, too?

What other explanation could there be for his action? He was not going to acknowledge that he knew her, not even when she was about to be married to another. He was staring at the floor, not daring to meet her gaze, willing to abandon her again. Acting like a dishonorable coward.

Endredi tried to collect her scattered thoughts and marshal her confused emotions. She wanted to run. To hide like a wounded animal and let herself moan in agony. Or perhaps worst of all, she wanted to beg him to look at her again.

"I am honored," Bayard said.

Adelar did not want her. Perhaps he never had. Perhaps she had only been swept away by his looks and his apparent need for her comfort.

Suddenly aware that they were waiting for her to speak, she said stiffly, "No, the honor is mine."

Bayard held out his hand, and she put hers into it. She was a woman now, and the dreams of her childhood were dead.

The wedding feast was a long and very rich one. Dagfinn and the other Danes gobbled up the abundant food as if they had not eaten in days—so greedily, in fact, that Endredi was quite ashamed. It was obvious that the Saxons were not impressed by their guests' lack of manners, either.

"That is my cousin, Adelar," Bayard said to his bride as the Saxon warrior rose and left the table with only the curtest of nods toward his host when the gleeman began to sing, signaling the end of the feast but not of the celebrations. Others stood and moved about the hall, filling it with hushed voices and muted whispers, giving the lord and his bride the occasional curious glance.

Cousins, Endredi thought, watching Adelar go out the door. That explained the resemblance between them and why Adelar would be in attendance here.

The cousins had the same fearless brown eyes, dark hair and muscular build, Endredi realized. Indeed, even now, Bayard reminded her of Adelar so much that she found it difficult to look at her husband without a pang of bitterness.

But she would have to find a way. The gifts had been exchanged, promises made, the priest had even said a blessing. Only the consummation remained to make them truly husband and wife. One more duty to fulfill.

And to her, it *was* a duty. She could not understand why men seemed to find such a thing a tremendous pleasure. Nonetheless, she did want to have children. A baby would surely bring her joy and fill the loneliness in her heart.

"Adelar is one of my finest warriors and one of the few men I trust. You must forgive his seeming rudeness. It is just his way," Bayard said with a look of concern.

"Is it?" she responded politely, but with growing dread. Bayard seemed all too ready to excuse Adelar's impertinence. What else would he excuse his cousin?

If Adelar was so capable of deceiving her when he was but a lad, was he now deceiving Bayard, who obviously trusted him enough to have him in his counsel? She would find out and warn her husband if she suspected any treachery at all.

With even more dismay she realized that Ranulf, her husband's nephew, was coming to sit in the space closest to her, away from his thin, sallow wife, who seemed not to notice.

"I trust, my lady, that you will not think we are all so lacking in our attentions to you, as my lord's wife,"

Ranulf said, attempting to sound polite but only succeeding in sounding the worse for too much ale.

She bowed her head toward Ranulf in slight acknowledgment.

Obviously taking Endredi's response to be encouragement, he said, "Adelar is an uncouth fellow. But of course if one believes those tales about his family—"

Bayard said, "I am pleased he has decided to remain here."

Ranulf returned to his wife.

Endredi fought to stay silent, although she was filled with curiosity. What did Ranulf know about Adelar's family? Did others know what Kendric had done? What had happened to Adelar and his father in the years since she had seen them? She dearly wanted to find out, but until she understood the natures of these men, she had best speak cautiously. She had sensed an undercurrent of hostility ever since she had set foot in Bayard's hall and had assumed it was the natural enmity between Saxon and Dane. Now, however, she realized all was not well within Bayard's ranks. Bayard did not like Ranulf, Ranulf sought eagerly to please in a way that roused her suspicions, and Ranulf did not approve of Adelar although Bayard did.

She twisted her hands in her lap. She was completely alone here among these men.

"Adelar's father is a wealthy thane, with lands and a *burh* further south," Bayard explained.

Endredi nearly knocked her goblet from the table. Adelar's father still possessed land after what he had done? What tales had Ranulf been speaking of, if not that Kendric himself had arranged for a Viking raiding party to attack his village, only too glad to see it destroyed? He had murdered his wife, too. It was not possible that his people could have forgiven such things—but once she would have said it was impossible that Adelar would ignore her, too. She would also have said it was impossible that Adelar could be like his father, but how else to explain his actions since she had arrived?

"If you will excuse me, my lord, I must prepare for evening prayers," the priest sitting near her said gravely.

"Good even, Father," Bayard replied, bowing his head.

Endredi watched the priest walk away. Before she had known a Christian, she had been told priests were evil men who would cast spells to send you to eternal torment if you didn't pay them to say special prayers. She had learned otherwise, but this gloomy man still added to her dread. She did not trust him, either, especially as he had been giving her harsh looks for the better part of the meal.

Bayard, seeing where she looked, patted her hand. "It is not you he disapproves of, Endredi. It is women in general."

"Women in general?"

"Yes. He suspects you all of being little more than demons sent to tempt honest men. You see the long tunic he wears? He began to dress like that after he went to Rome. He was there several years. Too many, I think. He was a kind enough fellow before he left, but easily swayed. I understand he joined with some rather strict priests. Ever since he has come home, he has spoken as if women were God's special punishment.'' Bayard smiled, his eyes twinkling rather mischievously for a powerful thane. "Fortunately, he leaves tomorrow on a journey to the monastery of his bishop for synod." He touched her hand. "I hope you will soon come to feel at home here. It will help that you speak our language."

"My...my family has Saxon blood," she replied, slipping her hand into her lap. Then, as she smiled with some sincerity, she began to hope that she might not find her marriage just a duty. Bayard seemed genuinely concerned about her.

Her response had caught Ordella's attention, as well as most of those seated around them. Ranulf said, "Cynath will surely be pleased to hear that you are part Saxon."

Endredi looked questioningly at Bayard. "Cynath?"

"My overlord, an *ealdorman* in the Witan."

"Cynath thinks very highly of your husband, my lady. Justly so, of course," Ranulf said.

"Of course," Ordella echoed.

The man who had been singing stopped and put down his harp. "What would be my lady's pleasure?" he asked, an infectious grin on his round face. "Another song? Another instrument? I can play pipes, horns and *fithele.* Perhaps you would care to dance?"

"This is my gleeman, Godwin, and a talented fellow," Bayard said by way of introduction. "He amuses me, for which privilege I pay him an extraordinary amount of silver."

"I assure you, my lady, I am worth every coin!" Godwin proclaimed, making a very deep bow.

His mien was so sincere and yet so comical, she knew he was trying hard to make her smile. She attempted to oblige him.

"I think we will dance another time," Bayard said. "Show her how you juggle."

Godwin responded with a roguish grin, then pulled out three knives, the shortest of which was twelve inches long. The Danes, seated just below Ranulf, half rose from their seats, until he threw the knives up into the air and began to juggle them.

"Look at him," Dagfinn said scornfully in his own language. "Saxon warriors have many skills, albeit useless ones."

"What did he say?" Bayard inquired of his bride, shifting closer to Endredi so that his body was against hers. She moved away.

"He says that Saxon warriors are very skilled."

Godwin picked up three heavy battle axes and juggled them, the blades flashing. This time, the Danes stared openmouthed. "I am not a Saxon," Godwin said without taking his attention from the whirling axes. "I am a Mercian."

"If other Danes act like these, we may use our skills to drive them right out of the Danelaw. They seem as attentive as a dog waiting for a bone from his master's table," Bayard remarked.

The Saxons around him smothered their laughter. Endredi stared at the fine white tablecloth. She had never liked Fenris's brother, who often made jests at the expense of those weaker than himself, but she did not enjoy hearing her countrymen insulted. Nor was she pleased to find that her husband so obviously wanted the Danes expelled from their lawful land. He had been attentive and polite to her thus far, but perhaps that would change when they were alone.

Godwin stopped juggling the axes and began to do other tricks with his knives. The Danes went back to drinking.

"Barbarous rabble, are they not?" Ranulf observed loudly. "And most unpleasant—yourself excluded, of course, my lady. No wonder Adelar hates them all."

Bayard darted an angry glance at his nephew. "Ranulf!" he said, an unmistakable tone of warning in his voice. "You must forgive his hasty words, Endredi," Bayard went on placatingly, as if she were no more than a child. But she knew only a fool would believe a *burh* full of Saxons would welcome a marriage between their thane and a Viking, and she was not a fool. "It is true that my cousin dislikes most Danes. He was abducted by Vikings when he was a boy. They killed his sister."

"*What?*" Too late Endredi realized that she had shown too much. Everyone stared at her. "How terrible, my lord," she said, fighting to keep her voice calm and not to proclaim to everyone that Adelar had told a base falsehood. "I am most dismayed that my countrymen may have caused a member of your family any anguish," she said after a moment. Despite the seeming regret in her voice, anger was boiling under Endredi's placid surface. If anyone had been to blame for Betha's death, it was Adelar, who had taken her from the Viking village during a snowstorm in an ill-fated attempt to make their way home. Even then, the little girl had died of an illness, an act of the gods, as she had tried to tell him. Then she had given him the silent companionship he seemed to find the greatest comfort. This lie was her reward?

She would make him correct that lie. Such falsehoods only inflamed the hatred between the Danes and Saxons. Many of the women she knew were as tired of the fighting and the bloodshed as she. If making Adelar confess the truth would prevent one skirmish, one more death, she would ensure that it happened.

"You had nothing to do with it," Bayard said kindly. "Godwin," he called out, "sing something else. Something pleasant."

Godwin complied. After his third song, Bayard turned to her and said solicitously, "You are so quiet. Are you weary? Do you wish to retire?"

Endredi glanced at her husband. Out of the corner of her eye she saw Helmi waiting patiently at the end of the hall.

"Yes, my lord," she said, rising. The time had come. She was this man's wife.

"I shall join you in a little while."

"Sleep well, my lady," Ranulf said, a leer on his impertinent face.

She was going to hate her husband's nephew. And she would make Adelar reveal the truth, at least to Bayard. As for how she would feel about her husband, she would find out soon enough, no doubt.

Helmi held open the door of the bower. Inside, someone had kindled a small, coal-fueled fire in one of the braziers, so that the building was warm against the cool night air of spring. The bed curtains of fine damask had been drawn back, as had the fur coverlet.

Endredi turned her back on the bed.

"Please sit, my lady," Helmi said, "and I will remove the ornaments from your hair."

"Leave me."

"But my lady!" the servant protested. "I should help you."

"I said, leave me."

Helmi shrugged and went to the far corner of the bower, where she had made a bed from a mattress filled with straw and some blankets.

"I would prefer you to sleep elsewhere tonight," Endredi said. She had no wish to have a servant's presence on her wedding night. She was nervous enough without that.

Helmi frowned deeply. "Where else? There are Saxons everywhere, like fleas on a dog!"

"There are other Danes in the hall. Sleep there tonight."

Helmi looked about to protest, but wisely, she did not. When she had gone out carrying her bed, Endredi sighed softly and sank down onto a stool, putting her hands over her face.

"Adelar, Adelar!" she moaned softly, finally allowing herself to express the hurt that had been fighting with her anger ever since she had seen him. She knew she should distrust him. All through the meal she had sought to convince herself that she could not have faith in him. He was not the boy she had known. He had changed.

Why was he here, and now of all times? Why could she not find strength in the fact that he had had years to come back to her, and had not? Why could she not keep anger in her heart when she thought of his lies? Why did something different, something stronger, intrude until her bitterness and anger were gone like a speck of dust upon a summer's breeze?

Why did she remember not the moment she knew he had abandoned her to her fate, but instead the one and only kiss they had shared? It had been early night, just like this, in the dimness of her father's house. They had been alone, two children on the edge of adulthood, sitting beside the fire, silent as usual. He had turned to her and spoken of—what? She had never been able to recall because of what had come after. He had talked and she had listened.

Then, slowly, wondrously, the expression in his dark, intense eyes had changed. Without even being aware of it, their bodies had moved closer. And closer. Until their lips had touched.

Even now, her heart raced at the thought of that gentle, tender kiss. She had changed into a woman then, with a woman's heart and a woman's dreams and a woman's passion.

And to think it had meant nothing at all to him.

She lowered her hands. She must put away these memories, once and for always. She must be strong and remember that her loyalty, and her body, belonged to another man. Adelar had done nothing to stop that, either. Yes, he had changed, and she must guard against her own weakness.

Resolving to be as good a wife to Bayard as she could, Endredi disrobed and climbed into the bed. She drew the curtains around it and waited, not afraid, but not with joyous anticipation.

Finally the door opened and someone entered. Her hands started to shake and her chest seemed tight, which was foolish. She was no tender virgin.

"Bayard?" she called out tentatively.

"Yes," came a low response.

Endredi closed her eyes. Oh, Freya, goddess of love and beauty, abandoned by Od and always mourning, help me! Even Bayard's voice is like Adelar's. Help me to forget! Please, Mary, mother of Jesus, give me strength to do what I must.

Then came the sounds of a man disrobing. Something metallic striking the stool. The dull thud of cloth on a chest.

The curtains parted, and Endredi opened her eyes.

Chapter Three

Bayard stood beside the bed. He was naked, his bearded face in shadow. He looked down at Endredi, and she tried to force a tentative smile to her lips, but oh, how his eyes were like Adelar's in this dim light!

Bayard got into the bed with her, yet he did not touch her. "You are sure Adelar's behavior did not offend you?" he asked softly. "Or Ranulf's? If so, tell me, and I will speak to them."

"No. I am unknown here, and drink can make men say things they themselves regret later."

"You are wise, Endredi. I am pleased you forgive him," he whispered. "Adelar is not only my cousin. He is my most trusted friend."

Was he deserving of such trust? she wondered. Did Bayard know what kind of man had sired his "trusted friend"? "These tales of Adelar's family that Ranulf spoke of," she began. "What did he mean?"

Bayard lay on his side and regarded her thoughtfully. "It was said that his father had somehow arranged the Viking attack on his village. That is what the leader of the Vikings claimed when he came seeking his wife and daughter, whom Kendric had stolen away in revenge when he came to take Adelar home.''

"Perhaps it was true."

"Kendric claimed otherwise. His own people believed him, and there was no proof of wrongdoing except for the word of a Viking."

"What do you believe?"

"Adelar is here, is he not? I have no doubt about his loyalty to me. Besides, I judge a man on his own merit, not his father's."

Endredi said nothing. She could not argue with Bayard's wish to judge a man for his own actions. Indeed, she knew how it was to be looked down upon for the unsavory actions of a parent. How many in her village had hinted that Endredi might be like her mother, who had slept with any man who asked her?

Bayard touched her cheek. "Are you afraid of me, Endredi?"

"No."

"You tremble." He moved closer to her.

"It is a chill night, my lord."

She could feel the heat from his body and was acutely aware of their nakedness as his arms encircled her. "I would warm you, then," he said. "And please, do not call me 'my lord' when we are here."

His hand touched her amulet. "What is this?" he asked, a hard note creeping into his voice. "Dagfinn assured me you were Christian."

"Truly I am, Bayard. It is a charm, nothing more."

"And what does this charm do?" he inquired, letting it fall. His fingers toyed with the chain, cool against her flesh.

"It is a sign of Freya."

"A goddess?"

"Yes."

"Goddess of what?"

"She watches over women getting married, or having babies. We used to pray to her to give us healthy children. Are you angry?"

"No." He chuckled, a low, pleasant sound that made her glad she had not told him more about Freya, who had taken lovers after being deserted by her husband. For her punishment, she had been made a goddess of death, too. "I would wear twenty such charms if I believed in their power. I am pleased, Endredi, that you hope for children."

"I do, very much."

"I will do my best," he whispered with a trace of wistfulness.

Before she had time to wonder at his tone, his body covered hers.

In a few short moments, the marriage was consummated. Without speaking, Bayard rolled away from her. Then she heard his slow, even breathing and realized he had fallen asleep.

Clasping her amulet, Endredi stared at the thatched roof. Not once had Bayard kissed her.

And despite all her prayers and resolutions, she was glad of it.

* * *

Adelar climbed out of the pile of fetid straw in which he had slept. His head throbbed, his mouth was as dry as old leather, and his tongue felt as if it was twice the normal size.

Sluggishly he brushed at the stray wisps that covered his clothes as he went outside, barely aware of the daily activity going on around him. The stable lads traded amused grins as the mighty warrior staggered out of the building, and the older women at the nearby well smiled condescendingly. Some of the younger girls giggled, but those of marriageable age sighed wistfully. They knew that a warrior like Adelar would probably never marry anyone but a thane's daughter. Still, they could look and admire and dream and sigh again.

Adelar saw none of this. All he knew was that he felt wretched, the air was chill, and there was a slight touch of frost on the ground he was staring at. He made his way to the nearest water trough and sluiced cold water over his head, which brought some relief.

He glanced at the hall, then up at the sky. It was a fine cloudless day and the sun was halfway to the zenith. The others had probably already broken the fast. Maybe not Endredi and Bayard...

Adelar threw more cold water on his head, then slowly walked toward the hall.

All through the wedding feast, he struggled not to stare at Endredi as she sat in the wide settle beside Bayard.

Of course he had recognized her at once. Her calm, quiet beauty, her bountiful red-gold hair and her unforgettable green eyes. She had seen him, too, and for a moment he had thought…hoped…been tempted to tell Bayard that the wedding must not be.

But who was he to go against his cousin's plans, especially when he could not be sure of Endredi's feelings? Once they had felt something for each other. They both had known it, and he, at least, had cherished it. Yet she had married another man.

It was as if she had confirmed his worst fear—that he was not worthy of her love. He was, after all, his father's son, and though he struggled constantly to prove that he was not the same as his traitorous sire, perhaps it only mattered that he was of Kendric's blood after what his father had tried to do to her.

The women at the well began to point, laugh and make jokes of the most bawdy kind. Adelar turned to see what they were talking of and saw Godwin at the door of the weaving shed bestowing a most impressive kiss and bold caress on Gleda. His breeches were half-fastened, and Gleda's garments could only be described as disheveled. Clearly Godwin had not spent the night in the hall, or the stable, or alone for that matter.

When the passionate couple realized they had an audience, Gleda pulled away, gave the women a saucy smile and sauntered off to the hall. With a dismissive flick of her hair, she passed Adelar. Her presence made absolutely no impression on him whatsoever. There was only one woman who occupied his thoughts today.

Godwin made the women an impressive bow. "Greetings, my dears," he said with great politeness. "I was not aware my every performance was to be observed. Ah, Adelar! Have we missed the meal?"

The women continued to chuckle among themselves while Godwin joined him.

"Greetings, Godwin. I believe you have already feasted," Adelar remarked sardonically as he continued toward the hall.

"And well, too," Godwin replied with a sly grin. "But then, you would know how well Gleda satisfies a man."

"Apparently any man will do, too."

"Is the mighty Adelar jealous of a humble gleeman?"

"Not at all. Take her, if she is willing. There are plenty of other women."

"Speaking of women, Bayard's new wife is not as lovely as they said, is she?"

"It is not for us to discuss Bayard's wife," Adelar replied coldly.

"You're in a terrible humor today, Adelar. What's the matter—not enough sleep last night, eh? Who were you with, if not Gleda? Let me think . . . I know! That little slave Ylla has had her eye on you. Or perhaps that servant of Bayard's wife. She is old, but you always say older women have a hoard of experience that they are only too willing to share—"

"My only companion last night was a cask of ale, and I am ruing that decision now."

"What? I don't believe it! And yet he admits it, too. Well, miracles do happen, after all. Adelar awakens alone for the first time in how many years? I must tell Father Derrick at once."

"Can you stop that wagging tongue of yours?" Adelar demanded. "You make my head ache."

"Speaking of tongues, is it not amazing what Gleda can do with hers?"

Adelar did not wish to have a complete recital of Gleda's abilities, so he began to walk faster. "I'm starving."

"Me, too. Shall we see what remains haven't already been thrown to the dogs?"

The door to Bayard's bower moved and Bayard strode briskly out. "Good day!" he called, his breath like puffs of smoke in the chill air as he approached. "I am going hunting this fine morning."

Adelar looked away from the bower where Endredi had spent her wedding night. "It is a fine day indeed, Bayard. I will fetch my horse."

"I had intended to ask you to remain behind. Endredi needs someone to show her about the *burh*."

"I am not fit for a lady's company this morning," Adelar answered. "What of Dagfinn and his men?"

"They are sleeping like rocks in my hall. I have left some men to guard them. I do not want to spend more time in their presence than I have to."

"I would be most happy to escort your bride about," Godwin interjected.

Bayard eyed Godwin. "Perhaps, but I would like you to escort Endredi, Adelar. You can speak to her in her own language, and I want to make her feel that this is her home."

His gaze was hard and firm, and Adelar knew he was as good as ordered to show Endredi the *burh*, although he would rather face ten armed Danes. "I will do as you ask, Cousin."

"Good. Since you seem particularly grim today, I think it would be wise to have Godwin go, too."

"I am only too happy, my lord," Godwin replied.

"Rouse the dog keeper. I believe three pair of hounds should be sufficient today. I leave Endredi in your hands, Adelar."

Adelar nodded as Bayard strode off toward the stable. The women at the well and the stable lads called out their good wishes, which the *burhware* acknowledged with a jovial response.

Godwin eyed his companion cautiously. "Bayard was not pleased by your reluctance."

Adelar did not bother to wait for Godwin, who trotted along behind him. "I have no wish to play nursemaid to his bride."

"Fine—but you should have been more tactful about it. You've annoyed him, and he looked happier this morning than he has for many a day."

"I know," Adelar replied softly. Indeed, he had thought the same thing. But he did not want to spend time with Endredi. He had no wish to see her look at him as she had yesterday—either the first time, when he had seen the unspoken feelings in her eyes, or later, when she had become as cold and distant as her homeland. Yet he dare not disobey his cousin, and Godwin was right about Bayard's good humor. It had been all too rare of late.

They paused at the entrance to the hall, and Godwin let out a low whistle. "Bayard spoke the truth. Look at these louts!"

The Danes were sleeping wherever they had fallen into a drunken stupor. Some slumbered with their heads on their arms slung over the table, some lay on the benches and some were even under the tables. More than one snored loudly. One or two of Bayard's dogs sniffed among the rushes, searching for food.

Adelar and Godwin stepped around them and went to Bayard's end of the lord's table.

"Not a morsel worth eating!" Godwin muttered in disgust, looking at the remnants of the feast.

Adelar picked up a crust of flat bread, then let it fall into the straw on the floor. One of the smaller hounds lunged for it and wolfed it down.

A deep voice from the nearest corner mumbled, "Who's botherin' the dogs?" Two human feet were barely visible beneath a pile of straw and dogs.

"Is that you, Baldric?" Godwin asked.

An affirmative growl answered them. "Can't you let a fellow sleep in peace?"

"Bayard wants to go hunting. He says bring three pair of dogs."

"This is no time for one of your jests, Godwin," the dog keeper mumbled.

Adelar kicked the fellow's feet. "Bayard wants to go hunting."

Baldric sat up when he heard Adelar's low, stern voice, his blond hair sticking out like so many pieces of straw. He shoved the dogs away from him and stood, scratching his flea bites. In the dim light, the short, burly fellow looked not unlike his charges. "It's you, eh? Then I believe it." With his rough voice, he sounded like a dog who had been taught speech, too. "Any food about?"

Godwin shrugged. "Duff's probably gone back to bed after serving Bayard."

"What time of day is it?" Baldric demanded. "I would have heard the ruckus if there'd been a proper meal. And so would they." He nodded at the slumbering Danes.

"They would probably sleep through a thunderstorm—and you, too. We could have cut off your legs and you wouldn't have noticed," Godwin said. "The food's been served and we've missed it."

"I will be happy to find you some," a young woman's voice said shyly. Adelar turned around to see the slave Ylla standing inside the door. "There is bread and meat in the salter's stores. If you like, I will bring it to you."

"Delightful creature, I am beholden to you," Godwin said with a courtly bow. "Bring enough for three starving men."

She gave a slight smile and hurried away. Baldric whistled, making the dogs come instantly alert. "Save some for me," he muttered as he led the dogs outside.

"She's not bringing it for *us,* you know," Godwin said quietly but pointedly to Adelar. "It's you she wants to make happy."

Adelar's only response was a Baldric-like grunt.

Godwin joined Adelar on a bench. "She's a pretty little thing, eh? And she's a virgin, or so the merchant who sold her to Bayard claimed."

"She is Bayard's property." Adelar eyed Godwin with some curiosity. "If you are so smitten with her, why are you pointing out her virtues to me?"

Godwin's surprise was comical to behold. "St. Swithins in a swamp, why *am* I? Too much ale has addled my wits. Forget everything I said!"

"Very well, but I would suggest you keep your eye on Ranulf. He is the one not to be trusted around virgins," Adelar warned.

Godwin's eyes widened. "It's true then, about Ranulf and that thane's daughter at Cynath's *burh?* How much did he have to pay?"

"You are much too interested in gossip, Godwin."

"It was you who first told me the tale," Godwin noted. "How much?"

"I do not know the exact amount, but let us hope Ordella never finds out. And," Adelar said sternly, "I believe she would never forgive the messenger, either."

"I think you are correct about that," Godwin agreed. "Still, Ranulf had best take better care, eh?"

Ylla returned. She eyed the still-sleeping Danes warily and gave them a wide berth as she quickly cleared a space at the table. When she set the bread and ale down in front of Adelar, she smiled shyly. "Anything else, my lord?"

"No. You may go."

One of the Danes stirred and snorted noisily, and Ylla scurried out of the hall as if she expected him to rise and give chase.

"You see, I was telling the truth. She likes you."

"She belongs to Bayard."

"Who never touches slaves." Suddenly Godwin smote himself on the forehead. "Ah, I am the biggest dolt in the kingdom! You are not interested in that little slave because you care for another!"

"And who might that be?"

"Gleda—no! You have but to crook your finger and she is in your lap. Someone who lives elsewhere, perhaps. Let me think...you haven't had her yet, or you would not be pining for her—a minor delay, I am sure."

"You seem confident of my charms."

"Are you going to try to deny that women find you irresistible? I tell you, Adelar, between you and Bayard, it is a wonder there is a virgin left in England."

"Who am I to disillusion you? But do you think I would wish to find myself in Ranulf's place? I am not as rich as he is, to risk my money seducing noblemen's daughters."

"Perfectly right. So, she must be married. And she must be beautiful, because everyone knows you would only want a beauty. That lets out Ordella—" Adelar sniffed derisively "—and I think Bayard's wife, who although not as ugly as Ordella, is no beauty, either."

Adelar did not reply. Endredi's beauty was not the kind that most men would see. It did not flaunt itself with bright eyes, pink cheeks and beguiling, empty smiles. It was far more subtle, in her intelligent eyes, in the slight flush that would steal over her soft cheeks when she was embarrassed, in the fullness of her lips when she smiled her shy, sweet smile.

The same smile she had given Bayard last night. He stabbed at the bread in front of him. "Why don't you stop talking and eat?"

"Careful! You nearly got my hand. I didn't realize you were *that* hungry. You are right. We mustn't tarry or Bayard will be even more angry. I do not want to be the one to further sour his mood."

"Where is the priest?" Endredi asked Helmi, who had been bustling about the bower trying to look busy for some time. She knew the serving woman was probably full of questions about her husband, but she was in no mood to satisfy a servant's need for gossip.

"That one? He has done their ceremony and gone already, I am happy to say. A more pompous, miserable, misguided man never lived, I believe. Do you know he actually thinks all women *evil?* Everyone knows the gods and goddesses are both good and bad. I think this Christianity is a Saxon plot to disrupt the natural relations between men and women. I hope your husband does not think you are evil, my lady? I trust he treats you well?"

Endredi did not answer Helmi's questions. "So I have missed Mass."

"The noon draws near, my lady," Helmi said with a knowing grin. "A good sign, being so tired. Your husband must be a virile man, eh?"

Again Endredi did not answer. Her husband had done what was necessary to consummate the relationship, no more, but that was no subject to be spoken of to another.

Helmi finally seemed to understand that she did not wish to discuss her husband or the wedding night. "Do you have any plans for today, my lady? Or would you rather rest?"

"I wish to meet all of the servants," she said thoughtfully. "Bayard said he would see to it that someone shows me about the *burh,* too."

"I should hope he would arrange an escort. We couldn't go by ourselves. It wouldn't be safe."

Endredi kept her smile to herself. Helmi thought all Saxon men were little removed from rutting rams, at least those who weren't vicious murderers. "Perhaps one of the thanes will escort us," she said, washing her face and reaching for the comb Helmi held out to her.

Helmi opened a chest of clothing. "This gown is a pretty one. I am sure your husband would like it."

"What of Dagfinn and the others?"

"Still snoring in the hall, no doubt."

"I believe you are right. It would be an act of the gods if they move before nightfall after the amount of ale they imbibed at the feast."

Helmi grinned slyly. "Perhaps you would rather wait here for your husband's return."

Endredi picked up her thin wool cloak and an intricately carved wooden box. "I will meet the servants of the hall now, and see to the preparations of the meals. Will you come with me?"

Helmi looked as if Endredi had suggested she run naked through the *burh*. "There will be Saxons in the hall."

"I expect so."

"I . . . I have too much to do here, my lady. I will eat later, when the men are gone. *All* of them."

Endredi suppressed a small smile as she went and crossed the yard, surveying the timber wall surrounding the *burh* as she did so. It was of stout oak trees, and the ends were sharpened to dangerous points. The gate they had entered yesterday had been thick, too, and the village that surrounded the thane's enclosure had been a large one, for Saxons. It was not as big as some of the Viking towns, and certainly not to be compared to Hedeby or one of the other Viking ports, but obviously Bayard kept a sizable force near him, and it was the workers who serviced warriors that no doubt made up most of the village trade.

She could hear the rhythmic clangs of more than one smith at work, and judging by the smell, knew the stables were being cleaned out.

A few women lingered by the well and made no secret of their curiosity as they stared at her. She bowed her head very slightly, acknowledging their presence but making it very clear that she was of superior rank to them.

Endredi entered the hall and at once she realized Adelar was there. He was sitting at the farthest end, near Bayard's seat, and the gleeman was beside him.

He was no more than any other warrior in her husband's service, she reminded herself. She turned her attention to the hall, which was now her concern. Her nose wrinkled with disgust as she picked her way through the soiled rushes. The fire in the large hearth was out, goblets and drinking horns lay scattered amid puddles of ale and mead, benches were overturned. Several men were still sleeping there, oblivious to the time of day and the activity outside. She spotted Dagfinn immediately, his loud snoring like the growl of a bear. A young female slave she recalled from last night appeared. "Where are the servants?"

"I . . . I don't know, my lady."

Endredi knew the girl was lying, but it was also obvious that she was frightened, so she spoke kindly. "What is your name?"

"Ylla, my lady."

"Where are the cook and the other servants, Ylla? They need not know how I discovered where they are."

"He, um, they... Duff is in the potter's shed."

"And Duff is...?"

"The cook, my lady."

"Ah. Can you point out the potter's shed?"

Ylla went to the door and did so.

Endredi handed her the wooden box. "Please hold this for me," she said, then she left the hall and marched toward the shed. Once there, she peered inside and saw a man and a woman, their half-clothed bodies intertwined.

Endredi turned away and went back to the hall, where she picked up one of the iron kettles and a spoon. She began to bang on the pot, the loud sound enough to wake all but the dead. Adelar and Godwin stared, and Ylla looked startled until Endredi smiled at her.

"By Odin's eye!" Dagfinn shouted. "What are you doing?"

"It is nearly noon. I thought you might want to eat."

He frowned as he adjusted his rumpled tunic. "Come," he barked at his men. "I have no wish to linger here. I want to be in my own longhouse."

Dagfinn ignored his curious men while he gathered his scattered belongings. His men staggered after him out the door, several of them barely able to stand.

In the next moment those still in the hall heard angry mumbling, then the cook came inside, pulling on his tunic. "What in the name of—"

Endredi put the kettle down.

Duff saw who was making the noise and smiled weakly. "Ah, my lady! What are you doing here? This is a...a surprise!"

"I would like something to eat," she said. "Our guests have already departed without eating. I am most displeased."

Duff blanched.

"Fortunately, I do not believe they were very hungry. However, *I* am."

"Of course, of course." The cook was a big man, but he bustled into the hall with surprising speed. "What would you like? Boiled fish? Fried eels? Some oatmeal?"

"Bread and boiled ham," Endredi answered.

"The baker—"

"Must also be found and set to work. I suggest you rekindle the hearth. Then I want the servants to help this girl clean the hall. It is a disgrace."

"Yes, my lady. At once, my lady."

The woman Endredi recognized from the shed came inside, adjusting her bodice, her eyes wide with surprise and dismay. "Merilda!" Duff barked, making her jump. "Get to work!"

"I have something here to use in the cooking," Endredi said, taking the wooden box from Ylla and approaching the cook.

"Oh, my lady?" he replied respectfully, if insincerely.

"Yes." She placed the box on the ground and opened it. Immediately a wonderful spicy aroma filled the air, and despite himself, Duff moved closer to look inside. The box was filled with a variety of small earthenware jars.

"It was a wedding gift from my grandmother's husband," Endredi explained. "He was a trader and these spices and herbs come from all over the known world." She glanced at Adelar. Surely he would remember Thorston, who had treated the boy so kindly and who had been repaid with thievery.

Duff gazed in awe as she lifted out a jar and gently opened the lid. "This comes from far in the East." She closed it and brought out another. "This is from Rome."

Duff looked as if he was being offered costly jewels until she closed the lid of the box. The maidservants no longer even pretended to work, but listened unabashedly. "Do you not intend them to be used, my lady?" he asked.

"Of course they will be used," she said. "By me, when I help you prepare the meals."

He regarded her with surprise. "But you are my lord's wife!"

"I like cooking."

"For having such a beautiful, accomplished lady who does not seek merely to be waited on, Bayard and the rest of us will be forever thankful," the gleeman said. Endredi turned to the young man with a small smile, which vanished when she caught Adelar's eye.

"Naturally I would welcome your help, my lady," Duff said, scowling at the gleeman, then smiling at Endredi.

Just as naturally she doubted his truthfulness, but she guessed, from the greedy expression in his eyes when he looked at the box, that he would have said anything to get his hands on some of those spices.

"Shall we start with some stew? I think a little of this will help," she said. She pulled out a jar.

Ordella's voice interrupted them. "Get to work, you lazy creatures!"

Everyone turned as Ordella stepped daintily toward them, her face wreathed in smiles distinctly at odds with the harsh order she had issued. "Servants can be so slothful," she explained sympathetically. "You shall have to take care that they fear you enough to obey you."

"It is a well-known fact that terror inspires loyalty," Adelar said gravely.

"Thank you for the advice," Endredi said to Ordella, fighting an urge to look at Adelar. "If I find I have any trouble with them, I shall certainly ask your opinion."

"What are *you* doing here?" Ordella asked of Adelar. She also gave Godwin a less than pleased look as the servants hurried to their work.

"Bayard has asked me to escort his bride through the *burh* today, if she is agreeable," Adelar replied quietly.

"That will not be necessary," Ordella said sharply. "I shall show Endredi what she needs to be shown."

"Of course, that is your privilege," Adelar responded. "But then I would be disobeying Bayard's order."

Endredi glanced at the two uneasily. She had no desire to spend time in Adelar's company. Indeed, it was a strain even now. Although she tried not to, she kept wondering what he was thinking about her and trying to read his inscrutable dark eyes. It was obvious he had no wish to be near her, either, if he was acting as her escort only on Bayard's orders.

How much better it would be to spend her time cooking, especially since the food Duff prepared was somewhat plain, if good. Then perhaps she could forget Adelar, Bayard and everyone else in this *burh*. However, she did not think it wise to go against Bayard's wishes. And although she did not want to be anywhere near Ordella, it was probably best that she come along.

"I see no reason I should not enjoy the company of you both," Endredi said at last.

"Bayard told Godwin and me to escort her, Ordella. You must have other things to do," Adelar said coldly.

"I assure you, Adelar," Ordella said even more coldly, "*some* of us earn our keep around here. I do have many things to do. I simply wanted to make Bayard's wife feel welcome.''

"You have," Endredi said quickly. "I see that Adelar and Godwin have already broken the fast. Please, Ordella, eat with me. You can tell me of the village while we break bread and before you must go. I am most interested to hear what you can tell me.''

Ordella gave Adelar a triumphant look and moved toward the high table.

"I shall leave the spices here for the present," Endredi said to Duff. "Use them sparingly. They are quite strong. Please bring us some bread and meat as soon as you can."

"Bring some ale," Ordella said to Gleda, who had only just arrived. The maidservant hurried off at once.

Endredi was now nearly alone with Adelar and Godwin. "Godwin, would you be so good as to fetch my warmer cloak from the bower? I feel a slight chill.''

"As you wish, my lady." He paused a moment, then went on seriously. "Perhaps you should give me a word of passage, lest your servant think I come to ravish her?''

Endredi had to smile at the gleeman's words. It seemed he understood Helmi rather well. "I think Helmi will not fear you, Godwin, if you smile at her as you do at me.''

The gleeman grinned and hurried out the door.

Endredi turned to Adelar, very aware that Ordella was watching them. "That wasn't very clever, Adelar," she said quietly but firmly. "There is no need to treat Ordella as an enemy."

"And you have no need to make jests with Godwin." He gazed at her with his penetrating brown eyes. "You know nothing of the people here, especially Ordella and Ranulf. Leave me to handle those two in my own way."

"There can be no harm in a little banter with Bayard's gleeman. You used to be a clever boy. Have your wits grown dim with age? My husband has plenty of enemies outside the *burh*. Why make more within?"

"Again, you do not understand."

Realizing that she should not spend any longer in conversation with him, she said, "We will speak of this later." Then she hurried toward Ordella, a smile on her face. "I am sorry, but I wanted Adelar to know that I cannot allow such disrespect in my hall."

Ordella's eyes widened with genuine pleasure. "I see Bayard has indeed chosen his wife wisely. Adelar has been too free with his ways."

The two women watched Adelar leave the hall. Gleda made her way past him, and Endredi saw the girl press against his body quite unnecessarily. He seemed to find nothing amiss, although he had chided *her* for exchanging a jest with Godwin. Still, his brow remained furrowed and he said nothing to the serving wench at all.

Endredi looked away. She should not be pleased that he ignored Gleda. It could be that he was oblivious to many things, for he also seemed not to care that he had angered Ranulf's wife. Ranulf was not worthy of respect, perhaps, but he *was* Bayard's kin.

Gleda poured the women some ale while Ylla brought bread and meat.

"I see you have managed to instill some proper respect in that harlot, too," Ordella said, her lips pursed as she watched Gleda stroll away.

"Harlot?"

"She goes with any man who looks at her, even that fool Godwin, probably. She will be with child again soon, and then you will have to find another to take her place."

"Again? She has children?"

"Two. They died during their birth."

"Oh, how sad for her!"

"It was a punishment from God, which unfortunately has not made her change her ways," Ordella said peevishly. "I think every man in this *burh* has been with her, except Bayard, of course. *He* has *some* discernment. I think Adelar's bedded her every night for nearly a month."

Endredi wished Ordella had stayed in her bower. She had seemed quiet enough before, but she was proving to have a wasp's tongue. Not that Adelar's women mattered to her.

"I suppose we can't expect Adelar to have any sense of discernment or discretion," Ordella went on, "considering that his mother was little better than a harlot herself, and such behavior runs in families." She reached for more food, so she did not see the way Endredi clutched the knife in her hand or the slight flush on her cheeks. "I do not mean to imply, my lady, that Bayard would behave so," she went on condescendingly. "Everyone knows that since Bertilde died he has not touched another woman." She sighed sadly. "Of course, Bertilde was quite a beauty."

After a brief moment of anger, Endredi set Ordella's insult aside. After all, Ordella knew nothing about her mother.

But her other words had pricked at Endredi like the tip of a knife. Endredi had always known she was not pretty. Indeed, in the still small hours of the night she had often wondered if Adelar would have come back to her if she had been more beautiful.

She also felt the beginnings of sympathy for Adelar. He, too, had lived with gossip and rumor—and not just for one parent, as she had, but for both. How difficult it must have been! No wonder he had left his father's village. Yet the gossip and the rumors followed.

"It was a great pity she did not give Bayard children. Or Magreth, or Adda."

"Bayard has had *three* wives?"

"Yes. Sad, is it not? Still, we all hope that Bayard will have children *now.*"

Endredi glanced at her companion. That was a lie, if Endredi was any judge, and she was. If Bayard died without issue, who would inherit his lands and his property? Ranulf, probably, as his nearest male heir, unless Bayard had written a will that stated otherwise.

She would ask him. She had no liking for either Ranulf or Ordella, whose eyes gleamed with greed like those of a rat in the dark.

Of course, should she bear Bayard a son, the child would inherit. A man like him deserved a son. Many of them.

She should be happy to have them. She would be. Please God and Freya, she would be.

Chapter Four

"Adelar!" Ranulf cried. He hurried to catch up with the Saxon as he strode toward the hall. Adelar did not stop or even slow his steps.

Arrogant bastard, Ranulf thought angrily. But he was in Bayard's favor, so Ranulf knew it would be wise to seem pleasant.

"Adelar!" Ranulf repeated insistently.

This time Adelar halted, because he had reached the door of the hall anyway. "What do you want?" he demanded. "Is there something of import you wished to say? I must show Bayard's wife the *burh*."

Ranulf nodded and drew Adelar aside, down a narrow way between two bowers. "I don't trust the Danes."

"Nor do I."

"Bayard appears to."

"For the moment, at least. I would not be certain that he trusts them completely."

"He married a Viking woman."

"He agreed to this marriage because it was prudent to do so. If the Danes break the bargain in any way, I am certain Bayard will not hesitate to strike."

"I don't trust *her,* either."

"I see no reason to distrust the woman. She is Bayard's wife now. If he comes to harm, so will she."

"Perhaps—or perhaps she is sent to spy upon us."

Adelar's eyes narrowed. "Do you have any proof of such a charge?"

"I make no formal accusation," Ranulf replied, remembering well the penalty for slander. He had no wish to lose his tongue. "I merely think the woman should be watched. Surely you must agree it would be a sensible precaution."

"Yes."

"Then you will help me?"

"To spy on her?"

"No," Ranulf said, a hint of frustration in his tone, "not spy. But if we find out anything—"

"Naturally Bayard will be told."

"Perhaps Bayard will not believe you. The woman seems to please him," he noted. "You are in your cousin's counsel. Do you think otherwise?"

"I think Bayard's marriage is none of my concern," Adelar replied gruffly.

"I hope for Bayard's sake he *is* happy. I suppose any wife is better than an empty bed."

Adelar gazed steadily at Ranulf, his dark eyes as sharp as the point of his dagger. "That tongue of yours is going to get you killed, Ranulf."

"I meant no harm," he said innocently, surprised by Adelar's vehemence. Indeed, he had expected Adelar to be only too willing to keep watch on the woman who was, after all, a Viking. Instead, Adelar seemed almost anxious to defend her.

Or only Bayard, perhaps.

"But what of you, Adelar? Are you quite well?"

Adelar looked at his interrogator with a raised eyebrow. "I mean no impertinence," Ranulf said, smiling. "It is just that you do not seem yourself."

"Yes, my lord," Godwin said, coming up behind them. "You used to be so jolly and now you are as grim as Father Derrick on All Soul's Day."

Adelar gave the gleeman a rueful grin. He had certainly never, ever been what could be described as "jolly."

"I was only wondering if he was ill," Ranulf said peevishly. "And should you not be elsewhere, gleeman—assisting the other servants?"

Godwin's eyes flashed with anger, and for a moment Adelar thought he was going to protest before leaving, but he did not. No doubt Endredi would say Godwin was the wiser for holding his tongue.

"Good day, Ranulf," Adelar said truculently as he turned away and proceeded on his errand.

Adelar had spoken the truth when he had told Endredi she did not understand the enmity he bore Ranulf.

When Adelar had arrived at Oakenbrook, he had realized immediately that he was not welcome to

Bayard's nephew. He guessed that Ranulf feared he had come to make some claim on his cousin or seek to take Ranulf's place in Bayard's esteem, although it was quite obvious that Bayard had little esteem for Ranulf anyway.

Immediately rumors started concerning Adelar's family, and Adelar did not doubt that they had come from Ranulf, or his wasp-tongued wife.

And then, one day, Ranulf chanced to speak of Adelar's mother when he did not realize Adelar was standing behind him, near enough to hear every word and understand every nuance.

As much as Adelar hated his father, he had loved his mother. He had heard the tales of her lover, and although he was loath to believe his mother capable of dishonor, he had learned enough about his father to allow him to sympathize with her actions.

When Ranulf saw the faces of those to whom he talked and slowly turned to face a furious Adelar, he looked as if he would gladly slither beneath the nearest building like the snake he was. There was a long moment of intense silence as Adelar came very near to drawing a weapon on the red-faced man, for not only had Ranulf insulted Adelar's mother, he had contrived to put his words in such a way as to blame all the women of the family, which included Bayard's mother. An insult from Bayard's nephew to himself was one thing; an insult to Bayard quite another.

Nonetheless, because the man was Bayard's nephew, Adelar kept his sword sheathed. His face betrayed every thought, every emotion, however, and he saw no need for it to be otherwise. Ranulf knew precisely what Adelar had been thinking, and Adelar was quite certain it was Ranulf's fear of Adelar's vengeance that kept him from being even more obvious in his greed.

If it aided Bayard to have Adelar as his watchdog, he would be as fierce as Baldric's most savage hound.

"This is the new chapel," Adelar said later that day. He gestured toward a building that was nearly complete.

Endredi looked at the impressive wooden structure with a high thatched roof located beside one of the rivers that bordered the village. Huge hardwood trees surrounded it, promising cool shade in the summer and protection from the snow in winter.

Like most of the buildings Adelar had shown her, it was very well-built, strong and solid. It was quite evident that Bayard expected this *burh* to be a permanent town, not just a temporary fortress. She could tell him about the large trading towns the Vikings visited and maybe even make some suggestions for this one. For instance, there was only one pier on the largest of the two rivers. They could easily build more to accommodate trade in the summer months, especially if there was going to be peace.

Yes, there were many improvements she could suggest, provided Bayard wanted to hear them.

"Father Derrick is anxious to obtain a holy relic for the chapel," Adelar remarked, breaking the silence.

"I think he expects a piece of the True Cross or a saint's bone to fall from the sky, for he certainly is loath to pay for them," Godwin noted.

"He can purchase such a thing?" Endredi asked incredulously.

"Certainly," Adelar replied, turning away from the chapel to look at her. "The question would be, though, was it real, or something made of chicken bones or old wood."

"Do you mean people sell false relics?"

"All the time," Adelar said. "To those foolish enough to trust whatever they are told."

Endredi did not reply. It was appalling, of course, to think that anyone would seek to profit by such a fraud. However, she was also struggling not to attach any significance to Adelar's words. She kept thinking he was speaking in riddles. For instance, was she foolish to trust his words long ago? Was she foolish to trust him now? Or was he speaking of trusting someone else? Or was he merely referring to the relics? Whatever he meant, she hoped they had seen all of the *burh* she needed to see. She was not anxious to spend more time in Adelar's company than she had to.

Godwin nodded toward the river. "Would you care for some water, my lady? I can fetch a cup from the workmen at the chapel."

"I would be grateful, Godwin."

The gleeman gave Adelar a grin. "Do not gossip about me when I am gone," he said, "unless it is only good things."

The gleeman trotted off toward the building, leaving Adelar and Endredi to stroll along the riverbank. They halted under the shelter of a large and ancient oak tree in an awkward silence. The trees were just coming into blossom and the air was heavy with the scent.

Endredi's gaze moved along the river. Nearby, a group of peasant boys laughed and unsuccessfully tried to shoot at birds with small bows and what appeared to be arrows of their own manufacture.

How happy and carefree they looked! She glanced at Adelar, remembering him at their age, although he had been less happy and certainly never so carefree.

He was tall now, and imposing and aloof. He had grown into the strong, lithe warrior she had always envisioned. The warrior she had often dreamed would come sailing back into the fjord at home and take her away with him, until she realized that he had abandoned her forever.

Her throat grew tight and she returned her attention to the boys.

"Where is your crucifix?"

His question in the Viking tongue made her start. Her hand flew to her chest as she realized he was staring at her. "The crucifix? I...I do not always wear it."

"Did your father give it to you?"

She shook her head. "Meradyce."

He turned away as if he was going to leave her there.

"Do you not wish to know how she fares?" Endredi demanded. She knew what Meradyce had been to him, nursemaid, friend, the first love of his boyish heart—and a traitor for becoming a Viking's wife and Endredi's stepmother. "She is well and happy."

"I did not ask. I only wanted to know about the crucifix because it was my mother's. Your father stole it." How harsh and hate-filled were his words!

"And what did *your* father do in return?" she retorted. "You may have the crucifix. I will fetch it at once. And later you can tell all here that my father is a thief. Or have you already? What is one more lie?"

He glared at her, his full lips drawn tight. "I have told no lies."

"Do not play the ignorant fool with me, Adelar."

"I have said nothing of my time in your village."

She eyed him skeptically. "Not even to Bayard?"

"He is the only one who knows anything at all, and then only what concerned my father. Others merely know that my sister died and I learned your language. Does it surprise you now that Bayard allows me to remain? That he trusts me as he does? As he *seems* to? I thought you were too clever to trust to appearances, Endredi. Perhaps he simply uses me to annoy Ranulf."

"If I *were* to trust to appearances, I would say you enjoy the role," she noted angrily. "Is that what you have become, Adelar? Some kind of gleeman whose purpose is not to entertain but to annoy? Is that why you questioned me about the crucifix? I suggest you take care, *gleeman*. I would not be so quick to insult and annoy Ranulf, who is Bayard's nephew and a rich thane."

"You do not understand about Ranulf."

"Then explain it to me, *gleeman*."

"It does not matter," he replied coldly.

She looked at him squarely and tried not to see in his face the boy she had known. "If it concerns Ranulf, it concerns Bayard. And if it concerns Bayard, it concerns his wife. Explain it to me."

Adelar's eyes grew wide for a brief moment, then he shrugged. "Very well, *Bayard's wife*. I do not have to hide my disgust for him, for he knows it well enough anyway."

"What has he done to make you hate him?"

"He said my mother was no better than a whore. I would have killed him then, except that he is Bayard's nephew and a wealthy thane," Adelar finished sarcastically.

He could not fool her with appearances now, either. She knew him too well, so she saw that Ranulf's insult had caused him bitter pain, a pain she herself had felt. Truly, she could believe it was only Adelar's loyalty to Bayard that had spared Ranulf's life.

"That I have no love for Northmen is no secret," he continued. "Why should it be? You know what they did to my people, my family."

"I *know* that my father treated you like a son." She made no effort to subdue the twinge of bitterness that knowledge always gave her. "I know that it was your own father who was a traitor, who paid to have your mother killed. I dare say you forgot to tell them that not one of your father's villagers was killed, yet when he came to *my* village seeking you, he and his men slaughtered many innocent women and old men. And then he was going to sell the rest of us—or have you conveniently forgotten that, too?"

"I remember everything. Especially your father's face when he told me what kind of man my father is."

"You had to know, and so did your people."

"Did we? Did *I*? Do you expect me to be grateful for the knowledge that the man who sired me was a base traitor? Whatever else he is, he is my father. But Einar thought nothing of a son's need for a father, or the loyalty owed to a parent. He was so completely sure he knew the right thing to do."

"Einar treated you like a warrior, Adelar. You had to know."

"I wish your father had never come to my village," he whispered fervently, his dark eyes full of pain and anger and, she thought, guilt. "I wish he had left me there, as he was supposed to. I wish I had never met you!"

His words stung her deeply. "And I wish you had not been a coward when your father took me to his hall to rape me. But you did not come to my rescue. You did not even try to help me!"

"Forgive my tardiness, my lady!" Godwin called out. He hurried up to them, a crude wooden cup in his hand. "Would you believe not one of them had anything to drink from? I had to go to the alehouse!"

Endredi tried to smile placidly at him, although her heart continued to beat as if it would burst. Finally she had been able to accuse Adelar to his face, to give voice to some of the pain she had harbored for so long!

She risked a glance at him. He stood casually, his weight on one leg, his arms crossed, his expression inscrutable. It was as if she had said nothing at all.

As they continued to walk through the *burh*, Godwin realized that Endredi had grown disinterested and Adelar distracted.

To be sure, they had not been the most loquacious of company, but the sudden change after he had left them alone together was most interesting.

Had Adelar said something to insult her? Perhaps, yet she did not seem overly offended. No, she appeared triumphant—but not happily so. And Adelar? His silence was nothing very unusual, for he was a grim and quiet fellow most of the time. But today he seemed pensive.

Something had gone on between the two of them. If the woman was more attractive, he might guess that Adelar had said something flattering that could be construed as an attempt at seduction. The woman would be mistaken, of course, for Adelar always kept away from other men's wives. Indeed, the Saxon's preference for willing serving wenches allowed Godwin to make much sport at the warrior's expense.

Nevertheless, something had changed between these two, and he would do his best to discover what.

Godwin was not the only one who was curious, at least about Bayard's new wife. The very next morning, Ordella sidled into the space beside Endredi that Bayard had vacated when he left to oversee the completion of a weapons storehouse. The others who usually dined in the hall lingered, finishing their bread and ale. Father Derrick, who had returned unexpectedly, complaining of obdurate priests—thereby unknowingly telling everyone he had quarrelled and left in a fit of temper—ate in stony silence. Gleda, Merilda and Ylla began clearing off the remains, and Baldric could be heard outside, already training a new brace of hounds.

Adelar had not been in the hall at all.

"I trust you were pleased with your walk yesterday," Ordella said, her lips smiling and her eyes displaying that avid curiosity Endredi had noted from the first.

"I was most impressed," she answered truthfully.

"I must say I was quite surprised at Bayard's choice of escort," Ordella replied, frowning slightly. "I hope the gleeman did not talk too much. He believes himself to be quite amusing—an unwarranted opinion, if you ask me, but then he is vain, like all the Mercians."

"I found him very entertaining," Endredi said coolly.

Ordella gave her a measuring stare. "Well, I suppose he would at least exert himself for Bayard's new wife. I don't suppose Adelar said more than ten words the whole time."

"He was very informative."

"Was he, indeed?"

"Yes."

"Beware a wagging tongue," Father Derrick suddenly warned. He rose majestically. "Especially the sly tongue of a woman or a man who dreams of becoming a bishop!" He gave them a malevolent glare before striding down the hall and outside.

"Ah, and to think he was once notorious for his bawdy verses," Godwin said loudly from his place below the salt. "There was one in particular, something about the Moist Nest of My Desire—"

"Gleeman! I am shocked!" Ordella said sharply.

"I have it on the best authority," he replied innocently. "I wonder what sent him scurrying to the priesthood?"

"Perhaps a woman broke his heart," Endredi said quietly.

"Perhaps," Godwin admitted, but he did not look convinced. "Perhaps several."

"Whatever happened to him," Ordella complained, "he is a most tiresome fellow, priest though he be! Really, I wonder that Bayard does not send him to some monastery, preferably back in Rome."

"He was born here," Godwin observed.

Ordella turned to him with a sour expression. "I do not recall asking your opinion, Godwin."

The gleeman shrugged, but when Ordella turned back to look at Endredi, he puckered his lips and frowned in a very accurate impersonation of Ranulf's wife. Endredi had to bite her lip to keep from laughing.

"Would you care to accompany me to the weaving shed?" Ordella asked. "Some of our women are very skilled."

"I would like that," Endredi answered. She should go there to see how the Saxon women managed this important task. An accomplished weaver herself, Helmi had managed the courage—or her curiosity had overwhelmed her fears enough—to have already ventured that far from Bayard's bower. She was quite contemptuous of the Saxon methods and design, but Endredi suspected that was only because of Helmi's belief that anyone else's work must be inferior.

Endredi would rather go by herself than with Ordella, but there was no way to refuse without making it look like an insult. Accordingly, she rose and waited for Ordella to follow suit.

The two women left the hall. Outside, the day was warm and the air humid. A low line of dark clouds on the horizon promised rain later in the day, and Endredi hoped sooner rather than later.

The weaving shed was part of a group of buildings just outside the walls of the *burh*. It was a long, low structure, part of which was used to store the washed fleece. Inside, especially on such a muggy day, there was a distinct odor of sheep.

Endredi spotted Helmi, who had set up her own loom a little distance from where the Saxon women worked. She was making a great show of ignoring them, but as they drew near, Endredi saw her glance toward the chattering Saxons more than once. Obviously Helmi wanted them to notice her work, and either they truly did not, or were similarly ignoring her.

It was probably just as well that Helmi could not speak to them, for otherwise she would never have accepted such a response in silence. She would have been telling them all how to do their work, too.

Helmi and the others caught sight of Endredi and Ordella. Helmi nodded a greeting, but the other women's expressions were considerably less favorable. They probably did not welcome a Viking, but the knowledge did little to dull the sadness Endredi felt when she saw the contempt in their eyes before they returned to their task.

As they continued to watch the women, Ordella shifted uncomfortably closer. "As much as I dislike being the bearer of bad tidings, I feel it is my duty to tell you what I have heard about a certain lady with whom Bayard has been, shall we say, very friendly— both before and *after* your arrival."

"Like Father Derrick, I have no liking for gossip, Ordella," Endredi replied. "Besides, I thought you said Bayard was an honorable man."

"Well, yes, I did. And I truly believed that. Unfortunately, Ranulf has since told me..."

"What?" Not bothering to keep her voice low, Endredi raised one eyebrow skeptically. If Bayard did have a mistress, that was not so surprising. He was a handsome, wealthy thane. Nor was it a surprise that he might continue to see her. Theirs had been an arranged marriage, for the sake of peace. Indeed, if there was any surprise at all, it was that she felt so little. She cared in a vague way, but she was certainly not upset. She was almost pleased to think that Bayard would not abandon the woman entirely.

"Does this lady have a name?"

Ordella flushed. "Ranulf would not tell me."

"I see," Endredi said, now suspicious that the woman was a spiteful fabrication. "Thank you for the information. I shall ask Bayard about this nameless woman."

Ordella looked horrified. "Oh, I would not do that, my lady! These are only rumors, you know. Perhaps merely malicious gossip, after all. I would not question Bayard."

"No?" Endredi said with a smile, convinced she had guessed correctly. There was no mistress. "Then I would suggest you keep such malicious gossip to yourself, lest you find yourself accused of slander."

Ordella blinked rapidly. Obviously Endredi had not reacted the way she had expected at all. "Yes, of course, my lady, of course."

The Saxon weavers, whose hands had grown much slower about their tasks, began to work quickly again.

After a long silence, Ordella cleared her throat awkwardly. "I think the men are in the field practicing their swordplay. If you have been here long enough, perhaps we could watch them?"

"I would rather not disturb them. And it might not be wise for me to take an interest in their preparations for war, since to many here I am still, and only, a Viking."

The women glanced at her, some with surprise, others contemptuous.

"Very well, then. We shall not go."

"I understand why the people here are suspicious of me, of course. I myself have to struggle to subdue my suspicions of Saxons."

Ordella and the others made no secret of their surprise at her blunt words.

"When I was a girl, my village was destroyed by Saxons," Endredi went on. "A band of Saxons took me and the women and children they had not killed back to their village. Fortunately, we managed to escape."

"Saxons do not venture onto Viking lands!" Ordella protested. "They only defend themselves."

"This Saxon band did."

"But how could women and children escape from a Saxon village?" Ordella's disbelieving tone matched the expression on the other women's faces, and Endredi knew they were all wondering the same thing.

"It was not so difficult," Endredi said, letting some measure of scorn creep into her voice. "They did not think us capable of tricking them. They were wrong."

"Were you . . . were you—"

"Raped?" Ordella had the grace to blush at Endredi's frank response. "No. But not because a Saxon brute did not think of it. I hit him and got away. By that time, the others had freed themselves. We stole a ship and sailed home."

"All by yourselves?" Ordella asked incredulously.

"We were Viking women," she answered simply.

"Oh, of course. But you had no help in the village?"

Endredi hesitated, then answered, "No. However, that is in the past. I am determined to make a home here," she said sincerely, "to show that Vikings and Saxons can live together in peace. I have had enough of fighting and bloodshed."

Some of the women nodded approvingly. But not all. Endredi suppressed a sigh. It was not going to be easy, living here.

"By the blessed Virgin, it seems incredible. I'm glad you were not hurt. Naturally Ranulf and I have felt all along that since Bayard has married you, you must be rather special. We have decided we must put aside our old feelings about the Danes and help you."

"How kind."

"It is a pity that *some people* are not so easily swayed. Adelar, for example. I was shocked that Bayard had him show you about. I hope he said nothing to upset you?"

"No."

"Perhaps when he hears what happened to you, he will think of you in kinder ways—as we all do." Her gesture encompassed the weaving shed.

"I do not care what Adelar thinks of me," Endredi said firmly.

"That is just as well, my lady. Indeed, I would not trouble yourself about him. He is not important enough to concern Bayard's wife."

Endredi gave her a slightly bored, quizzical look. "Oh?"

"Considering that he will never amount to much."

Never amount to much? Ordella must be blind and stupid. Adelar could be anything, even a king.

"It is no secret his father is a feeble old man. Yet Adelar will not take over his land, as he should."

"Why not?" Endredi told herself this was of import to Bayard.

"I have no idea, unless it has something to do with his mother. She was the sister of Bayard's mother and an *adulteress*. His father could have been a great man, but for her. After her death, he never remarried. Who could blame him for wanting to avoid such a thing again? But Adelar will not hear a word said against his mother. There are rumors Kendric plans to will everything to an illegitimate son. Why not, I say, if his own son is going to ignore him and defend a woman like that? And then, of course, there's the question of Adelar's time among the Vikings."

"What of that?"

"Not that I'm saying anything against you, my lady, but I think we can guess how he might have been treated. He left home after staying with his poor father only five years after his return. He went first to one *burh,* then another, and finally here, to his cousin's."

"I am certain Bayard is pleased by his company."

"Of course. It is still a great pity that he hates Vikings. I doubt there is anything you could do or say to change his mind."

"I realize several people are not happy with my presence and I shall do my best to prove to them that as Bayard's wife, my first loyalty is to him and to his people. As for Adelar's opinion of me, he is but one man."

"He is Bayard's cousin."

"And I am Bayard's wife."

Chapter Five

In spite of himself, Adelar once again found his gaze drawn to Endredi, seated beside his cousin in the hall. He watched her delicate, graceful movements as she lifted her food to her lovely lips, admired the soft pink paleness of her smooth cheeks and sought to catch a glimpse of her beautiful eyes beneath her demurely lowered lids.

And all the while he cursed himself for a weak-willed fool.

For days he had avoided being anywhere near her, and his desire for her was not the only reason. He had no wish to reveal the shameful act of violence he had very nearly committed, even though it would have been for her defense. Why should he admit to it, if she held him in such contempt? Besides, she was married to his cousin. Let her believe the worst of him, as long as she made Bayard happy.

Which she apparently did.

He noticed that a strand of her hair had escaped the scarf over her head. She had lovely hair, darker than when he first knew her. How much he longed to touch it again! To kiss her again—but not as before. That had been the questioning, tentative kiss of a boy. He wanted to kiss her with a man's lips, and a man's passion.

But what would she do if he did? Slap his face? Denounce him to Bayard?

It did not matter, because it would never happen.

He rose to leave the hall, determined to get away from the sight of her. Then Bayard called out his name.

"Yes, my lord?" he replied, purposefully avoiding Endredi's eyes.

Bayard gestured for him to come forward. "I must see to the sentries. Endredi has no wish to retire, so I would ask that you play a game with her."

He saw the surprise on Endredi's face. "Perhaps someone else, my lord. I have no skill at games."

Bayard frowned slightly, and Adelar realized he should not have been so swift to demur. "If you command it, my lord, naturally I will be happy to play."

"Please, Bayard," Endredi said quietly, letting her hand rest gently on her husband's arm, "if he has no wish to linger, he need not."

Bayard patted her hand. "Oh, pay no heed to Adelar's charmless ways," he said. He darted a swift, sharp look at his cousin that was as good as an order. "He will enjoy it. It will do him good to think of something besides his belly and fighting and wenching. I shall return shortly." He stood up. "I warn you, though, Adelar. She is no novice. I have yet to win a game."

Once Bayard departed the hall, others followed suit. Ranulf and Ordella remained, ostensibly still eating. Endredi thought it was more likely that they were curious to see how Adelar acted with Bayard's wife.

Ylla and Gleda moved quickly to fold the cloth that covered the half of the table where the nobles sat. Some of the men helped take down the long trestle table and lay it against the wall. Ylla brought forward a smaller round table for the game. Endredi picked up a stool and set it down, then sat wordlessly, her gaze fastened on the board.

Godwin, who had watched all that had passed while he played his *fithele,* struck up a cheerful tune. Those who remained began to clap and sing the familiar words to the song.

Adelar strode over to a chest in the corner and took out the game pieces. He put them on the table before her and drew up a bench on the opposite side.

The music danced about them and it annoyed her, like the chattering of a bird when you wish to sleep.

"You do not have to stay," Endredi said when he took his seat, her voice as cold as the harsh winter's wind across an open field.

"Bayard wished it."

"What shall we play, then, my lord?" she inquired with great politeness.

"Do you know capture and escape, my lady?"

She glanced at him, wondering if there was a hidden reference to the way they had first met, but his face revealed nothing. "Very well," she said. "I shall be red."

"Then I will be black." He reached for his pieces, his hand momentarily brushing hers. She held her breath, felt the color rising to her cheeks, told herself it was nothing, nothing! It was the first time he had touched her in years. That was all. That was why that brief contact of flesh to flesh seemed to sear her skin like a red-hot coal.

With quick, sure, yet self-conscious movements, she set out her red pieces. The first person to get their chieftain across the squares of the board without getting captured would win. Ready to begin and determined to beat him, she glanced up at him.

To encounter that intense, dark gaze she knew so well. "You first, my lady."

She had no voice to refuse his offer. She slowly pushed her corner piece, a churl, forward.

With a swiftness that startled her, he shoved out his center piece. The chieftain. She chewed her lip. A direct attack was an unconventional move, but probably not for Adelar.

Her chieftain ventured forth. He countered with one of the thanes of the right side. She moved another churl. His chieftain, one space toward her. Direct for her chieftain. A foolish, bold move—or a trap.

Trapped—that was how she felt, with Ranulf and Ordella watching her. That was how she had felt ever since she had arrived. It was clear Adelar did not share her dread of these two, but he should. It was never wise to underestimate an enemy.

It would not be wise to underestimate Adelar if she was to win.

Adelar moved his pieces swiftly, as if he was already anticipating what she would do. She tried to concentrate on the game, wanting—needing—to win. But she couldn't. Her traitorous gaze strayed to his long slender fingers. Different now. Callused from weapons. Hard and older. A man's hands. His muscular forearms. He had always been good with a bow. Was he still, or had he abandoned it as a weapon for churls and foot soldiers, not nobles?

The music kept on, and the low murmur of other voices constantly reminded her that they were not alone. They would never be alone together again.

She moved her left-most thane to protect her chieftain. His was still alone, vulnerable in the center of the board. Adelar was no fool. Surely he would move other pieces to protect it. She must be wary of being drawn into an entrapped position.

A stray wisp of dark hair caressed his forehead, which furrowed with thought.

Who soothed his worried brow when his troubles were more than a game? Once, she had been the one he turned to for solace. Had another woman taken that place?

Godwin paused in his playing and saluted them with his drinking horn. "Although I have the greatest respect for Bayard's wisdom, I do not believe she will vanquish you, eh, Adelar?''

He darted a glance at her. "Only if I allow it."

She forced herself to smile at Godwin. "He has a fine opinion of himself, this bold fellow.''

"With some good reason, my lady," Godwin replied cheerfully before striking up another tune. "Yet he was ever a hasty fellow, and sometimes haste is a mistake.''

Endredi turned back to the game board. It was Adelar's move, but his hand hesitated. She glanced up at his face, and the intense expression in his eyes shocked her.

"I did not abandon you, Endredi," he whispered fervently in the Viking tongue. He was simply no longer able to keep silent in the face of her cold and distant green eyes. Before, he had thought he could ignore her harsh words. Here, now, he could not.

"I was there," he went on, his voice full of insistent passion. "Hiding in my father's hall. I would have killed him before I let him hurt you. I was ready to do it. My arrow was on the bowstring! But there was no need. You hit him and ran away.''

Her eyes widened, yet she did not speak.

"He told you that he thought you were thin, and that he liked thin women," he went on quickly. "He told you that all Viking women were little better than harlots and that living in your village had even corrupted Meradyce. You begged him to let you return to the barn with the other women. You kept backing away from him toward the hearth. He said he would let you go—" he paused and took a deep breath, the words agonizing to say "—when he was finished with you. Then he grabbed you by the shoulders. I raised my bow, preparing to shoot him, my own father! Ready to murder him to save you." Still she said nothing, the expression in her green eyes uncertain. "Did you never wonder how I came to be on the shore at the same time you were making your escape?"

Suddenly they both realized the hall had grown silent and that most of the people were looking at them.

Endredi made a brief smile in Godwin's direction and spoke in Saxon. "I should have been forewarned of his skill."

Adelar cleared his throat and shrugged, then addressed the others. "She is very clever. I see why Bayard has yet to beat her at this game."

He looked at her, and her gaze faltered, then fell. "Then why did you never come back to me?" she whispered. The anguish in her voice pained him, and yet it thrilled him, too. She had *not* forgotten him, or their feelings for each other.

"I wanted to come back for you, Endredi, very much. But—"

"But?"

"I was afraid."

"Of what? The few villagers your father did not slaughter? Or your father's rage if he found out?"

"Oh, no," he answered, his gaze flicking to her face. "It was never my father I feared." He took a deep breath. "I was afraid of you."

"Me?"

"I was afraid that I had misjudged your feelings for me. I was afraid you would hate me because I was my father's son, especially after what he tried to do to you in his hall." He looked at her steadily. "I was afraid you would not wait for me. And you did not."

"What was I to do? Wait and wait for a boy who had apparently forgotten me? I *did* wait, a very long time, but there was nothing. Not a message, not one word."

"I could not sail into a Viking village," he protested.

"You could have found a way, Adelar." Again he saw the anguish in her tear-filled eyes and heard the sorrow in her voice. "If you truly cared for me, you could have found a way."

"She is going to take all your churls." Bayard's hearty voice cut through the air.

Startled, Endredi gasped, then stared at the board. She had forgotten the existence of everyone except Adelar.

"No, she is not," Adelar replied. With great effort he kept his voice calm. Then he finished his move, capturing her chieftain.

Bayard put his hand upon Endredi's shoulder. She moved quickly, standing so that his hand fell away. She stared at the rushes on the floor and summoned the strength to show nothing on her face when he said,

"Come, Endredi, the hour grows late. Sleep well, Adelar."

"Sleep well, my lord," Adelar answered coolly.

She let Bayard lead her from the hall, aware of his hand upon her arm, his nearness in the dark, and Adelar's distance. He might as well have been on the moon. It would be better if he were.

"Were you crying?" Bayard said quietly.

"I do not like to lose," she answered, which was the truth, although it had nothing to do with her true state of mind.

The full meaning of Adelar's words was finding its way past the carefully constructed barriers about her heart. He had been in his father's hall that terrible night, prepared to kill to save her!

She should never have doubted him. She should have kept faith in their feelings for each other. Her heart soared, then fell to earth like a lump of clay. Because his revelation, and her answering emotions, had come too late.

"I am happy to hear you are loath to lose, even though it be only a game," Bayard said. "So am I. And so is Adelar. I am also pleased that you allowed him to win."

"I did not let him win."

He chuckled softly. "I saw your final moves. They were so bad, a child could have defeated you. Yet you seemed truly distraught."

"I thought it was better to act the way men expect women to act when they are losing. I . . . there are so many here who do not like me, and I know Adelar is important to you."

"Yes, he is. But I do not fear Adelar's disapproval."

"Ranulf's?"

Bayard chuckled again, but this time with scorn more than true gaiety. He held open the door to the bower and she entered, realizing at once that something was not right.

"Helmi? Why is it so cold here?" she demanded.

Helmi stood up, setting aside the gown she had been mending. "Because that stupid Saxon slave hasn't brought any coal for the braziers yet."

Bayard followed Endredi inside, but he didn't say anything. He simply went to the small table and poured himself some ale.

"You could not fetch it?" Endredi asked calmly.

Helmi glanced from her mistress to Bayard and back again, her annoyance changed to uncertainty. "That is a job for slaves," she answered.

"Or a servant," Endredi countered. "I suggest you get some at once."

At that moment, Ylla appeared at the door, a basket of coal on her arm. She hesitated, her eyes wide with fear when she encountered Helmi's hostile gaze. Endredi stepped forward and took the coal. "You may go," she said, and the girl scurried off like a terrified mouse. Endredi turned to Helmi. "You, too."

"But, my lady, I should make up the fire—"

"Leave us."

Helmi frowned, but she did as she was told.

Bayard watched as Endredi placed the coals in the brazier on a bed of tinder that Helmi had prepared. Using a flint, she struck a spark and made the fire. "You do that well," he commented.

"I am not used to servants," she confessed. "In truth, I wish Helmi was not here."

"I will send her back, if that would please you."

"That will not be necessary."

"But if she troubles you..."

"It is not Helmi's fault."

"I could send Helmi home and you could have Ylla for your servant."

"She is a slave."

"I will make her free, if you would like it."

Why must he be so kind to her?

"They would think Helmi has offended us, and perhaps she would suffer for it."

"As you wish. But what of Ylla?"

Endredi thought a moment. "Helmi is not young. She should have someone to help her. Ylla seems a clever girl and she could learn much from Helmi if she was given the chance to learn."

"It shall be as you wish."

Endredi smiled at him, the first genuine smile she had given him. "Thank you." She suddenly realized that he looked fatigued and perhaps even ill. She went toward him. "What is it, Bayard? Are you sick?"

He grinned, and because of her concern for him, this time she did not note the resemblance to Adelar. "It is nothing. I am merely tired."

She sat on the stool beside him. "Perhaps I can help you, Bayard. I have been taught healing."

"I am only tired."

"And troubled? Is it Dagfinn?"

"He is one. You know him—is he to be trusted?"

"No."

He looked at her with some surprise. "No? Just like that? And you are so sure?"

"He can be trusted to be true to a bargain as long as the bargain continues to be in his favor. While the Saxons of Wessex are strong, he will abide by his word. But if the Danes show sign of defeating the Saxons and their allies, that will surely change."

"You give me hope and despair at the same time."

"I give you the truth. There is one other thing I would tell you, Bayard. My father is a rich and powerful Viking in the land across the sea. Dagfinn would not be eager to attack his daughter's home, so I do not believe he would unless he was very sure of success."

"Then I must ensure that Dagfinn has no such hopes."

"An attack does not always come from without. What of your own men? What of Ranulf?"

"Ranulf is a fool. Unfortunately, he is also my nearest blood kin. And because he has much wealth, he has many friends."

"Send him back to his own land."

"It is not so simple. How can I force him to go while I let Adelar stay?"

"Does Adelar have land, then?"

"Alfred decreed that a man need only serve his lord as a soldier in the *fyrd* for half of the year. Adelar lingers because he has no wish to see his father. I agree because I enjoy having one truly loyal person near me."

Endredi rose slowly and took his hands in hers. Adelar could never be hers. Never. Bayard deserved a loyal wife. "I have sworn my loyalty to you, Bayard."

He gave her a strange look. "Have you?"

"Yes." She bent and kissed him, moving her mouth over his in a slow, sensuous movement.

Bayard rose and his arms encircled her. Strong arms, holding her as she had so often dreamed....

Bayard drew back and smiled warmly. "I believe you, Endredi."

She fought the tears that came to her eyes and smiled tremulously. "That pleases me so much, my lord." She leaned into him, determined to fulfil her oath. Determined to forget.

He blew out the feeble flame of the nearby candles before pressing hot kisses to her cheeks and neck. His fingers undid the brooches at her shoulders, and her tunic slid to the floor. With a low growl of desire, Bayard lifted her in his arms and carried her to their bed.

"I want to be a good wife to you," she whispered in the darkness.

"You are." She felt him untying the drawstring of her shift.

"I want to please you."

His hand reached into the loosened garment. "You do."

He slipped the shift from her shoulders, and his hand continued its slow exploration. "I want you to have children."

"Yes," she replied honestly. Yes, let her do her duty.

He caressed her body skillfully, his hands sure. He stroked her breasts, her stomach, her thighs. She did not fight the arousal he caused, but let him take her beyond her fears and worries to some other place composed of sensation and lust. His tongue swirled over her breasts, teasing the rigid peaks until she moaned and arched with desire. Responding, wanting, she grabbed his broad shoulders and wrapped her legs about him. *This* man was her husband. This man alone had the right to do this with her. It would be different with Bayard. It must be.

But when he entered her, her blood throbbed with the rhythm of another man's name.

Adelar, Adelar, Adelar...

"I think Bayard's a lovesick fool," Ordella said decisively as she disrobed.

Lying in the bed, Ranulf gave his wife a disgruntled frown. "I don't see anything to suspect. Bayard's happy, she seems loyal. And she's *quiet*."

Ordella's expression turned even more spiteful at his last word, which was so obviously aimed at her. "Yes, she *seems* loyal. For now. Who's to say what might happen if the Danes attack?"

"You've been with her more than I have. What do *you* think?"

"I think she's very clever and very good at hiding her true thoughts."

"In other words, you couldn't find out anything."

"Yes, I did. She was taken prisoner by Saxons once. She hates us as much as we hate the Danes."

"Then why would she marry one?"

"Because Dagfinn wanted the alliance, fool. She's only a woman—what say would she have? But maybe she's harboring a secret grudge against us all. Maybe she's conspiring to have us murdered in the night. She could be up to any number of things."

"Bayard does not share your fears."

"Maybe Bayard does not know of her hatred. She is a sly creature, Ranulf. It could be that he has no idea of her true feelings."

Ranulf continued to look at his wife skeptically. "Has she traveled outside the *burh*?"

"Yes."

"Alone?"

"No. I was with her."

"Then how is she arranging this murderous attack, Ordella? Witchcraft?"

"It could be. I don't believe she's a Christian, for all Dagfinn said."

"She goes to Mass."

"That means nothing. She could be using some Viking magic." Seeing that Ranulf was still dismissive of her concerns, she said, "And there is something not right between Endredi and Adelar."

"Something? What 'something'?"

With all the frustration she felt, Ordella said, "I don't know exactly!"

"Then maybe you're imagining that, too. Or maybe Endredi's cast a spell on him."

"I would not be so quick to make a jest of such a thing. He acts like a man enchanted. You saw him in the hall tonight. He could hardly take his eyes from her."

"They were just playing a game. A game Bayard *ordered* him to play."

"They were in very earnest conversation for another man's wife and a man ordered to play. If only I could understand the Viking language!"

"They were probably discussing the game, nothing more."

Ordella gave him another disgusted look. "He is the comeliest man in Wessex, barring Bayard—and you, of course. Maybe she was talking about another kind of game entirely."

"Didn't you see her face? He upset her. He *is* a Saxon, after all, and you say she hates us. Possibly she is not flattered by his attention. Maybe she thinks someone will start rumors." He looked pointedly at Ordella. "It could be she finds his attention suspicious. Or even repulsive. And aren't you forgetting that Adelar, of all men, would never try to seduce Bayard's wife?''

"But she does not know that."

Weary of trying to follow the currents of Ordella's mind, Ranulf muttered, "How much better for us all if Adelar would go!"

"That is most unlikely. Where else would he go, especially since Bayard treats him so well? If only there was a way to be rid of both of them!" Naked now, Ordella slipped her thin body under the bedclothes. Ranulf made no move to touch her, but let himself drift toward sleep.

"I have it!" Ordella exclaimed suddenly.

"What?" Ranulf demanded with a start.

"If Endredi bears Bayard a son, we will get nothing. If Adelar remains close to Bayard, we may get nothing. Supposing Adelar *were* to seduce Bayard's wife and they were found out, they would both cease to trouble us. And Bayard would be so ashamed, he would take himself to a monastery!"

Scowling, Ranulf twisted to confront his wife in the darkness of the bower. "We cannot force Adelar and Endredi to commit adultery. And if we accuse Adelar and the woman and it is not true, we could have our tongues cut out for slander."

"Who speaks of force?"

"What are you talking about?"

"We must find a way to encourage them, that's all. Adelar is handsome. She must be lonely. Bayard keeps making them spend time together, probably hoping to persuade Adelar to lose his prejudice against Vikings. But he may be encouraging more than that!''

"Adelar is completely loyal to Bayard."

"Perhaps. That loyalty has never been tested, not really. Who knows what Adelar might do if he thought no one suspected? If he believed himself to be safe? I tell you, Ranulf," she said, growing more excited at the possibilities, "I saw the way he looked at her tonight. It is not so farfetched."

Ranulf nodded slowly. "You are a clever woman, Ordella. You may be right. If this comes about, no one will stand in my way."

"*Our* way." Ordella ran her fingers along Ranulf's body, letting the tips brush ever so lightly over his nipples.

Aroused herself, she pushed her hips against his body, a small smile playing about her lips as she thought of the ease with which she manipulated him. And certain that any woman would be easy prey for Adelar, if he wanted her.

The only question was, could they make Adelar want Bayard's wife?

Chapter Six

Bayard rode slowly behind the other men as they moved through the forest. Up ahead, he could hear Ranulf trying to tell Baldric how to deploy the hounds for the hunt.

Because no one was nearby, Bayard allowed the full measure of his dislike for Ranulf to show on his face. His nephew was a fool. Baldric knew more about dogs than Ranulf ever would, or could.

Worse, Ranulf was a greedy fool who did not even have the slightest notion of masking that greed effectively. Indeed, he was so covetous of Bayard's lands and goods he put up with innumerable insults that would have sent a more perceptive and less avaricious man away long ago.

Unfortunately, Ranulf did not leave, not even when Bayard had so pointedly put Adelar's advice and company above Ranulf's.

Bayard's gaze traveled to Adelar, a short way ahead. His cousin rode as he always did, although this was but a hunt, with his back straight and his head ever moving, seeking anything out of place.

Adelar was everything a warrior should be, and would be a fine leader, too, if only he would have confidence in himself. He was brave but not foolhardy, and could be subtle in his wisdom.

Bayard silently cursed Adelar's father again. Kendric had poisoned Adelar's boyhood and youth, and threatened to spoil the rest of his son's life, as well. Adelar thought he was tainted because of his father's sins. Despite Bayard's trust, Adelar continued to believe that he bore dishonor.

Bayard sighed deeply. Perhaps that was just as well, if Adelar was to play the part in his plans that Bayard intended. A man who considered himself totally honorable would never agree to what Bayard had to ask.

However, his plan also depended on Endredi's opinion of the Saxon warrior. Again he wondered what had happened during the game between Endredi and Adelar. She had been truly upset, despite her denials. Adelar, too, had been disturbed, more disturbed than Bayard had ever seen him.

It was a good sign that they felt something for each other, but he didn't want it to be anger or suspicion or contempt. It was important that his wife and his cousin at least *like* each other, or his plan would never work.

Endredi was a quiet, clever woman. That should have made a favorable impression on Adelar. She was no beauty, yet there was a serenity about her that was most appealing. She handled the servants well and was making the people accept her as his wife.

Perhaps he should ignore Endredi a little. Make Adelar pity her. That might draw them together. Or perhaps Adelar would think Endredi was responsible for her husband's disinterest. Yet surely even Adelar could see that Endredi would make almost any thane the perfect wife.

As for what Endredi thought, that would be harder to gauge. She was able to keep her feelings well hidden.

Nonetheless, Adelar was a handsome man and a good one. And always rather aloof. She must find him an object of some curiosity, if nothing else.

Maybe the best way to proceed was as he had been, simply forcing them to spend time in each other's company. Adelar would surely come to see Endredi's merits, and Endredi would come to recognize Adelar's loneliness. That would appeal to her kind heart.

His brow furrowed in concentration. He remembered that Endredi had said she wanted to learn to ride. Apparently the Vikings did not teach their women as a matter of course, and Endredi's father had been somewhat protective of his daughter. Bayard opened his mouth, prepared to order Adelar to instruct his wife, when he caught sight of Ranulf.

He had been even harder on Ranulf than usual lately, and it might be better to be a little more circumspect in his treatment of his nephew, in case his plan did not work.

Indeed, Adelar felt so much contempt for Ranulf, surely he would think it would be a terrible fate to have to spend much time in the man's company. That would make him have some sympathy for Endredi.

Bayard summoned Ranulf to his side and ordered him to show his wife how to ride, as soon as she was ready to learn.

"I shall be honored," Ranulf gushed, obviously only too happy to have this small mark of a return to favor. "I shall begin this very afternoon, if she is willing."

"Good," Bayard said, very aware that Adelar had halted his mount to listen to the two men. He drew closer to Bayard as Ranulf rode ahead, a beaming smile on his lean face.

"Ranulf?" he questioned.

"I thought it best not to give Ranulf any more cause for annoyance," Bayard replied, "at least for the moment."

He grinned at his cousin, who nodded, his expression grim. "I suppose Endredi will understand that, even if she does not relish Ranulf for a teacher," Adelar remarked.

"Oh? Why do you think she will not?"

"It was . . . something she said during the game."

"Something?"

"She does not like him. She sees his covetous nature."

"As do I. But I am surprised she spoke of him to you. She is not one to share her thoughts."

"She warned me that it was unwise of me to make my dislike so obvious."

"Do you think she is right?"

Adelar raised an eyebrow questioningly. "Ranulf knows how I feel. There would be no point to feign affection."

"However, Cousin, I must agree with Endredi. Things may change rapidly, Adelar, if we go to battle. I have no desire to leave my lands to Ranulf, but there may be no help for it, so perhaps a little more respect might be warranted. Come, don't look so angry. I think I would do better to appease Ranulf somewhat myself," he finished ruefully. "That is why I asked him to teach Endredi. Or would you rather have that task?"

"No."

"There—then I made a good decision. Tell me, Adelar, how does Endredi seem to you?"

"I don't know what you mean."

"Would you say she is happy?"

"I have no idea. What do you think? She's your wife."

"I think she is somewhat homesick. I wish you would spend more time with her."

Adelar frowned, and Bayard wondered if he had said too much. "Well, when you can. I'm sure Endredi will come to feel at home here soon enough." He paused and heard the baying of the hounds. "Baldric's loosed the dogs. Let us hunt and hope Ranulf gets lost again."

"I won't do it!" Ranulf glared at Ordella, who stood in their bower with her hands on her hips and her shoulders thrust forward.

"Don't be a fool, Ranulf!" she said angrily. "This is precisely the opportunity we were speaking of. You simply ask Adelar to take your place. Tell him you hurt your foot hunting."

"This is the first time in days that Bayard has given me any sign of his favor, and you expect me to give it away?"

"Are you forgetting that we have more to aim for than Bayard's favor? Besides, what kind of task is this that he assigns you? There is no honor befitting your rank in being a riding master."

"But he *asked* me," Ranulf whined like a thwarted child.

"Are you a thane or a servant?" Ordella demanded.

One of their slaves, carrying fresh rushes, appeared at the entrance to their bower.

"Get out, oaf!" Ordella ordered harshly.

"You cannot speak to me that way!" Ranulf said.

"I wasn't speaking to you. It was Olrith."

Nonetheless, Ranulf continued to pout. "Bayard asked me," he reiterated.

"I tell you, Bayard insults you with this request, although I believe you acted wisely," Ordella lied. "You kindly agreed to do this thing so obviously beneath you, until you were injured." She hesitated. "You were alone at some point on the hunt, were you not, so that no one will question your excuse?"

"Yes. They went into that thicket again and I got separated from the rest of them."

In other words, he had gotten lost, Ordella thought with disgust. "Now you must regretfully ask Adelar to take your place."

Ranulf sighed wearily. "Very well, I will do as you say."

Adelar watched Ranulf limp away. Simpleton! He had finally gotten a chance to be of service to Bayard, and he had injured himself. At least Ranulf might not be so quick to demand responsibilities for a little while.

Adelar turned and walked toward the stable, telling himself he had agreed to take Ranulf's place out of concern for Endredi. She did not like Bayard's cousin and would surely welcome any replacement. Now that she knew he had not deserted her, it pleased him to think they could be friends. Friends, and nothing more.

He looked about the *burh*. It was a fine, warm day. The scent of the damp earth drifted to him on a slight breeze from the newly plowed fields. The growing grass added its own particular perfume to the air. When he entered the dim stables, a shaft of sunlight illuminated the bits of chaff and straw floating there. A horse whinnied, and Adelar went toward the mare, a gentle animal he thought would be perfect for Endredi.

He stroked the beast's smooth head and whispered soft words of praise.

"Where is Ranulf?"

He spun around to see Endredi standing inside the door, her brow furrowed. "He hurt himself and regrets that he will be unable to give you a lesson. He asked me to take his place."

Adelar smiled. Not the sardonic grin he gave the others, but the smile Endredi remembered. Happiness diffused through her, radiating from the secret place in her heart that was his alone.

But she must not allow such feelings. They were wrong. Sinful and shameful when she was married to another. Yet knowing that he had been prepared to kill Kendric to protect her had made her struggle to subdue her feelings all the more difficult.

Even when he was not before her, she could not rid herself of thoughts of Adelar. She could not look at Bayard without thinking that he stood between herself and the man she truly wanted. She feared she might be tempted to speak of her confused emotions to Adelar, or even Helmi, rather than keep them bottled up inside her.

Adelar was at this *burh* because he was his cousin's trusted friend, and so he would surely remain here. She must learn to deal with his presence.

"If you would rather have another teacher," he said quietly, coming toward her, "I will find you one."

She knew the best course was to stay away from him, and yet at this moment she could not find it in her heart to tell Adelar to leave the stable. She shook her head wordlessly and watched while he saddled two horses, trying not to stare at his bare, muscular arms or his long, lean legs encased in breeches that hugged his thighs or the way his hair brushed against his broad shoulders.

At last he finished and led the way to the meadow.

"Shall we begin?" he said, his voice matter-of-fact, as if she were anybody. Or nobody.

Good. It would help her treat him as if he were anybody, or nobody. "Yes."

"Put your foot in my hand and I shall boost you onto the horse. Grab hold there—" he pointed at the wide stiff part at the front of the saddle "—and swing your leg over the horse."

He linked his hands and waited expectantly.

She paused uncertainly. "Where...how...?"

"You can put your hands on my shoulders first to steady yourself."

She did, aware at once of the muscles beneath his tunic and her own rapidly beating heart. When he raised his hands, she moved her leg and she was in the saddle, uncomfortably high, she thought. At least the horse stood still.

Effortlessly and with catlike grace he swung onto his own mount beside her. "Now take your reins in your hands and hold them like this."

He demonstrated, and she did her best to follow his example. "Not so tight," he admonished. "You grip with your knees."

She glanced at his legs and taut muscles. Swallowing hard, she tried to concentrate on the reins.

"That's better. Let's try a walk. Just lift the reins a little higher, and the mare will understand."

She did, and they walked slowly around the field. It took some time before she felt that she wasn't about to slip off, or that her insides would never recover from the jostling.

Adelar halted his horse and began to instruct her in the way to signal a change of direction, taking hold of her hands to better teach her.

His touch was firm and his skin rough against hers, yet he was gentle, too. She felt the heat of a blush flooding her face, but she did not wish him to stop. She wanted to take his hand and press it to her lips.

When he was finished, he let go of her, then suddenly looked at her intently. "Bayard agrees that I should treat Ranulf with more respect. He appreciates your wisdom."

"That pleases me," she answered softly, her eyes downcast.

"You are making him happy, Endredi. He is fortunate to have you for his wife."

She shifted uncomfortably. The mare mistook her action for a signal to gallop. Endredi's shriek filled the air as the mare made straight for the brambles at the edge of the nearby wood.

Mercifully, the mare halted before colliding with the thorny bushes. Endredi clutched the saddle and drew in a deep shuddering breath as she realized that Adelar was beside her.

"Are you hurt?" he asked, dismounting quickly and coming to her side.

"No. However, I think the lesson should cease for the present," she replied shakily.

He nodded and reached up to help her dismount. "I don't know what you did, but the mare thought you wanted to go fast. Are you certain you are all right?"

"Yes." She placed her hands on his strong forearms and slid from the saddle. He was close, so close that she could almost count each dark eyelash above his earnest eyes and feel the beating of his pulse within her own body.

"Good." He smiled at her warmly, with affection and relief. She reddened, but couldn't take her gaze from him.

Suddenly his expression changed and he pulled her into a break in the bushes, away from the meadow. "Endredi," he said softly.

"Adelar," she whispered. She felt as if she was treading on the thin ice of the river in winter and it had started to give way.

"Are you truly happy with Bayard?"

She prepared to speak, ready to lie again. Ready to remind him that she was wed to another. Ready to shut the gate of her prison.

But the look in his dark eyes! The longing, the desire—everything answered the feelings in her own heart, and she could only speak the truth. "I am as happy as I can ever be."

"I am wretched, always seeing you and never being near you. Never being able to touch you, to kiss you..."

He bent his head toward hers, and she pulled away, the bonds of honor strong. "I am the wife of another. Please, say no more."

He took her gently in his arms and held her, not so much as a lover but as a comforter who sought to share her pain. Who perhaps already did. She lay her face against his chest and allowed herself to feel his strength and warmth surrounding her.

"I am miserable, Endredi," he said huskily. "Every moment I see you with Bayard fills me with pain."

"There is nothing we can do."

"Isn't there?" He looked into her eyes, his own asking her a question that she had not dared to contemplate. Now, here, alone with him, it did not seem so wrong to give in to her passion. To be with him. To share their love and their desires.

There was a movement in the trees nearby. Startled, she looked over Adelar's shoulder, peering into the woods. She stepped away from him briskly. "Get away from me," she said loudly. "I shall tell Bayard what you sought to do."

His face filled with shock and surprise.

"It is a good thing no one saw you," she went on. "I shall keep this secret, because of Bayard's regard for you. But I tell you this, Adelar, try to seduce me again, and I shall certainly tell my husband."

With that, she marched away, leaving him staring after her.

"Adelar, what in God's name did you think you were doing? Bayard would kill you if he knew!"

Adelar pivoted at Godwin's words. "How long have you been spying on me?"

"Spying? I was doing nothing of the kind. I was simply walking through the woods trying to make up a song about larks and nightingales and instead I find you trying to defile Bayard's wife!" Godwin frowned with dismay as he approached. "I thought better of you than that."

Adelar tried not to look overly concerned or watch Endredi's hasty departure. "Her horse bolted and she was frightened. I was only comforting her. She misunderstood."

Godwin's expression grew skeptical, and he shifted the cloak he carried from one hand to the other. "Comforting, Adelar? Who do you think you speak to? I know you too well. You should be thankful it was I who saw you, and not Ranulf."

"Ranulf was supposed to be instructing her, but he hurt his foot." Adelar shrugged. "I admit it was not a wise thing to do. Consider me warned—although you saw her response."

"Yes. You should also be grateful she will say nothing to Bayard. If he thought you were doing anything other than comforting, he would never forgive you. Come, I will walk back with you."

Adelar picked up the reins of the waiting horses. In the distance he could see Endredi disappearing inside the gate of the *burh*.

Godwin fell into step beside him. "She might decide to tell Bayard, after all," he said thoughtfully.

"I do not think so."

Godwin halted. "Did she see me? Were you really trying to seduce her? Were you *succeeding?* Is that why she stopped?" he demanded suspiciously.

"She stopped because she does not find *me* fascinating."

"Then she is truly a most remarkable, perceptive woman, which is a good thing, I must say."

"For the last time, Godwin, I was not trying to seduce Bayard's wife." He had been swept away by his own burning need and her answering response. He knew full well what might have happened then, but it would not have been a seduction.

It would have been a fulfillment of all his hopes and dreams.

Yet if Endredi had not noticed Godwin, or had it been anyone else, they would be in grave danger. He dare not put her in such a situation again.

There was but one way to make sure he did not give in to the overpowering temptation to be with her, and he would take it. For her sake, and for his.

Chapter Seven

Adelar adjusted the strap of the pack behind his saddle in the early morning light that made its way through the chinks in the stable walls. His baggage contained little save his weapons, his *byrnie,* made of small, interwoven iron rings, and some articles of clothing.

In the wood beyond the *burh,* a lark greeted the dawn. The boys whose duties were to feed, water and clean the stables still slumbered, while around him, horses stamped and shuffled in the straw.

Whistling quietly in imitation of the bird, Godwin stood nearby, his arms crossed and leaning his weight against a support post. "What are you doing?"

"What brings you to the stable this early in the day? Where is Gleda?"

"Sleeping elsewhere. It seems we have both tired of the other's charms."

"Ah. So you were but lonely and thought to amuse the animals with your wit?"

"I was but curious, when I saw you leaving the hall with that bundle beneath your arm. Has Bayard sent you elsewhere to convey a message?"

"I am leaving."

"I can see that, obviously. Where do you go, and why?"

"You would make a fine interrogator, Godwin. I believe you should leave off being a gleeman and offer for such a post."

"Does Bayard send you on a secret journey?" The gleeman's eyes glimmered with interest.

"No. I have spent more than the necessary time in the *fyrd*. I wish to go."

"You have given no hint that you are dissatisfied. And others may think you must have a good reason for leaving so suddenly. Do you?"

Adelar paused to give the gleeman a stern look that would have been worthy of Father Derrick. "What are you suggesting?"

"Bayard's wife—is she the reason you are going?"

"No."

"Are you worried she will cause a rift between you and Bayard?"

"No."

"Then why *are* you leaving? Your time in the *fyrd* was ended long ago, and you never hinted at leaving before."

"Perhaps I am tired of your endless chatter."

"You like my endless chatter. Now, if you said you were sick of Ranulf's ugly face, to that I could give credence. Or is it another woman?"

"Why is it you always attribute everything I do to women?"

"Because so many of them like you. And you, I thought, liked them."

"It is not a woman," Adelar lied.

"You are blushing like a boy."

"It is not a woman."

"Very well, I believe you. But maybe you should give that as your reason to Bayard. Surely it is better to give some excuse other than simply your time is ended, as if you only just discovered a year had passed."

Adelar scowled, but he supposed Godwin was right that he should give some explanation to Bayard, just as he was right to leave before anyone suspected the feelings he harbored for the wife of his lord were not what they should be. He had been a fool, deluding himself into believing he could mask his feelings from them all, and from himself. Yet it had taken only one moment alone with Endredi to call forth all the passion he felt.

"And if you don't give some creditable explanation, others may wonder if you have learned something to turn you against Bayard. They might decide to desert Bayard, too. Then Cynath will hear of it. How will it be for Bayard if Cynath is angry?

"Bayard may feel betrayed. After all, he has treated you better than Ranulf, to his peril, too. And think, Adelar, that there will be no one to give him wise counsel. Everyone knows that all Ranulf thinks about are his own interests.''

"Bayard has his wife to give him counsel.''

"She is but a woman. How wise can her counsel be, unless he asks her of clothes and jewelry?''

"Other men will come to his hall. Bayard is a fine lord, as Cynath knows. You are seeing troubles that will not come to pass.''

"Perhaps leaving so soon after the wedding will make Bayard wonder at the wisdom of his choice. He seems happy now, but maybe he will blame his wife for your going.''

Adelar faced Godwin. "Unlike some, I do not believe Bayard would think any such stupid thing.''

"Will you return to your father's *burh*?''

"I seem to recall telling you that I would sooner die than be in the same place as he.''

"Then where?''

"Anywhere a man can earn a living fighting. Or perhaps I feel the need for a religious pilgrimage. Maybe I will visit Rome.''

"You? A religious pilgrimage?'' Godwin scoffed. "That would last until you came upon a comely wench.''

"So what would be wrong with that?'' Adelar asked sardonically.

"It will not ease your pain,'' Godwin said, his usually jovial voice suddenly serious.

Adelar glanced at his friend. "What pain?''

"I don't know. Something from your past. Is it because Bayard's wife is a Viking?"

"I say again, Godwin, Endredi has nothing to do with my decision."

"It seems there is nothing I can say to change your mind. Gleda will miss you."

"You can console her."

"And Ylla. She'll cry herself to sleep when you are gone."

"Now that Bayard has set her free, I think she will have other things to think about."

The sound of horses' hooves and the jingle of harness interrupted them. The two men looked at each other. "Bayard expects no visitors," Adelar said shortly. They rushed to the door of the stable.

"They're from Cynath," Godwin said, clearly awed as he stared at the standard one of the mounted men carried. They rode very fine horses, and several well-bred hounds ran beside them.

"I know that fellow," Adelar said, nodding toward a well-dressed, black-haired man bearing ornate weapons. "He's Dunstan."

"Cynath's eldest son?"

"Yes."

"No wonder he looks as if he thinks he should be the *Britwalda*. What an ass!"

"His father has been in the Witan for over twenty years, and he is Bayard's overlord, so you had best take care what you say about Dunstan."

"I hope I will have little to do with him other than keep a smile on his fat face. He could use that belly of his as a weapon."

"Godwin, take care. He may be plump, but he is quite a fighter. I've seen him. I would hate to see you run through."

"Thank you for your kind words, my lord. But you will not be here to see it if he does."

Dunstan leapt from his horse and tossed his reins in the direction of one of Bayard's men.

Adelar watched as the retinue continued to arrive. "It must be important business, if Dunstan comes, and with so many men," he said thoughtfully. "Perhaps I should delay my departure until we know what it is that brings him here, and so early in the day."

If Bayard was concerned about Dunstan's presence, he was not showing it, Adelar realized when he entered the hall. Most of the warriors and thanes were still inside finishing the first meal of the day. Father Derrick, who no doubt believed his presence warranted at any meeting of importance, sat close to Bayard's right.

Endredi was not there.

Adelar watched as Bayard greeted Dunstan with the correct amount of protocol and deference, then offered him a seat to his right and invited him to eat.

Adelar silently took a place below the salt, not wanting to draw attention to himself. He was curious to know what had brought Dunstan, and that was all.

Then he would go. Godwin sat beside him and reached for some boiled meat.

Duff, obviously nonplussed by the unexpected arrival of this important visitor, rushed about giving sharp orders to the rest of the servants, who seemed to be somewhat dazzled. Gleda, especially, moved as if she was wading through water.

Bayard didn't look troubled, and Adelar wondered if he had known Dunstan would be arriving. As he watched the two, Bayard happened to glance in his direction. "Adelar!" he called out. "I have been wondering at your absence. You should not be skulking there! Come, join us."

Reluctantly, Adelar did, because although Bayard's tone was friendly, there was a reprimand in it, too. He made a place for himself on the far side of Ranulf, who would not have yielded to even an angel if one had tried to sit between Bayard and him.

"What I have to say is only for your most trusted men," Dunstan announced without preamble when the meal was nearly over.

Bayard nodded, apparently unoffended by the man's officious tone. "Adelar," he said, "Father Derrick and Ranulf, stay." He named a few of his other warriors. "The rest, outside. Gleda, fetch my wife."

There were a few mumbles of discontent from those not chosen, particularly when it became obvious that Dunstan's retinue had no intention of leaving. Nonetheless, Bayard's men slowly filed out of the hall.

"So, it is true. You are wed," Dunstan said with no attempt to hide his displeasure.

"Yes," Bayard replied, a smile on his lips. "A man cannot live alone forever."

"A man is never alone, if he trusts in God," Father Derrick intoned. Dunstan darted a startled glance in the holy man's direction.

"Very true, Father," Bayard said calmly.

"Is it also true, the other rumor we have heard—since you did not request my father's permission to make this marriage—that she is a Dane?"

"Cynath has never found it necessary to interfere in Bayard's decisions. There was no need to trouble him with this one, either," Adelar said.

Dunstan eyed him coldly. "I do not talk to you, Kendric's son." He turned back to speak to Bayard, but fell silent when Endredi came into the hall.

Adelar's breath caught in his throat when she hesitated at the sight of the visitors. Her green eyes seemed to glitter in the flame of the torches. Her pale smooth cheeks grew slightly pink, and her lips parted as if about to ask a question. He knew she would not, though. She would stay silent and listen . . . well.

When she drew near, his eyes roved over her thick, red-gold hair, which was covered by a thin scarf of the finest silk he had ever seen. The rest of her garments fell about her body with a fluidity that bespoke quality.

Dunstan was surveying her, too, but with none of the deference due a noblewoman and the wife of his father's ally. He looked at her as if she was nothing more than a serving wench. Or a slave. "This is the woman?" he asked insolently.

Endredi's face reddened and she bowed her head. It was all Adelar could do to remain silent. Even Father Derrick seemed taken aback at the conspicuous slight to a woman who was, after all, wedded to a thane.

"This is my wife, Endredi." Bayard also was clearly affronted by Dunstan's manner, for his tone was reproving as he rose and escorted Endredi to sit beside him.

"What I have to say is not for a woman's ears."

"Whatever you have to say, you may say in front of my wife."

Bayard was worthy of her, Adelar thought, and she of him. What did *he* have to offer her? No land, no wealth.

Nothing but his heart.

She deserved more. And Bayard deserved the kind of wife Endredi would be.

"I will not speak of the king's business with a Dane in the hall."

Adelar flushed hotly, anger flying through his body at the rebuff, although had it been any other Dane, he would have been the first to agree. However, Dunstan spoke thus of Endredi.

But it was not his place to defend her. Not his place.

"I am sure that it was not your intention to cast doubt upon my wisdom," Bayard said coolly, "for of course an insult to my wife is an insult to me."

"You are playing a dangerous game, Bayard," Dunstan warned.

"And an insult is anything but a jest, Dunstan. My wife will stay, or I will go."

"My father—"

"*Your father* knows he has my devotion and he always will have. *Your father* knows I am one of the king's *burhwares* because my loyalty is without question. *Your father* knows that I have been leading men for him since you were a babe at your mother's breast. *Your father* would not take kindly to an insult made to me, either."

Endredi stood up. "Bayard, I thank you for your faith in me. Nevertheless, if my presence is not welcome, I will return to our bower."

Dunstan stared at her, slack-jawed.

"Are you so surprised I speak your language, sir? I am part Saxon myself, but I see that piece of gossip did not reach you. Nonetheless—" she turned to Bayard "—I have no wish to remain where my presence is cause for disagreement."

Her head held high, she swept down the hall. She paused on the threshold and flashed a smile that was at once scornful and proud. "I hope you will be able to remain for the night, Dunstan. You are always welcome here."

Bayard looked surprised and delighted, until Dunstan turned to him. "Now that I have seen her, I can understand your desire to wed," Cynath's son admitted with a sly and knowing grin. "I did not know she had Saxon blood. Pray forgive my hasty words."

He was still impudent, the scoundrel, for there was no contrition in his tone or looks. Adelar wanted to kill him even more.

"Shall we get to the purpose of your journey here?" Bayard said, demonstrating once again why he was such a good leader. He had the ability to put away from him personal affronts and deal with the important issue at hand.

"It's Aethelwold," Dunstan replied, his manner wisely subdued.

"What now? Has he moved to strike?"

"He continues to send small bands out of Essex to harass the countryside. However, Edward fears that he will lead a major attack either this summer or next spring. Edward has called a meeting of the Witan and all his loyal thanes. My father has sent me to bring you."

"My *fyrd?* Where and when?"

"Cynath's *burh.* In five days' time. He does not require your whole *fyrd.* Just you and a few of your men, to discuss our plans."

Gleda and Ylla entered the hall. Gleda carried a vessel of wine, Ylla a tray bearing silver chalices. Dunstan eyed the maidservants as they handed the filled chalices to the men.

Gleda gazed quite boldly at the finely attired Dunstan, but he was staring at the younger and prettier

Ylla. Ylla accomplished her task quickly and competently, never once meeting anyone's eyes.

Gleda moved more slowly, and when the women left the hall, Gleda's hips swung even more provocatively than usual.

"Your hall does you credit, Bayard," Dunstan said.

"I am pleased to hear the son of Cynath say so." Bayard leaned back in his chair. "Edward does not give his allies much time to muster."

"That is why he does not request the *fyrds*. He prefers to only make plans, for the present."

"And to discover if any men of Wessex will follow Aethelwold, probably. We can be ready to leave in two days. Will you enjoy our hospitality until then?"

"Yes, and I thank you."

"Ranulf, you will choose five men to go with me to Cynath's *burh*. Father Derrick, I am sure to need your wisdom and faith. I will leave Adelar in command here."

Dunstan nodded his approval, and Ranulf smiled smugly.

"Cousin!" Adelar began in protest.

"I know you would prefer to go with me, Adelar, but I will feel better if you are guarding my possessions," Bayard replied.

Adelar said nothing. He wanted to tell Bayard here and now that he was leaving right away, but Dunstan's presence and Ranulf's smug complacency silenced him.

"I was planning to go hunting today," Bayard remarked. "Would you care to join us, Dunstan? I understand one of my people has seen a snow-white stag in the wood. Surely such a beast should afford us fine sport."

"Nothing would give me more pleasure—except hunting Aethelwold!" Dunstan replied with a loud guffaw. "My dogs are anxious for a chase."

"Baldric!" Bayard shouted.

"Here, my lord!" came Baldric's deep voice from outside the hall. He stuck his head in the door.

"All the dogs who are able will hunt today."

"Aye, my lord. Tom'll have to—"

"Make sure my men's horses are taken care of," Dunstan ordered.

"Can't do that, my lord. That bitch is whelpin' and it's goin' to be a rough time." With that, Baldric's head disappeared again.

Dunstan eyed Bayard with surprise. "You allow this fellow to speak thus to me?"

"I will have the lads see to your horses for the present. And yes, I do allow the finest dog keeper in all of Wessex, Mercia, Kent and Essex to speak so, when the finest bitch I possess is having pups."

Not mollified, but obviously deciding it was better not to speak, Dunstan rose, followed by his entourage.

"Would you care to have the pick of the litter?" Bayard offered. "I assure you, these are the finest hunting dogs you will ever see." There was no servile conciliation in his tone, but the offer proved his wisdom. Dunstan nodded and made his obeisance with better grace than he had demonstrated thus far.

"I shall join you shortly," Bayard said, also getting to his feet, "after I fetch my cloak."

The rest of the men in the hall stood up and began to gather their weapons, while Dunstan and his followers departed.

"Bayard, I would have a word with you," Adelar said quietly, but not quietly enough.

Ranulf came beside them. "What can Adelar have to say that needs such secrecy?" he demanded.

"It is enough that he seeks it, Ranulf," Bayard replied calmly. "Leave us now and wait for me at the stables."

Ranulf darted a suspicious look at Adelar, but he joined the others as they headed for the door.

Adelar turned toward his cousin and suddenly noticed how tired Bayard seemed today. His face was drawn, and there were dark circles beneath his eyes.

"Now, Cousin," Bayard said, "as Ranulf remarked, what is it that requires such secrecy?"

"I cannot remain here."

"I am sorry if you are offended that I did not ask you to ride with me to Cynath's counsel."

"No, you misunderstand me, Cousin. I was planning to go from this *burh* today."

"Why? What has happened? Have I or any of my men done something to anger you?"

"No, Bayard."

His cousin frowned. "There must have been some-thing to prompt this sudden decision. Do you think I would let my kinsman—who is also my finest war-rior—leave without a word of explanation?"

"I have served my time in the *fyrd.*"

"I did not expect *you* to act like the men who aban-doned Thorney Island when the Danes were nearly ready to surrender just because their time of service was at an end," Bayard said reproachfully.

"You have others to take my place."

"There is no one I trust as much as you."

"You have your wife."

"Who is, whatever I may say to Dunstan, a Dane."

"But you *do* trust her, do you not? If I were to stay while you were at Cynath's *burh,* it would not be to act as a prison guard." And certainly never for Endredi.

"Then I will have to leave Ranulf here. Or Father Derrick. I do not wish to have Endredi under either man's rule, but..."

Bayard had given Adelar the one reason he should stay. Ranulf would never dare to harm Endredi, but he was as sly as a snake. He would find a thousand subtle ways to make her life miserable. Father Derrick's low opinion of women was enough to try the patience of even Endredi. "Very well, Bayard. I will stay until you return."

Bayard smiled, his pleasure lighting his face. "Thank you, Adelar. I need you, and so does Endredi."

Adelar nodded, realizing he knew exactly how a fly feels when it discovers it is trapped in honey.

* * *

Dagfinn frowned as he regarded the spy. "You are certain of this? The full Witan as well as other thanes and warriors?"

"Yes. The king requested a partial muster at Cynath's *burh* in five days' time. The thanes and *ealdormen* have much to discuss."

"You will find out everything you can, especially about the building of *burhs*. And a description of Cynath's. I also need to know about Mercia and Kent. Will they follow Edward, or is there a chance they will leave the men of Wessex to fight alone?"

"If Aethelwold is wise, he will choose to fight Wessex first. The Mercians and Kentish men may wait to see what happens, and Edward will be deprived of their help. It would be even better, of course, if Edward was killed. Then Ethelred of Mercia would be the best choice for king. Even those arrogant simpletons in the Witan would have to agree."

Dagfinn scowled. "I admit that what you say sounds a good course, but it is ambition that moves Aethelwold, not wisdom. Still, I shall pass on your advice."

"Good. There is another thing."

"What?"

"It is about Endredi. And Bayard's cousin, Adelar."

"The arrogant one who speaks our language? What of them?"

"He attempted to seduce her."

"By Odin's eye! Is this true?"

"I have said so."

"He did not succeed," Dagfinn stated with conviction.

The spy's eyes widened. "You knew of this? How?"

Dagfinn's laugh was more like a harsh grunt. "I did not—but I know Endredi. Her heart is as full of ice as the northern seas in winter. I have no liking for my brother's widow, but she would never betray a husband."

"*I* know Adelar, and I would not be so swift to dismiss him. If he wants a woman..."

"If he does, he can have her."

"Bayard may decide to send her back."

"He wouldn't dare!" Dagfinn's eyes narrowed slightly. "The marriage *is* consummated, is it not?"

"I am not privy to *that* kind of information, but I believe so, yes."

"Then he must keep her. Or do what you Christians do with unfaithful wives. It matters not to me."

"But a possible adultery should. Bayard would be disgraced."

"So?"

"So it is a sign of weakness. Some of his thanes might be persuaded to abandon him. He—and his *burh*—would be less protected."

Dagfinn put a purse heavy with silver coins down on the table in front of him. Women's bracelets jangled on the arm of the traitor who reached for it. "Find proof of an adultery and Bayard's disgrace, and there will be more. In the meantime, discover everything you can about this meeting."

"That may take some time, and it will be more difficult to leave the *burh* when Bayard has returned."

"Even with such a fine disguise?" Dagfinn replied. "I would not have taken you for anything but an ancient crone myself." He handed the traitor a drinking horn. "Why do you do this?" he asked, unable to stifle his burning curiosity.

"Because I hate the thought of a Saxon of Wessex ruling over my country."

"England?" the Dane asked, suspicion in his voice.

His companion's expression was scornful. "Mercia. The rest of the country doesn't matter a whit to me except as provinces under the rule of a Mercian king."

Dagfinn frowned. "You do not include the Danelaw?"

"Of course not. You Northmen are too established here to be driven out. Better we should work with you than against you. There will be plenty for both the Danes and the Mercians when we have Wessex."

"Edward will not be easy to beat. And the men of Kent will fight hard to prevent another Mercian ruling them."

"They have been nursing their wounds for so long, surely they are too weak to fight."

"Beornwulf never should have humiliated Eadbert Praen that way."

"He led a rebellion. It was only fit that his eyes be put out and his hands cut off."

"And if you are caught fomenting rebellion against your king, will you think that fitting punishment then?" Dagfinn asked.

"I will not get caught," the traitor replied.

At the evening meal, Dunstan made every effort to show Bayard and Endredi that he harbored no ill will toward them, and indeed regretted his earlier doubts about Endredi's loyalty. To most of those watching, it would have seemed that Bayard was pleased and Endredi mollified. Adelar knew it was not so, for Endredi's carefully guarded expression did not fool him. She did not trust Dunstan, she did not like him and she certainly wasn't going to be duped into believing he had changed his mind so radically after the forceful words he had uttered that morning. However, clearly she recognized Dunstan was, unfortunately, a powerful man, and that it would not be wise to offend him.

Dunstan was also all too interested in the women of the hall. He surveyed each one with his slow, impertinent, arrogant gaze. Gleda smiled enticingly and looked boldly back. Ordella gave him a vacuous stare, a fit response to the slight curl of Dunstan's lips when he looked at the very slender, hook-nosed woman. Ylla reddened and hurried so at her task that she spilled the wine she was pouring into Ordella's goblet. Ordella rebuked her with a swift, harsh word.

Ylla's eyes filled with tears as she hurried outside to fetch more ale from the storehouse. Ordella had a sharp tongue, and she had better learn to curb it,

Adelar thought. Endredi had made it very clear that she liked Ylla. Indeed, everyone guessed that it had been Endredi's request that Bayard give the girl her freedom.

Dunstan rose and belched loudly. "If you will pardon me, my lord," he said. "My cask needs emptying."

Bayard nodded and returned to whatever he was saying to the fellow on the other side of Endredi. He leaned close to his wife, his smile warm as he looked at her.

Godwin took his place in the center of the hall. "A song for your amusement, nobles? A game? A joke? What say you, my lady? My lord?"

"A song," Bayard said. "Something new."

"I have composed one in honor of your wife," Godwin said. "I call it, 'The Lady of the Lovely Eyes.'"

Bayard beamed his approval, and Endredi flushed prettily.

Adelar couldn't bear to stay another moment. He rose abruptly.

"Leaving?" Ranulf asked, his voice thick with drink.

"I am tired. I am going to sleep."

"Alone?" he said with a grotesque leer.

"Jealous, Ranulf?"

"Not of you. Not of a man who beds nothing but servants or slaves."

Adelar grinned slowly. "At least I do not have to pay any penalties for my indiscretions."

"I do not think Gleda will be waiting for you this time."

"That is nothing to me. Sleep well, Ranulf. With your charming wife."

With a bow toward Bayard, Adelar excused himself and went outside. The haunting, beautiful melody of Godwin's song followed him into the stillness of the night. From habit, he surveyed the outer wall of the *burh* and checked that the sentries were patrolling the perimeter. Although Dagfinn's Danes would probably honor the alliance, there were other bands of Vikings who would not. And the men of Kent had only joined with the West Saxons within recent memory; they might yet be planning a revolt of their own.

He sauntered toward the stable, away from the music. The bowers around the hall were silent, most of the inhabitants being in the hall. They would continue to drink and listen to Godwin for some time yet.

He passed the hut where Baldric keep the bitches when they gave birth. He heard the dog keeper's low, rough voice crooning what sounded like some kind of melody of praise. Bayard's best bitch had outdone herself that day, producing a litter of ten puppies, most of which looked strong enough to survive.

Adelar continued toward the stable. It would be warm, and he could lie on the straw and try to sleep, or at least think of something other than Endredi. He would not meditate on everyone's apparent happiness and his own extreme distress.

Then, from inside the building, he heard the sounds of a struggle and a woman's stifled scream.

Chapter Eight

Adelar pushed open the stable door. From the shadows came whimpers and a low, insistent, guttural voice. A man's voice. Then a whisper—a young woman, saying, "No, please, my lord!"

Adelar shoved the door so that it hit the wall with a crash. "Who is here?" he demanded while his eyes adjusted to the darkness.

Dunstan stepped out of the shadows. "Leave us!"

"Who else?"

"It is none of your concern."

Adelar smiled coolly. "If you have a servant of my lord and you have injured her, then it most certainly is my concern."

Ylla appeared, holding the torn bodice of her gown together with trembling fingers. Her cheeks were stained with tears, and her shoulders shook with sobs.

"She is not injured."

"You may go," Adelar said to the young woman. With a lowered head but grateful eyes, she hurried past him and outside.

"You had no cause to do that," Dunstan protested. "Everyone knows women struggle only to increase a man's ardor."

"Perhaps," Adelar replied with a shrug. "But she is a favorite of Bayard's wife. If she claimed you hurt her, Endredi would not be pleased." He let his words hang in the air, hoping Dunstan would understand the implication that if Endredi was not pleased, Bayard would not be, either.

"My father said Bayard's hall would be hospitable," Dunstan muttered as he reached for his belt.

Adelar waited for the man to join him at the door. "I will tell you this in confidence, Dunstan, only because I am certain I can trust your discretion," he said, his tone serious. "Endredi's father is a very fierce man. I think Bayard is wise to keep her happy, at least for the time being."

"I am not afraid of any Dane, and I am surprised to hear that Bayard is."

"Bayard is merely being cautious. Endredi's father is not one of the tamer Norsemen of the Danelaw. Bayard, and your father, would not want to have to fight him and his men, I can assure you. They make the men who attacked Alfred look like children only playing at war. Should his daughter be made unhappy, I have no doubt the fellow would come himself."

Dunstan eyed Adelar as they crossed the yard together. "Is that why Bayard married her? To keep her father from his lands?"

"As you know, Bayard keeps his own counsel, so he has not *said* so. But you and I also know that Bayard is a far-seeing man. Perhaps he has heard rumors of impending trouble, which this call to counsel by your father seems to confirm. With this marriage, he insures he will have one less enemy to fight."

Dunstan let his breath out slowly. "I see." He glanced at Adelar. "I am glad you told me of this. I never would have touched that woman had I known."

Adelar chuckled. "I like a woman to warm my nights as much as you, so I will give you one other small piece of advice. That serving wench with the mountainous breasts has been casting her gaze at you all night. I think you have but to crook your finger to have her."

"She is not so pretty."

"She is very skilled, Dunstan. In a variety of ways."

"Is that so?"

"Yes."

Dunstan grinned lustfully. "My thanks to you, Adelar," he said as he entered the hall.

What a fool, Adelar thought scornfully, turning away.

"My thanks to you, too, my lord," Ylla said softly from the shadows nearby.

He pivoted toward her voice as she stepped out into the moonlight. "He came upon me after I left the storehouse and dragged me to the stable. I was too frightened to call out."

"Your mistress would have been very angry if he had hurt you."

She put her hands on his arm and pressed against him. "I am very glad you came."

Suddenly he was aware of the sensation of the young woman's breasts against his arm and the desire gleaming in her eyes.

He could not have Endredi. Why should he not have this willing wench instead? With a low chuckle, he pulled Ylla into his arms. "Grateful, eh? But perhaps you are too young for a warrior's ways."

She smiled at him. "I am older than I look, my lord. It is to a woman's advantage to appear a child when she has no rights."

"You are a clever girl—woman, Ylla."

"I am happy to hear you say so."

She pressed against him again, this time with more of her body. Why not? Why not? He picked her up easily and strode across the yard toward a building used for storing grain, pushed open the door and kicked it shut after they entered.

The smell of barley and oats filled his nostrils as Adelar let Ylla slip down in the darkness. She was shorter than Endredi and thinner, but as he ran his hands over Ylla's body, he did not doubt that this was a woman in his arms. Her brown hair was long and thick, and he buried his hands in it.

She put her arms around him, embracing him. "I am a virgin, my lord," she whispered tremulously.

Endredi was no longer a virgin. She had given that to another man.

He would not think of Endredi now. He would enjoy himself. He bent and kissed Ylla fiercely, letting his needs rule his actions. He caressed her expertly and felt her relax into his arms.

Still kissing her, he lifted her and carried her to the back of the building, laying her on a pile of coarse sacks. His eyes now used to the dark, he looked down at her and smiled to see the hunger in her face as his body covered hers.

She wanted him, and there was no reason he could not have this woman. With slow, undulating movements he sought to increase her yearning for him. He kissed her again, this time tenderly to ease whatever fears might lurk beneath her want, and let his lips journey slowly across her cheek and down her neck. She whimpered when he licked her collarbone while his hips thrust against her, letting her feel his arousal.

His mouth continued to make slow progress down her body to her breasts exposed by her torn gown. He paused for a long moment to tease the hardened peaks with his tongue. His hand meandered between her legs, upward, pushing her skirt toward her waist. He loosened his breeches, raised himself up and—she was not Endredi.

His ardor died, and with a low groan of despair, he rolled away.

"What is it, my lord?" Ylla asked, her voice small in the darkness.

"It is not for me to take what you offer," he muttered. The lack was in him, not Ylla, and he did not want her to blame herself. Nor could he reveal the true cause of his tribulation.

"My lord," she whispered, moving close to him in the stuffy little building. She ran her hand over his chest. "Please, my lord," she persisted. "I want you to take me." Her cool fingers entered the warmth of his tunic.

He didn't reply, so she went on, her words heartfelt and unmistakably sincere. "I am a virgin only because most men, like you, thought I was a child yet. But that safe ruse is clearly at an end. When Dunstan seized me, I feared the time had finally come when a man would take me against my will. I have often dreaded that day."

"You are no longer a slave. You can refuse."

"How many servants have refused you, my lord?"

"None, but—"

"But you are a nobleman and they were nothing but servants."

He lay back against the grain sacks, suddenly ashamed. He had always arrogantly assumed . . . Oh, dear God, how like his father that sounded!

"I am a servant still," Ylla continued. "I knew in my mind that Dunstan could do what he liked, but I found I could not simply lie still and let him. And then you came." Her voice grew softer, and she laid her head against Adelar's chest. "I have long admired you, my lord. I wanted . . . I hoped you would be the one. If I could have a choice, I would choose you."

"Ylla, I—"

She pressed a kiss to his lips. "Please, my lord, let me finish. I know that you are a nobleman and I am but a servant. I know that I can ask nothing of you. But I will, this once. Please, my lord, I would like you to be my first. Then, no matter what happens or who else forces me, I will have one memory that I can cherish." Her voice caught in her throat. "One choice *I* made."

Adelar gently brushed Ylla's hair from her damp cheeks. "Things may change for the better for you," he said softly.

"Or they may change for the worse," she replied bitterly. "I was not born a slave, my lord. I was stolen as a child and sold. Endredi is a good woman, and Bayard a just lord, but they may die. And then my fate would rest in other hands."

Adelar gasped at her matter-of-fact words, because they were true. Endredi might die—and then so would his heart.

"I am sorry to say such things of your cousin," she said quickly, misinterpreting his reaction. "But we both know that war may come, and battles, and so death." She raised herself to look upon him, her gaze intense. "Please, my lord, please. Take me. It need be only this once."

He shook his head. "Ylla, what you offer is a gift I cannot take. I . . . I do not deserve it."

The door opened suddenly, and on the threshold he could see a woman's shape illuminated by the weak flame of a lamp. Before he could move away from Ylla, Endredi called the girl's name.

"My lady!" Ylla gasped.

Endredi strained to see the two figures who moved apart hastily.

One was Ylla, hurriedly getting to her feet. As the other person rose beside her in the dimness, Endredi's hand went to her throat as if to strangle the cry of pain building there, for it was Adelar, his naked chest gleaming in the lamplight.

Her gaze darted from him to Ylla, noting her flushed face and slightly swollen lips. Adelar had taken Ylla, made love to her here, on a pile of grain sacks!

"Endredi," Adelar whispered, stepping toward her.

His action and the sound of his voice saying her name jolted her. "Ylla, you have been remiss in your duties," she snapped.

"I am sorry, my lady—"

"Go."

The girl hurried past her as Endredi turned to leave.

"Endredi!"

She ignored Adelar's pleading tone. She could not look at him. Could not bear to think what must have happened here. He grabbed her arm. "Endredi!"

"Let me go, Adelar, or I will tell Bayard you dared to lay a hand on me."

He did as she asked.

She ran out of the hut, clutching the lamp in her numbed fingers, running away from him. Not to the bower. Ylla would be there.

She shoved open the stable door and closed it be-hind her. Her throat ached from the struggle to sub-due her sobs, and now that she was alone, she gave up the fight. Tears spilled from her eyes, and the flame danced from the trembling of her fingers. She blew it out, then sank to the floor, her shoulders heaving and her breaths coming in great, shuddering gasps.

She had no right to feel the jealousy coursing through her body, filling her mind with anger and her heart with pain. She was married to another, sworn to be loyal to him, to bear his children. To do otherwise was unthinkable to her, and yet—and yet she craved Adelar to the very marrow of her bones. Long ago, he had listened to her, spoken to her, treated her with re-spect and allowed her to feel that he needed her, too. He was like a part of her too long absent from her life. Now he was there again, but his presence gave her no comfort. How could it, when having him near was to feel like a man dying for lack of water who finds a poisoned stream?

The stable door creaked open. Swiftly, Endredi put her fist in her mouth to still her sobs and blinked back the tears to see who entered. Adelar, now fully clothed and wearing a cloak.

"Endredi?" His deep voice reached out to her, but she did not answer.

He found her anyway. She scrambled to her feet, moving away quickly from his outstretched hand. "Adelar, leave me."

He drew off his cloak and held it out to her. "You are cold."

She was shivering, so there was no point in denying his observation, but she did not take the cloak. She wrapped her arms around herself. "I will go to my bower." She could not prevent the trace of bitterness that crept into her voice. "It should be ready now."

"Nothing happened between Ylla and me. Dunstan accosted her and—"

"Do you think I have grown foolish with age? Was it in defending her from Dunstan that your tunic came to be on the ground? I am not a child anymore, Adelar."

"I know," he said softly.

"She should have been at her work, that's all. If you desire Ylla and she is agreeable, there is nothing I will do or say to stop you. Unless it interferes with her duties."

"I do not desire Ylla. There is only one woman who touches my heart."

At his softly spoken words, her heart thundered against her ribs like a charge of mounted men. Still, she could not deny what she had seen with her own eyes, in spite of her growing need to believe otherwise.

He came close and put his cloak around her. For a moment, she allowed herself to feel the intimacy surrounding them the way the fur-lined cloak surrounded her with warmth. But only for a moment. "I am your lord's wife," she whispered, looking up into his piercing dark eyes.

"Yes."

"Then there is no more to be said between us."

"No." He regarded her steadily, his expression inscrutable.

"I will not betray him." She felt the soft brush of the fur against her skin.

"Nor will I."

His breath stroked her cheek. She glimpsed the flesh of his chest where he had not laced his tunic. He placed his strong hands on her shoulders. "I must go," she whispered.

"Yes," he replied quietly, pulling her into his embrace. Her hands pressed against him as if she would push him away even while she lifted her face for his kiss.

She thrust herself back. "This is wrong! Do not touch me, Adelar!" She ran to the door and grabbed the handle, then bent her head and whispered, "Please, for both our sakes, do not ever touch me!" She pushed open the door, yanked his cloak from her shoulders and threw it at him.

Then she was gone.

Adelar stood in the stables. Lost in thought, he made no move to retrieve his discarded cloak. Or to follow Endredi again.

She was right. She belonged to Bayard, her husband and his lord. And more than that, she was Endredi, who would sooner die than betray her loyalty. He knew that as well as anyone could, for it had been one of the first things he had admired in her. She had never said one word against her father, even when Einar had paid no attention to her. Instead, she had sought to win his approval.

As she was probably seeking to win Bayard's approval now. Fool, he should have thought of that.

Judging by his cousin's good humor, she was obviously succeeding. He had no right to jeopardize her marriage. He had no right to come between Endredi and her husband. He must put aside his desire for her and remember his oath of loyalty to Bayard.

So, to please Bayard and for Endredi's sake, he would stay while Bayard went to the meeting of the king, the *ealdormen* and the other thanes. Then, when Bayard returned, he would go. He simply did not dare to remain here another day, for although Endredi was forbidden him, in his heart he could not be sure he would remember that.

Determined to do his duty, too, Adelar strode from the stables.

Ranulf staggered into his bower and nearly fell over Ordella, who had been peering out the door. "Stupid oaf!" she muttered, tugging the corner of her cloak from beneath his feet, which made him reel into the room.

"Wha' in the name of Sin—Saint Alcuin are you doing?" Ranulf slurred angrily.

Ordella turned to him and closed the door, leaning against it with a peevish expression on her shrewish face. She gestured toward the two servants sleeping in the corner. "Lower your voice, you dolt!"

"Lower your own," he muttered. "They'll sleep through a thunderstorm, those two." Then he leered at her. "Waiting for me, eh?"

"Stupid sot!" she hissed. "I've been keeping an eye on some very fascinating things."

"In the dark?" Ranulf made his way toward the table where a goblet stood partly filled with mead.

"Haven't you had enough?" his wife demanded.

"I'm still standing, aren't I?" He downed the dregs and belched.

She sniffed derisively. "You smell like you've been sitting in the ale barrel."

He didn't reply, but sat down heavily on a stool. "So what have you seen? Dunstan and that wench? It was no secret what they were thinking about."

"Something far more interesting, I assure you."

Ranulf's eyes appeared a little less glazed. "Oh?"

"I'll tell you in the morning." Ordella took off her cloak and laid it on a nearby chest. She walked toward the bed, ignoring her husband.

Ranulf got to his feet. "What did you see?" he demanded. "Was it important?"

She continued to undress, her thin lips a disapproving line in her long face. With a scowl, Ranulf went to his wife and stood in front of her. "What did you see?"

"I said, I will tell you in the morning. You are drunk."

Through his haze, Ranulf glared at the homely woman who treated him as if he was a servant at her beck and call. The same way Adelar treated him. And Bayard, and most of the other men. But he was no dog—he was a man of noble blood, and he would show this woman that she had best remember that. He raised his hand and struck her hard across the cheek. "Tell me!"

Ordella fell back, startled, her eyes wide with fright. He clutched his hand, which stung from the blow, but he was vastly pleased to see her fear, and somewhat more sober. He raised his hand again in an obvious threat. "Tell me what I want to know!"

"It was Endredi. And Adelar," Ordella said tremulously, and with new respect.

Ranulf's eyes gleamed. "Together?"

"Yes," she said, a note of triumph in her voice. "We could not have planned things better ourselves."

"Tell me what you saw."

"I was looking out for you—"

Ranulf thought that was true enough. She had often waited for him and then plied him with a thousand questions about this man and that, their alliances, their weaknesses, seeking any little morsel she might be able to use in her schemes.

"—and I saw Endredi come rushing out of her bower. She was looking for someone, that much I could tell. I remembered that Ylla had left the hall some time before and wondered if she was seeking her.

She began going to the sheds and outbuildings, searching.''

"You did not offer to help," Ranulf observed.

"No, I did not. I will have nothing to do with that slave. But Adelar does not feel that way," she added slyly.

Ranulf appeared slightly less hostile, and Ordella continued eagerly. "I saw Endredi go to the grain stores. She was inside a few moments, then Ylla ran out. She went at once to the bower. Then Endredi left, but she didn't go to her quarters. I thought it was odd and was going to see what was the matter—"

Ranulf saw through those words. To be sure, Ordella was probably telling the truth, but she would have wanted to find out what was going on. Sympathy for Endredi would not be her motive.

"—when *Adelar* came out of the storehouse." Ordella dropped her voice to a conspiratorial whisper. "He was obviously finishing getting dressed!"

"Then he was with Ylla, not Endredi," Ranulf grumbled. "I see nothing so exciting in that."

"I have not finished! Adelar followed Endredi to the stable."

"And?"

"They were *alone* together."

"For a long time?"

"No," Ordella said regretfully. "But when she left, she stood for a moment at the door, and I saw that she was wearing a cloak. She hadn't been before, and I'm sure it was Adelar's. Then she took it off and threw it back into the barn. I think she was *jealous*."

"Well, well, well," Ranulf said thoughtfully, a wicked smile on his face. "Bayard's wife jealous of Adelar's dalliance with a mere serving wench. This is indeed welcome news."

"Yes," Ordella agreed, but her tone had grown more thoughtful.

"What is it now?"

"They may not have committed adultery...yet. And we are going to need proof."

"Surely the word of a thane—"

"Do you honestly think Bayard will take your word over Adelar's?" she demanded sarcastically. She saw the anger in her husband's eyes and added, "He should, of course. But he would not. No, we are going to need other witnesses."

Ranulf smiled cruelly. "That may not be so difficult, since Bayard is leaving them alone here."

Ordella's smile was even more vicious. "I think it is a good thing that I do not go with you to Cynath's *burh*."

Chapter Nine

"As you can see, my lord, my father has spent much effort and money on the fortifications," Dunstan boasted as Bayard and the rest of the mounted troop crested the wooded hill near Cynath's *burh*.

The fortress was large, commanding a view of the river and surrounding downs. There were several well-made buildings inside the walls and also a fair number of other structures outside the fortress.

When they paused to survey the *burh*, Bayard noticed a stream babbling beside the well-kept roadway as it headed for the river that wound around the fortress. On the banks of the stream, bedstraw and purple scabious, rush, lady fern and long, slender grasses nodded in the breeze. Red campion and bluebells, hawthorn and broom graced its edges, their tints of pink, blue, purple and yellow making splashes of color against the browns and greens of the sprouting trees close by. The oak and alder blossoms dangled overhead, and Bayard could see small yellow flowers against the sharp, dark leaves of holly bushes. Birds twittered in the trees, and a red squirrel scampered overhead, for the May day was a fine one. White, thin clouds littered the sky. As always upon the downs, soft breezes rustled through the wood, blending with the jingling of the harness and the panting of the dogs.

"He has built well indeed," Bayard replied, impressed more by what he saw than by Dunstan's bragging.

Dunstan nudged his horse forward. Behind him, Bayard and his cortege did the same, riding slowly toward the fortress.

Bayard could not wonder at Edward's choice of sites for an important meeting of the Witan and other followers of the king. Cynath was fiercely loyal to Edward, who had been named successor by the Witan according to Saxon custom. Alfred, with his exceptional wisdom, had refrained from naming an heir in his will, although there would have been few who would have protested. Unfortunately Aethelwold, his nephew, had foolishly ignored the Witan, demanding the right to rule because of an older will, which stated Alfred and his brothers were to rule in turn. Alfred, being the youngest, had ruled last, and obviously Aethelwold, the son of Alfred's elder brother, had expected the succession to pass to the son of the older sibling.

If Aethelwold had even a smattering of intelligence, he would have followed Edward's example and made a name for himself in battle, so that should anything befall Edward—and considering the constant threat of

warfare, that was not an unlikely circumstance—
Aethelwold would have a chance to be chosen successor. Instead, Aethelwold had declared himself king,
kidnapped a nun, seized a *burh* and announced that he
would fight or die there. Then Aethelwold abandoned
the nun and deserted his followers in the dark of night.
No Saxon warrior had any respect at all for the fellow
now, and it was surely only because the Danes welcomed the division between the Saxons that they had
decided to declare Aethelwold king.

Cynath, Bayard and several other thanes were certain Aethelwold was not a great threat. It was the
Danes they worried about, and their eagerness to attack and plunder. Everyone wanted them gone, or at
least under Saxon control. Let the Danes pay for the
privilege of living on Saxon land, rather than Saxons
bribing the Danes not to make war.

Unfortunately, Alfred had not the strength or the
means to keep back the Viking horde when he had first
come to power, and so had sought to prevent them
from seizing all the Saxon land in the only way he
could, by giving them the Danelaw. But much had
changed and much had been learned during Alfred's
reign.

Edward was not a man to buy off his enemies. Most
of the Saxon lords had no doubt that it was Edward's
intention to take on the Danes and force them to sub-
mit to Saxon rule. Edward had distinguished himself
as a leader and as a warrior, so there were many who

would gladly follow him into battle, Bayard among them.

Bayard could hear Ranulf and the others talking behind him, obviously making comments about Cynath's *burh*. Even Father Derrick was impressed, to judge from his remarks. A better compliment Cynath could not have. The priest was well read, thanks to Alfred's encouragement of learning that had sent Derrick and others like him to school in Rome, and he had found much to criticize about Bayard's *burh*, citing this example and that from the *Iliad* and seemingly every other classical reference he had ever read. The man was intelligent, tiresome and fiercely convinced he was always in the right. Endredi would surely welcome his absence.

As for the absence of her husband... Bayard still had little clear idea what Endredi actually thought of him. She did not dislike him, and more than that he could not guess.

Bayard fought a twinge of jealousy as he thought of Endredi and Adelar sitting together in the hall while he was gone.

The cortege drew to a halt, and Dunstan leapt from his horse. Bayard and his men dismounted. Lads hurried out from the stables and took hold of the horses. Several servants and slaves hurried about, so that the air was filled with the noise of voices and activity. The sounds of weapons being made were discernible, too, and the shouts of men practising for battle.

With a wave of his hand, Dunstan led his guests inside the hall. A servant waited to take their weapons, then they proceeded toward Cynath, who sat in a heavy, ornately carved chair at the far end of the well-appointed building. A fire burned in the long central hearth, and smoke-stained tapestries lined the walls. Many swords, shields, battle-axes and spears also hung there, a silent reminder of the impressive force Cynath commanded.

"Greetings, my lord Cynath!" Bayard called out warmly to the man who had been more than his overlord in his youth. Cynath had been mentor, teacher and friend, and still was, although he had risen to a position of great power within the Witan.

Cynath rose and hurried forward with a pleased smile on his face, and they exchanged the kiss of greeting. Cynath's white hair brushed his still-muscular shoulders and his equally white beard fell upon his powerful chest. In all, he was a finer formed man than his son, whom he now greeted. Indeed, Dunstan was already far too fat to be a great warrior, while Cynath gave every indication that he could still beat several men in battle before he was winded.

The *ealdorman* greeted the others in Bayard's party with lordly dignity. "Father Derrick," he said reverently when he came to the priest. "I am honored to have you in my hall. Do you recall Father Absalom from your time in Rome?"

"Indeed I do!" Father Derrick answered with more enthusiasm than Bayard had ever seen him express. "A very learned, devoted man of God."

"He has recently arrived here. Perhaps you would care to meet with him?"

"That would be most excellent, my lord. Where might I find him?"

"He is in the chapel."

"With your leave, then, my lord." Father Derrick did not wait for Cynath's permission, but strode out of the hall.

Cynath turned to Bayard with a serious expression, although his shrewd old eyes were dancing with laughter. "A priest is, of course, a necessary thing for a lord, to remind us that we are mere pawns to the will of God. However, sometimes it is better for men of war to think of the battle first, and then pray for help." Cynath smiled broadly. "Besides, that fellow makes the ale sour in my belly."

Bayard and the rest chuckled, for most of them felt that way, too. For a man who had never actually wielded a sword or commanded a host of warriors, Father Derrick was quick to suggest ways and means, often without considering that men must eat or that a day's march could be twenty miles at most.

"You are looking well, my lord," Bayard said as he took a seat on the bench nearby and Cynath returned to his chair.

"And you, too, Bayard," Cynath replied jovially. Nevertheless, his eyes regarded his former pupil in the arts of war with some slight wariness. "I suppose I must infer, then, that this marriage does you good." He gestured for the rest of the party to sit. Dunstan strode to the fore and sat before anyone else, throwing himself into the chair at his father's right hand. Cynath glanced at his son, but said nothing.

"All men want sons," Bayard answered.

"That is true," his overlord conceded.

"And by marrying this woman, I hope to keep Viking raiders from my land."

"If they abide by your agreement."

"They will. Their leader appears to have no stomach for a battle."

Cynath handed Bayard a drinking horn. "Against you, at any rate." Ranulf, Dunstan and the others also picked up vessels, which had been lying on the table, as a serving girl came around with mead. "You seem very sure you understand these Vikings."

"I understand Dagfinn. And I have seen no cause to distrust my wife."

"You were always wise, Bayard."

"Thank you, my lord." The two men exchanged knowing looks and let the silence of shared memories pass between them. "When does the king arrive?"

"Two days. Until then, you and your men are welcome to stay in my hall. I am preparing another bower for your use when the king comes."

"You are a good host, Cynath."

"I am pleased to hear you say so."

"Does anyone know of Aethelwold's plans?"

"Not yet, but Edward still seems disposed to wait for Aethelwold to move first. There are too many places he might strike. If everyone is prepared, we can move swiftly to overtake him when he does."

"Let us hope they choose a land attack. We cannot hope to beat the Danes on the sea."

Cynath nodded. "It is unfortunate they have taken Essex."

"What of the men of Mercia?" Dunstan demanded. "Have you heard anything of them?"

"They are still with us."

Ranulf and the others exchanged skeptical looks. Alfred's wife had been the daughter of an *ealdorman* of Mercia, and he had married his daughter to Ethelred, the most powerful of the Mercian *ealdormen*. However, it was possible there remained some bitterness that a man of Wessex was ruling over Mercia, rather than their own king.

"Surely they realize they will simply fall to the Danes without us," Bayard said thoughtfully. "We must stand united to have any hope of defeating them."

"Yes. But now," Cynath said, "I am sure you are all hungry and thirsty after your journey. Eat, drink and listen to my gleeman. He has just come back from Agincourt with some new riddles."

Some time later, Bayard and Cynath sat beside each other in the hushed hall. The gleeman had been excused, the serving women sent away. A few of the men still remained awake, but they spoke softly among themselves at the far end of the hall where they were preparing to bed down for the night. Dunstan was already sleeping, his loud snores clearly audible.

"It is good to have you near me again, Bayard," Cynath said quietly.

"I am always glad to come to your *burh*," he replied with a smile, "although this time I was not sure of your reception. Your son made it sound as if you considered me a traitor."

Cynath sighed wearily. "He is his mother's son, that one. Outspoken as a simpleton." He gave Bayard a wry grin. "Can you imagine what it is like to live with a woman who says whatever is on her mind all the time?"

"You would appreciate Endredi, then, Cynath. She is a quiet woman."

"Think yourself lucky, Bayard."

"You used to have a serving maid here, named Janeth."

"She lives in the *burh* still." Cynath regarded him shrewdly. "I did not think you knew her well enough to remember her name. I seem to recall it was Adelar who enjoyed her favors."

"It was."

"Then he may be disappointed to hear she is wed to my armorer."

"There was a child, I thought. A son?"

"Yes. He died not three months ago. Janeth never named the father."

"You have seen Adelar. What do you think?"

"It is possible, I suppose. But Janeth was a friendly girl. The child also looked rather like *me*." There was a touch of pride in Cynath's voice that brought a slight smile to Bayard's face and a twinge of jealousy to his heart.

"It could have been Adelar's son?"

"Is it important to know?"

"No. I had heard rumors and wondered."

"We sound like two old women gossiping at the well," Cynath noted wryly. "Next we shall take to bragging about our warriors, like women do of their children."

"Dunstan is a good fighter."

"Because he has not got the sense to realize what might happen to him in battle. I say it even if he is my own son." Cynath looked fondly at Bayard, and then at the sword hanging nearby, exactly like the one hanging behind him. "I would rather you were my son."

"He asked about the weapon," Bayard said, following Cynath's gaze.

"What did you tell him?"

"I told him it was a gift from you. He thought it was extremely generous of you to give me a replica of your own sword."

"Perhaps I should be glad my son lacks an imagination. He would have never forgiven me if he.knew I had given you my sword and had the replica made for myself."

"Still, Cynath, at least you have sons."

"True enough, Bayard, and so I cannot be angry that you married again even though you did not seek my permission or ask my advice. And if what you say about this woman is true, then I believe you have chosen wisely. I know how much you yearn for a child." Cynath and Bayard both glanced at Ranulf, who slept with his head upon a table and a goblet in his hand, having passed out some time before. "I can understand why you would not wish to leave your property to that one."

"Yes," Bayard said coldly.

"I see you have not forgiven him yet."

"His insult was unconscionable."

"You were children."

"Young men."

"It was before you came to me," Cynath reminded him.

"Yes, but not much." Bayard turned to Cynath with a hard and fixed expression. "Would you ever forgive anyone who called your mother's sister a whore and implied that the rest of the women in the family probably shared the same morals?"

"No, I would not."

Bayard smiled slowly. "We are very much alike, Cynath. We recognized that at once about each other, did we not?"

"But he did not actually accuse your mother of immorality."

"That was the only thing that saved his life. Yet if you had seen his face, Cynath, you would have known, as I did, that he thought the whole family less than honorable."

"Does your cousin Adelar know of this accusation against his mother?"

"Ranulf would be dead if he did."

"Yet you keep them both near you."

"Ranulf is not a complete fool. He knows it would be death to insult Adelar's mother, even if she has been dead for a long time."

"What about his father?"

"That is a more difficult question to answer. That Adelar has no love for his father is clear by his refusal to remain with him. Considering the sort of man Kendric is..."

"Those accusations were never proved. It might only be rumors about his wife's death. And as for leading the Vikings to his own *burh,* that is simply ludicrous."

Bayard did not reply. Cynath had never met Kendric, but Bayard had. A sly snake of a man he was, with Adelar's good looks and none of his principles. Bayard could believe Kendric capable of nearly anything, and remembering Adelar's words, he knew that what was said of Kendric was true.

"I thought you would have Adelar with you."

"No. I left him in command of my *burh.*"

"Do you intend to will it to him? If anything were to happen to you in battle, I would not be happy to have to put Ranulf in command."

"Nor would I."

"You would be dead," Cynath pointed out.

"It would be enough to make my spirit rise from the grave."

"Why do you persist in having Ranulf about you, then? He obviously thinks you intend to bequeath all your property and goods to him."

"Perhaps I let him remain with me the way a cat toys with a mouse, until I can snatch what he wants from his very grasp."

"You may be playing a dangerous game." Cynath looked at Bayard shrewdly. "It would be even more dangerous to toy with Adelar."

Bayard shifted uncomfortably. "What do you mean?"

"He is the best-looking fellow I've ever seen. Women like a good-looking man."

"As you well know?"

Cynath took another drink. "Is this a test of your wife?" he said at last. "Leave her with the most attractive yet loyal man you have and see if she tries to entice him while you are gone?"

"No."

"Oh, did that thought not enter your mind at all?" Cynath asked quietly.

"If I were going to do such a thing, I would have made certain Ordella came with us. The woman has the eyes of a hawk and the tongue of a snake."

"True," Cynath conceded. "Unless you wished to ensure that nothing happened between the two. Like putting a mare and stallion in separate pens, but close enough to smell each other."

Bayard frowned at Cynath's earthy comparison, but admitted to himself that it was rather accurate. Nonetheless, he repeated, "I am certain of their loyalty to me."

"Then if you have such faith in Adelar and such loathing for Ranulf, why do you not name Adelar in your will as your successor?"

"If I name Adelar in my will, Ranulf will surely come to know of it, and then he would make trouble."

"Yes, he does have many friends. There is also the matter of Kendric's *burh*," Cynath remarked thoughtfully. "Adelar may stand to inherit that."

"That I doubt. Kendric shares his son's animosity, and Kendric has other sons."

"None of them legitimate," Cynath noted.

"Still, I think he would name one of them over Adelar, since his son has so little use for him."

"Ordella is quite capable of using her influence, as well."

"Yes, the only real hope I have of preventing Ranulf from taking everything is to have a child of my own. Then all the force of law will be on my side, as well as Adelar. And I have married a woman who will surely fight for what she believes is right, whether for herself or her children."

"Ah!" Cynath sighed as the pieces of the puzzle fell neatly into place. Nonetheless, he gave Bayard a sidelong glance. "Let us hope that happens, then."

Bayard smiled somewhat wistfully. "I am doing my best to ensure it."

"But if not?"

"Adelar has made it clear he has absolutely no ambition or desire for command. I shall have no choice but to name Ranulf."

Cynath yawned and got up. "You are right. Things would be much simpler if this new wife of yours gives you a son. Now, the hour grows late. I bid you good night.

"What is wrong, Bayard?" the older man asked as Bayard rose slowly, a grimace on his face.

"A stiffness is all, my lord. I am not the youth I was," Bayard replied with a somewhat forced smile. "Sleep well, my lord."

"Time touches us all, Bayard. Sleep well."

"What sour apple have you bitten into this morning?" Godwin inquired cheerfully as Adelar rose from the bed of straw laid upon a bench in the hall. "Have you the toothache? Is that why we have seen almost nothing of you these past few days?"

Adelar's only response was a darker scowl.

"I see no swelling on your handsome face—ah! Is it Ylla?"

"I have been hunting."

"Is she angry with you? Or are you angry with her? Or are you sulking because Bayard has chosen to leave you behind?"

"Do you never cease your idle prattling?" Adelar grumbled. He yawned and surveyed the hall.

"Idle prattling? Is that how you interpret my concern for your health? A fine thank-you, I must say! Perhaps I shall see if the master of that new *burh* in the valley requires a gleeman."

"Now who is sulking? Come, let us see what Duff has prepared this morning."

"You have reminded me of the best reason for staying here. His cooking has improved immensely." Godwin followed Adelar to the table and sat beside him. "So, this new *burh*. Who will be put in command of it? Is it too much to hope it will be Ranulf?"

"Bayard told me Cynath will decide later. Perhaps Oswald, if he continues to do a good job with the building."

"He is rather young, is he not?"

"I think that is the only reason Bayard hesitates."

"And he has little wealth. I really do have no choice but to remain here."

Adelar wasn't fooled for a moment. Bayard generously gave Godwin money and gifts. The gleeman would be stupid to seek another lord's patronage.

"What about you?" Godwin asked. "You have but to ask, and Bayard would put you in command."

"I have no aspirations to be in command of anything."

"By the saints, you are a stubborn fellow."

"And you are full of questions."

"Here comes Ylla," Godwin said, nodding as the young woman entered the hall. "See? She doesn't even look at you."

"So?"

Godwin gestured at the cook, bustling about preparing the first meal of the day. "And Gleda spent the night with Duff. Merilda is going to fall into a fit when she finds out."

"Jealous?"

"Not about Gleda. Ylla is a pretty girl and a Mercian, too, like me. If you no longer desire her..."

"I am in no mood for your chatter today, Godwin."

Godwin shrugged dismissively. "Very well. I shall simply take my prattling tongue elsewhere."

"Good." Adelar watched Godwin saunter toward Ylla and begin to talk to the young woman.

He raked his fingers through his hair and rotated his stiff neck.

Then Endredi entered the hall. How lovely she looked, with her large, questioning eyes, her unruffled calm, her grave demeanor. Today her gown was of a somber brown, her jewelry plain and simple. She did not look like a *burhware*'s wife, but rather like the girl she had been.

Was it wrong to ignore the demands of his heart? And what of her heart? She had wanted him before, that night in the stable. Did she still? Or was she strong enough to deny the yearning that seemed to burn in the air between them that night and ever since?

Ordella arrived to break the fast, her manner subdued. She had been taken ill, so she had not stirred from her bower since yesterday morn. The illness was not serious, which Adelar considered rather unfortunate.

Baldric, the dogs not far from him, sat at the far end of the hall. The animals waited patiently for the fine bits of meat he would feed them. Indeed, Baldric kept all the best portion of his meals for his charges, which he treated considerably better than many men did their children.

Helmi also sat below the salt, watching the Saxon men and taking care that she was as far away from them as possible. After she had eaten, she would leave at once for the weaving shed, where she seemed to be spending most of her time since Ylla had become Endredi's servant.

Moving forward, Adelar took Bayard's place on the other side of Endredi, ignoring Ordella's disdainful expression. It was his right to take that place when Bayard had made him second in command.

Duff, Merilda and Gleda were speaking together, or, it appeared, arguing over something. The sounds of their quarrel grew louder, and Endredi's frowns were nearly as disapproving as Ordella's.

Suddenly, Gleda shoved Merilda. Without warning, the argument became a fight, the women hurling shrieks, screams and vile epithets at each other. Some of the warriors began to shout encouragement to the combatants. Adelar half-rose from his seat until he remembered that he was not responsible for the servants' behavior. That was Endredi's charge.

At once Endredi strode toward the women, who were rolling around in the straw pummeling each other. Broken dishes littered the floor and foodstuffs were scattered about. The lovely wooden spice box was a shattered wreck.

"Stop!" she shouted, clearly enraged, although the others would perhaps believe she was merely annoyed. Adelar knew better.

The men fell silent. The battling women ignored her until Endredi went to Gleda and dragged her off Merilda. "I said, stop this!"

Gleda, panting, glared at Merilda. "She started it!"

Merilda, glaring back, rose slowly to her feet. "She hit me first!"

"She called me a whore!"

"She is!"

"You're just jealous because Duff won't have you anymore!"

"You'd even sleep with Baldric if he offered you a coin!"

"Liar!"

"Slut!"

Endredi stepped between them. "Enough of this."

Suddenly Merilda's chin began to tremble. "She *is* a whore, my lady! She took my man from me!"

Endredi had no great liking for Gleda, but Merilda had no claim on Duff. They were not married, nor even pledged, as far as she knew. If they were, then Gleda would be the one at fault.

Duff shifted uncomfortably a short distance away. Endredi looked at him. "Well?"

"Well, my lady, I…that is, she…Merilda, I mean, she took it in her head that I said I'd marry her—"

"You told me that, you wretch! I never would have let you lay a hand on me but for that!"

"Did you say you would marry her?" Endredi demanded.

"No."

Gleda smiled smugly until Endredi asked, "Are you intending to marry Gleda?" and Duff shook his head.

"What?" the girl screeched. "You promised!"

"I said I *might*." Duff scowled.

"Gleda and Merilda, if either one of you ever puts on such a display again, I will see that you are sent far from here." Endredi reached down and picked up the ruined spice box. "As for you, Merilda, I suggest you listen less to men's promises. Duff, I give you a choice. Marry Merilda or marry Gleda or get out of this *burh*."

"But my lord Adelar—" Gleda began plaintively, looking at him with dismay. She started to snivel again.

"Bayard will be angry," Duff whined.

Adelar held up his hand for silence. "The *burhware*'s wife decides such matters," he said coolly.

Endredi felt a flash of gratitude, then told herself that she should not be so pleased. She was quite capable of controlling her own servants and did not need his help.

But this was finished, and she had no wish to prolong it, so she returned to her seat.

Merilda, pale and with a baleful expression, sidled silently away, followed by a repentant Duff and a sobbing Gleda.

When the meal resumed, Adelar cleared his throat, drawing Endredi's attention. "I understand you wish help distributing the alms."

"I can manage myself," she said calmly.

"It is no trouble."

"I am at your disposal, my lady," Godwin remarked pleasantly.

"Thank you, Godwin. I will accept your assistance. It will save time."

Endredi next spoke to Ordella, whose face displayed avid interest in their conversation. "How do you fare this morning?"

"Much better," Ordella said. "The medicine you prepared has helped."

"I am happy to hear it."

"Is she not a clever woman?" Ordella demanded of Adelar.

He did not respond, and Endredi was glad he kept silent. She could see the suspicion on his face, and wondered that Ordella apparently did not. She, too, found this solicitousness dubious.

For a time she talked to Ordella of medicines, then plants that made dyes, then how various fabrics took the hues. Anything that would prevent Adelar from taking part.

At last Adelar rose to leave. Endredi watched him depart, then looked down at the table to hide her eyes. No one must see how troubled she was.

Troubled? No, it was more than that. She knew only too well how deeply Adelar cared for her and that they both must force themselves to disregard their feelings.

It seemed he was attempting to do so. Ever since that night in the stable, he had stayed as far away from her as it was possible to stay. His aloofness pained her, although there could be no alternative. His attention and his championing her as he had before the servants only added to her misery.

She had hoped that the more time she spent here, the easier it would be to treat Adelar as simply another one of her husband's men. That was impossible. Whenever she entered the hall, the first thing she did was see if he was there. When he was, she had to fight to keep from looking at him. When he was not, she felt a dismay that was nearly overwhelming.

But she must fight her passion, her needs. She must not give in to temptation. And she must betray nothing to the others, not just for her sake, but for Adelar's. And Bayard's. Adultery would give Ranulf the power to destroy them all, and that must never be.

She told herself that her denial must make her strong, over and over again.

Yet every night she committed adultery in her dreams, imagining that it was Adelar in her bed. Was that so very wrong? Could she help her wayward thoughts?

Was it her fault that the man she desired so much was the very image of her husband? Did it harm anyone to let her have this small recompense?

Surely not.

She sighed raggedly. She felt so weak, so helpless.

So alone.

Adelar approached Godwin as the gleeman prepared to help distribute the alms. "Let me know of the old women to whom you give alms," he said.

"Since what time have you been interested in *old* women?" Godwin asked with a chuckle. "Is it not the younger ones you would like me to note?"

Adelar scowled. "This is a serious matter, Godwin. There has been talk of a strange woman in the woods. I myself have seen such a person while I was out hunting."

"You did not recognize her?"

"No, I was too far away. But I do not like the thought of anyone hiding in the forest, not even an old woman."

"Perhaps she belongs to someone in the *burh?*"

"No one is claiming her if she does. She may only be a harmless old woman, but I want to know."

"I shall keep my eyes and ears open," Godwin said solemnly.

Chapter Ten

Adelar was both relieved and sorry to see Bayard, Father Derrick, Ranulf and the rest of the retinue ride through the gates of Oakenbrook over a fortnight later. His command had been somewhat easier for the absence of Ranulf, but it had been a tense and anxious time.

He would have preferred waiting for a battle to begin. At least then you knew exactly how to fight the enemy.

How did one fight a foe like Ordella, who was the eyes and ears of the less intelligent Ranulf? She had shadowed Endredi like a malevolent spirit. He would have put a stop to it had he not been certain that such an act would only arouse Ordella's curiosity. He would have risked that, however, if he had not also been sure that Endredi could hold her own with a woman like Ordella.

Yet neither Ranulf nor Ordella nor even the army of the Danes was his worst enemy. That name belonged to himself, or rather, his traitorous, tumultuous feelings.

There could be no mistaking the passion he felt for Endredi, and no release. He would not act as his father might, ignoring the bonds of loyalty and honor to satisfy his own needs.

Now, as he watched Bayard greet Endredi and follow her into their bower, he hated himself anew for the jealousy he could not subdue. He could ignore Ranulf's boasting about the thanes they had met and the important churchmen with whom they had dined. In the hall, he could smile at Godwin's jokes and pay attention to Father Derrick's long-winded accounts of his meeting with Father Absalom and the news from the Church in Rome. But he could not stop imagining Bayard and Endredi alone together.

Worse was yet to come. At the meal to celebrate Bayard's return, he insisted that Adelar sit to his left between himself and Endredi, so that Adelar was closest to Bayard.

"We have business to discuss," Bayard explained when Adelar looked about to protest.

Adelar took his place beside Endredi. She wore a gown of fine wool in a lovely blue color that made her eyes appear even more green, although she did not look directly at him. Her hair was covered by a filmy silk scarf that brushed her smooth cheeks. Two brooches of ornate silver that he had never seen before were at her shoulders. Probably gifts from Bayard, he thought. He watched her slender hands reach out for her goblet and remembered how she used to slap his fingers playfully when he would try to grab food in the days when they were youngsters together. She would look sternly at him, but there was always a smile lurking in the depths of her eyes.

"Adelar, I did not mean to offend you by having you on my left," Bayard said quietly when the meal was under way.

With a guilty start, Adelar glanced at his cousin. "I am not offended," he answered honestly. "I am honored to be at your table."

"Good," Bayard said. He sounded listless, but Adelar supposed listening to interminable discussions on political matters would have that effect, as well as the journey home. "I take it nothing untoward happened during my absence?"

"No, my lord."

"Endredi tells me you were a good commander."

"I am pleased for your wife's commendation," he replied, flushing slightly and wishing he was not.

"Endredi has made a conquest!" Bayard said knowingly.

Adelar looked quickly at Bayard, then at Endredi, who appeared shocked. "A conquest, Bayard?" she asked hesitantly. "I do not understand you."

"It's Adelar."

"My lord!" Adelar protested.

"Come, Adelar, everyone can see it. Confess it—you no longer think I made a mistake marrying a Viking."

"My lord, I—"

"If you did, you would have ignored her completely while I was gone, and I know for a fact you did not.

Now, contradict me at your peril," he challenged jovially.

Adelar sensed Endredi's relief, which matched his own. "You may have found one Viking worthy of your trust," he replied.

"Not quite the answer I hoped for, but it is a start." Bayard leaned back and laid down his knife. "It is a relief to me to hear that at least my small part of the kingdom has few troubles. Marriage is a good thing, Adelar."

"In your case, I must agree."

"Several other thanes were asking about you. The ones with daughters, particularly."

Adelar merely grunted and reached for more meat, acutely aware of the silent Endredi beside him. "You are still considered a worthy article on the marriage market, Adelar."

"That is not my trouble."

"Do you intend never to marry?"

"Why should I? I won't have any land to bequeath."

"Your father—"

"Can rot in hell as far as I'm concerned, as you well know, Bayard."

"Don't you want sons?"

"I have no great desire to bring a child into the world." He saw Bayard's frown and realized that this was not the time to voice his opinion. Bayard, after all, made no secret of his obsession to have sons. Adelar forced himself to grin. "If it meant chaining myself to only one woman."

Bayard chuckled, and Adelar felt the tension pass.

"What do you think of my fine cousin, Endredi, eh?" Bayard asked cheerfully. "Him and his talk of chains!"

"If he considers marriage vows chains," Endredi said softly, "perhaps it is better that he not wed. For the woman's sake."

Adelar regarded her steadily. He did feel chained by marriage vows, but not because *he* was married.

"Well answered," Bayard cried. "Don't stare at her like that, Adelar. She's right, after all. Did you hear what Endredi said, Ranulf? And you tried to convince me not to marry her!"

Ranulf smiled halfheartedly. "From all I have seen and heard, my lord, it is evident I was mistaken. I most humbly beg your pardon."

Still later that night, Bayard eyed Adelar as they sat together in the hall. The men who had not yet retired sat upon benches, talking among themselves, drinking and occasionally singing snatches of song. Godwin was attempting to juggle stools, without much success. The fire had burned down so that the only light in the hall was the glow from the coals and the feeble flames of some oil lamps burning upon the table.

"I am glad to think that most of the thanes agree with Edward's plans. We do not need more dissension among us," Adelar said thoughtfully, running his fingers along his smoothly carved drinking horn.

"Yes. It is a good thing Alfred also married a daughter to a Mercian, though, or perhaps we would not be so united."

"The Mercians need us."

"The Kentish men continue to complain."

"Only to voice their hatred of the Mercians, it seems to me. I am certain when it comes to a battle, they will all unite with us against the Danes."

"I hope so." Bayard sighed wearily.

"Are you tired?"

"No." Bayard reached for his drinking horn. "Endredi told me today that she is not with child."

"Unhappy news for you, Bayard."

"Yes. It may be that this collection of buildings is all that will be left to show I ever lived."

Surprised by his cousin's unusual melancholy, Adelar said, "Cynath is pleased, is he not?"

"Yes. But the *burh* is still nothing more than a collection of wood and stone, easily destroyed."

"You are keeping your people safe with this collection of wood and stone," Adelar pointed out. "And it is more than I shall leave behind me."

Bayard smiled at his cousin, his face ruddy in the firelight. "That is the reward of duty and responsibility, Adelar. The knowledge that the world has been made a little different for your presence in it."

"You have made more than a little difference, Bayard."

"Perhaps. It pleases my vanity to think so, just as it disturbs me to know that I may have to turn all this over to a man who sees only the power he will be able to wield, not the obligations that attend it. You are still certain, Adelar, that you have no wish to command?"

"I have no desire to be so burdened."

"But the rewards—" Bayard's gesture encompassed his vast hall. "They can be worth it."

"No."

Bayard toyed with his chalice. "Perhaps you are right. I would give all this away to have a son, Adelar. A legacy of warm flesh and blood, not cold stone and hard wood."

Adelar looked at his uncharacteristically serious cousin and wished he did not have to say what he must, but he had already delayed too long. He spoke slowly, raising his gaze to Bayard's face. "Bayard, I am leaving."

"Why? I thought you had gotten over your objections to my wife."

"It has nothing to do with her. She is my lord's wife, and as such, I must accept her. I leave because my time in the *fyrd* is at an end. I wish to go tomorrow, at first light."

"How have I offended you?"

"You have not, Bayard. Believe me, you have not."

"Then why go?"

Adelar hesitated, more torn than ever by his decision. Bayard was different tonight, so sad and seemingly filled with dark thoughts.

Bayard eyed him shrewdly. "Adelar, I know you well enough to understand that you have made this decision and will seek to abide by it. I . . . I wanted to wait a while yet before I say what I must, but you seem so determined, you give me little choice." He leaned closer and spoke in a whisper. "I have a great favor I must ask of you, and I can ask it of no other man."

Adelar saw the intense expression in Bayard's face and wondered what need could put it there. "You know you have but to ask, cousin."

With his eyes downcast, Bayard said, "I want you to make love with my wife."

"*What?*"

"I want you to make love with Endredi."

"Are you mad?" Adelar fought to keep his voice low even as his mind struggled to comprehend what Bayard was saying.

"I am dying."

Bayard meant it, believed it. His conviction was there in his eyes, plain to be seen. "I . . . I do not understand," Adelar said haltingly, hoping that there could yet be some mistake.

"I have been ill a long time and I have seen more doctors and monks and even reputed witches than I care to remember. There is no hope for me. I want Endredi to bear a child before I die, and you are my only hope."

"I do not believe it! You do not even look sick."

Bayard smiled sardonically. "How many times in the past weeks have you told me I look tired? I was well-

rested. Adelar, you know how much I have wanted
sons. Now, more than ever, I need one."

"What are you saying? That you are too sick to. . ."
He hesitated, not willing to broach the sanctity of
Bayard's bower.

"Make love to my wife? I have, Adelar." He emp-
tied the drinking glass, which gave Adelar time to fight
both the moment of elation and then the disappoint-
ment of Bayard's response. "I do not believe I was ever
capable of fathering children. You know that I have
loved many women, Adelar. But I have never fathered
a child."

"How can you be sure?"

"Because I promised every woman I bedded that if
she was to bear my child, I would reward her hand-
somely. Some tried to collect, but there was always evidence that the child might not be mine. Now I am sure
I cannot, because of the illness." His expression grew
hard and determined. "I have no wish to leave my
lands and my possessions to Ranulf. I would leave them
to you, Adelar."

"I do not want them!" he protested at once.

"I know, as I also know Ranulf would never rest
until he had taken them from you. So, if I cannot will
you my possessions, I will give them to a son. Your
son, who will look enough like me that no man will
dare to question his parentage, should anyone ever
suspect."

"Bayard..." Adelar wanted nothing more than to be able to love Endredi, but not this way. By all the saints and martyrs, not this way.

"There is another reason I have chosen you. Do you remember that serving wench at Cynath's *burh*, Janeth?"

"Janeth? No."

"You should—she gave you a son three years ago."

"This is the first time I have heard of it," Adelar said warily.

"I had heard a rumor of the babe and thought you knew. Since you never spoke of it, I wondered if they were simply rumors and nothing more, so I questioned Cynath about her. Cynath is not sure who the sire was, but there is no doubt in my mind that the child could be yours."

"You think I have a son?"

"You *had* a son. The child fell ill and died."

"Oh." Strange it was to have a child, then to lose it in such a short space of time. But no more strange, perhaps, than anything else Bayard was saying.

"At least you know you can sire sons," Bayard said softly. "I would give anything, pay any price, to know that I could. But I cannot."

"You can't be sure of this, just as I cannot be sure Janeth's child was mine."

"I have no time left to waste in vain hopes, Adelar, or vague dissembling. I need a son—and so does Endredi. I think you are our last, best chance. Think what might happen when I am dead if Ranulf inherits. He will have no compunction about sending her back to that lout Dagfinn, or even something worse. If she has what everyone believes to be my child, she will have some security. I am certain she will fight for that child's rights as fiercely as a mother bear protecting her cubs.''

"That is why you asked Dagfinn if she was strong-willed.''

"Yes. I had been thinking of marrying again for some time, but I wanted a woman who could, and would, fight for herself. I believe I have got her.''

An image flashed unwanted into Adelar's mind, of the night Endredi and the others escaped his father. She had been so strong, so determined to get home. Fight for her child? She would, unto death.

"Then Dagfinn made his proposal. I believed it was a sign from God and dared to hope that my bride would answer my other prayers. That has not happened. I do not know how much time God will give to me, Adelar, so I must ask this of you. If you come to care for her, you might even consider marrying her yourself when I am gone. But I want to be certain Ranulf's greed is thwarted before that.''

"Endredi—does she know of this...this proposal?''

"No. I would rather she did not know I asked you.''

"You want me to *seduce* her?''

He smiled wistfully. "To leave myself a little pride. That is another reason you are my choice, Adelar. You have no trouble charming women.''

"I will if the woman is Endredi. Her loyalty to you will be beyond my skills." Even as he said it, he knew it was true. And that—God help him—he wished it wasn't. "Tell her about your sickness. She might be able to help."

"Does the thought of sleeping with Endredi hold so little appeal for you?"

"Bayard, I have no wish to be a stallion to service another man's needs," Adelar said truthfully, fighting the temptation. "And you are asking me—us—to commit adultery."

"I know."

"What if Ranulf or someone else finds out? You will have to punish us."

"If they do, obviously I will not condemn you. If you have a child by her, I will claim it for my own. No man would dare to question me, not even Ranulf."

"Is confession and absolution supposed to make up for such a sin? What if I die unshriven? I could go to hell."

"I have thought of that too, Adelar, and so I will understand if you refuse. Believe me when I say I wish things were not as they are. I would give nearly everything for a child of my body, but God has seen fit to deny me. Perhaps I am doing wrong to try to change that. I have spent much time thinking about it, and all I can say is, if you agree, you would be giving me a great gift and protecting Endredi."

"Godwin saw us together, and he has been watching me like a nursemaid ever since. As for Endredi, she avoids me entirely. It is simply impossible."

He waited for Bayard to respond, noting his drawn and haggard appearance. Some of the men said that Bayard had fallen ill on the journey. Adelar guessed it was the illness Bayard thought was killing him worsening.

Bayard sighed deeply. "I have one final plan," he said at last. "It is a trick, but I think it is my only hope."

"What is it?"

"We look alike, Adelar. Not enough to fool anyone in the daytime, but at night, in a dark bower, with the bed curtains drawn..."

"You want me to pretend I am you?"

"It seems to be the only solution."

"We are not that much alike, Bayard. Endredi would surely guess. And have you forgotten you have a beard and I do not?"

"If I am willing to let another man make love with my wife, do you think I would hesitate to rid myself of my beard? It will be gone by the morrow." He gave Adelar the ghost of a grin. "And I suspect that a man of your skill could distract even Endredi enough that she would forget whatever suspicions may occur."

"Where will you be, while I am distracting her? You cannot be in two places at once."

"I will wait in one of the storage sheds. When you are finished, mumble something about having to go outside and then come and fetch me."

"What if I am seen going in and out of the bower?"

"Wear my cloak. We are the same height."

"Bayard, I have no liking for anything about this deception."

"Neither do I, Adelar. And if this ruse does not work, I shall agree to give up. But don't answer me tonight. Think on it, as I have for many a day. If you decide against it, so be it."

Adelar did think about it, the whole of the long, sleepless night. And in the morning, when Bayard appeared in the hall without his beard and with anxious eyes, Adelar told his cousin the answer was yes.

Chapter Eleven

Endredi lay alone in her bed. Bayard had suggested that both Ylla and Helmi sleep in the hall now, and she had not objected. Sometimes, when she could no longer contain her misery, she allowed herself the luxury of tears when Bayard lingered in the hall, as he had tonight. She knew it was a weakness and each time vowed it would be the last.

After all, there were other things to occupy her mind. Bayard had much to tell the thanes and warriors about the plans that had been discussed at Cynath's *burh*. He had told her some of it, and for his trust she was grateful.

Bayard and Cynath agreed that Oakenbrook would be an obvious site for a first strike. Dagfinn seemed ready to abide by his oaths and promises regarding Bayard's land, but they were not certain he would keep them.

Nor was she. She knew Dagfinn too well. He was, above all, greedy, and if he felt confident enough in the Danes' ability to triumph, he would disregard any and all promises. Even if Dagfinn himself was reluctant, there were too many among his men who still believed that the Saxons were weak. Dagfinn might be forced to go to war against his better judgment, lest he lose everything.

Wasn't she a fine one, she thought bitterly, to be so harsh in her estimation of Dagfinn's trustworthiness? Her feelings and desire for Adelar could only be considered traitorous. She found it all too easy to forget her own oaths, sworn when she became Bayard's wife.

It might be different if her husband was a cruel, brutal man. Or a stupid, blundering fool. But he was none of these things. He was kind, generous, honorable—as fine a husband as a woman could desire.

Yet all *she* wished for was another man, a man who looked too much like her husband. She had noticed a similarity between Adelar and his cousin before, but now that Bayard had removed his beard, the resemblance was quite startling.

She heard the door of the bower open and close and snuggled down deeper under the covers, pretending to be asleep. Confused and uncertain, she simply wanted to be left alone. She kept her eyes closed and made her breathing deep and regular while her husband disrobed and blew out the slight flame from the oil lamp she had left lit on the table. Without making a sound, he got into the bed beside her.

His hand moved slowly along her upper arm to her shoulder, then across to caress her cheek. He shifted closer. She felt his naked skin against her. His hand moved lower, traveling along her leg and stroking her thigh.

This leisurely action was different from Bayard's usual quick ways, she realized vaguely. Different, too, from Fenris's fumbling under the sheets.

Delightfully different. She rolled onto her back, aware of the naked man beside her in the darkness. "Bayard?" she whispered questioningly.

He did not answer with words. Instead, firm lips pressed down upon hers in a heated kiss. His fingers grazed her skin ever so lightly, teasing her nipples. Then his strong, rough hands gripped her shoulders while his hair brushed her skin as she moaned softly, senses reeling.

"Bayard," she sighed, reaching up to touch his face.

It was not Bayard's face. These were not Bayard's lips, or his hands upon her flesh.

She sat up abruptly, staring. She yanked the coverings to hide her nakedness and tried to see the intruder's face in the dark. "Adelar!" she cried softly, suddenly sure. "What are you doing? Get out at once!"

"Endredi, please! I want you so much!"

"I am Bayard's wife. Get out, or I shall scream." She scrambled out of the bed, stumbling in the shadows, horrified that he would dare do this. She reached for her shift, drawing it on swiftly.

He was still in the bed. Bayard's bed. "Are you mad, Adelar?" she said, her tone between a demand and a plea. "Get out at once, before Bayard finds you here!"

With trembling fingers she tried to light the wick of the oil lamp, but could not. Suddenly, a warm, strong hand closed on her wrist. "Let me go!" she entreated, twisting away.

"Endredi," he pleaded. "Endredi!"

She knew she should flee even as he embraced her. "Endredi, I have tried to stay away from you. You, of all people, know this. Even tonight, I told myself I only wanted to speak with you. But I am too weak. I could not resist. God help me, I cannot."

"I will not betray my husband!" she whispered urgently, willing herself to be strong despite the desire in her heart.

"I have no wish to betray my cousin. My lord."

"He is all those things, Adelar—as well as my husband."

"I know. I have told myself so a hundred times. I even tried to go from here."

"You should have. Please, go now."

"I need you, Endredi. So much I am willing to risk anything."

She drew in a great, shuddering breath, touched by his words whispered in the dark. Hearing the truth of them. Feeling an answering truth in her own heart. "Adelar, I...I..."

He let go of her and lit the lamp. The flame sent flickering shadows over his broad naked chest and hid his dark eyes. "Endredi, look at me now and tell me you do not want me. Tell me to go, and I will."

She shook her head. "Adelar..."

"Tell me you do not want me, and I will leave this very night. Tell me that you have never wanted me, not in your father's village the first time we kissed. Not the last time we saw each other at my father's *burh*. Or the first time we stood together in Bayard's hall. I have never stopped wanting you, Endredi. All these years, I have dreamed of you, desired you, needed you. There is nothing else I want in all my life but you."

She stared at him, the boy she loved, the man she desired. She had been fighting her feelings for him for days and she had subdued her longing for him for years. Now, here, she could not fight any more. "Oh, Adelar," she cried, sinking down onto the ground, "I want you with all my heart and I wish I did not! We have our duty and our honor. If we lose that, what is there left?"

He knelt in front of her and took her cheeks gently between the palms of his hands. "In the long nights of our lives, will duty and honor give us comfort? If we deny what we so strongly feel, what is there left for us?"

Her silence emboldened him. "What we feel for each other cannot be wrong, Endredi. It is good. It is right. It is what was meant to be. Tell me you agree, and answer me not as Bayard's wife, but as the Endredi I knew." He kissed her again, tenderly, gently, with such yearning and hope and desire that she was helpless to protest any more.

Their kiss deepened as undeniable desire took hold of them both like an entwining vine. Endredi had one brief moment when she knew she should pull away before it was too late. It passed, and still she kissed Adelar, all thoughts of betrayal and sin consumed by the need to be with him. He, too, hesitated for an instant—until her hands began to press him closer.

Then they were lost to everything except each other in the dim darkness of the bower.

Their tongues touched, drew back, touched again and joined. She caressed him slowly, coming alive in his arms as he stroked her. Heat possessed her and fire burned in her limbs. Her breathing quickened, matching the throbbing of the blood coursing through her veins. She was no virgin, but no other man had ever inspired such explosive desire in her.

Adelar lifted her and took her to the bed. Without even breaking the kiss, he laid her down and joined her. He had had many women, but this time, it was as if she was the first. Gently, he ran his hand through her bountiful hair as he had dreamed of doing so many times. He could feel her chest rising and falling beneath him, feel her heart pounding in a rhythm that matched his own.

Breaking the kiss with a long sigh, his lips trailed slowly down her smooth skin. He marveled as she reached up and with trembling fingers undid the drawstring of her shift. He stared into the green depths of her eyes and saw her trust, and love. "Endredi," he whispered, certain they had always been destined for each other. God had wanted it, or He would not have brought her back to him. But he would still stop if she asked it of him.

"Adelar," she whispered. She pressed a kiss to his hot, naked chest.

It was a blessing, an agreement, a plea. The last constraint withered and died within him, annihilated by the flames of his desire.

They kissed again. And again. He tasted what remained of the salt of her tears. Her hands gripped his shoulders as his lips found her breasts, teasing her taut nipples. She undulated under him, her sensual movements increasing the speed of his own.

Yet because this was Endredi, he would not make haste. He would savor every moment in her arms. As if she agreed, she, too, continued to explore him slowly with her eyes, with her lips and with her hands.

He was everything she had dreamed of, and more. He touched her as no man ever had, as if his pleasure was not to be considered, only hers. And pleasure was what he gave. No, more. Excitement, ecstasy, delight beyond anything she could imagine. Desperate for him, she arched against him and reached, guiding him to her. Slowly, slowly, he met her. Then they journeyed together, until two stifled cries broke the silence of the bower.

"Adelar!"

He felt gentle hands shaking him and awakened at once, the memory of where he was and with whom flooding into his consciousness. "Endredi?" he whispered.

"Yes. You must go now, Adelar, before Bayard comes."

He rose at her urgent words and looked at her. She was so beautiful, clad in a white shift that seemed to shimmer in the flickering light of the one candle she had lit. Her hair flowed over her slim shoulders. Her slender, trembling hands reminded him of the incredible power she had to arouse him.

He wanted to pull her down beside him and kiss her until the morning birds began singing, until the sun was high in the sky, until it was too late for the evening meal, until it was time to sleep once more.

But her trembling told him she was afraid, too. "It is getting late," she said again. "Bayard may be here any moment, and if he should find you here, he will kill you."

"No, he would not," he replied quietly. Nonetheless, he reached for his breeches and tugged them on. He tried to think of some way to reassure her that would leave Bayard his pride.

"He would not care that you were his cousin. He is a proud man. He could not overlook adultery." He heard the anguish in her voice and went to her, taking her perfumed body in his arms.

"I am not sorry," she whispered fervently, her cheek against his chest. "I do not regret my feelings for you, or what we did."

"Nor do I, Endredi. Please, do not worry."

"How can I not? What we have done is wrong in law, if not in our hearts. If Ranulf should find out—"

"Leave Ranulf to me. And anyone else who may trouble you. I will protect you with my life."

"Oh, Adelar!" She sighed raggedly and her shoulders slumped, but only for a brief moment. "You *must* leave. Go carefully, my love," she urged, "lest you be seen."

"I will."

He drew back and they gazed at each other, remembering their desire and their pleasure. "Go at once!" she urged again, tugging him toward the door.

He slipped into the covering darkness of the cloudy night and moved into the shadows when the moon shone through. The breeze bespoke rain before morning and a warm day ahead.

He stopped and inhaled the scents on the summer wind deeply, allowing himself this moment of precious happiness.

He did not regret what had happened. Endredi was his, and he was hers. Their bond was forged too strong for anyone to break. Not Bayard. Not Ranulf. Not the Danes.

Although it would mean trouble if Ranulf found out. Even Bayard, despite his assurances, would not be able to overlook Ranulf completely, especially if the man went to Cynath with his suspicions.

Ever since the day of the riding lesson, when he had the first real evidence of Endredi's feelings, Adelar had considered what to do if that happened, and he was prepared. Godwin had given him the key. He would say that he forced Endredi against her will and he would take whatever consequences happened. Endredi would be disgraced, but no one would want her death. She could go to a convent where she would be alive, at least.

He continued toward the hall. What had Endredi meant, there at the last when she urged him to go? Did she want him to leave the bower... or the *burh?* Now that he knew the depth of her feelings for him, he would never leave her again unless ordered into battle. He would risk anything to stay near her and to be with her, to love her and protect her until the end of his life.

The hall was dim, the only light coming from the glowing coals in the hearth. One of Baldric's hounds growled a greeting and got to his feet. Before the dog could disturb his slumbering master, Adelar reached out and stroked it, surveying the hall. Bayard sat on the settle at the far end. His cousin was not asleep, but waiting with a questioning look upon his face. His grip on the arm of his chair tightened as Adelar went casually toward him. "It is done?" he whispered anxiously.

"Yes."

Bayard sighed and looked away. Adelar's heart ached for his noble, proud cousin who had helped him to his heart's desire. "She thought it was you."

There came the ghost of a smile to Bayard's face, and Adelar was glad he had lied and returned to Bayard some small measure of the dignity he deserved.

Bayard gestured toward Ylla as she slept on a straw mattress not far away. "Have you had her?"

Exhaustion stealing over him, Adelar gave his cousin a puzzled look. "Why do you ask?"

"Because it's obvious to any man with eyes that she wants you, and I wondered if you had taken advantage of it."

Adelar looked down at the rushes on the floor. "No, I have not."

"Ask her to meet you in the weaving shed tomorrow night."

Adelar raised his eyes to his cousin and frowned darkly. "Why?"

"I am only thinking that if you did, I could be with Ylla, pretending I was you. If others thought Adelar with her, it would divert any possible suspicion. Don't you see, Adelar?" he went on. "If anyone does come to think that you have been with Endredi, Ylla will say Adelar has been with her. She is only a servant, of course, but with you saying the same thing, it will have the ring of truth. Besides, then we would both be gone from the hall at the same time."

Adelar gazed at his cousin whose face now so closely resembled his own and saw that he was perfectly serious. Shocking though the suggestion was, Adelar could not disagree with the notion that the deception might allay suspicions.

Oh, dear God, he never should have lied and said that Endredi had been successfully deceived.

But to admit that Endredi had known it was not her husband... Despite the fact that the ploy was Bayard's own plan, Adelar could not be sure his cousin would actually welcome the news that his wife had committed adultery knowingly.

Yet how could he agree to this added subterfuge? What if Ylla realized it was Bayard as swiftly as Endredi had known it was not her husband in her bed? "Suppose Ylla guesses?"

"If Endredi did not, Ylla will not," Bayard said firmly, obviously believing it would be so.

Because Endredi's safety was the most important thing, Adelar finally nodded. Nonetheless, he said, "I do not like it."

"Nor do I, but it will keep others from being suspicious."

"Tomorrow night, then, Bayard."

Adelar sat at the table beside Godwin as Gleda and Merilda set out the food for the evening meal. "Where have you been all day?" he asked the gleeman. "You were gone before first light."

"You know I like to walk in the woods when I compose my music," Godwin answered glibly.

Out of the corner of his eye, Adelar watched as Endredi spoke to Father Derrick. How beautiful she looked to him! Lovelier even than she had by candlelight, which had made her skin seem to glow with the warmth of new-forged gold. Today, her pale skin had the bright luminosity of the full moon. How much he wanted to speak to her, but he knew he had to content himself with only looking, for now.

"I thought I saw that snow-white stag," Godwin remarked.

The gleeman's words made Adelar look away from Endredi. "Did you see that woman I spoke of?"

Godwin shook his head.

"Did you ask about an old woman when you helped with the alms?" he inquired.

"Yes. No one else has seen a stranger, either."

"I *did* see a woman, Godwin."

"What did she look like?"

"She was too far away and she wore a cloak, so I could not make out her features."

"That was unfortunate. Maybe it was Helmi."

"I wondered that, too."

"Why would she be in the woods, though?"

"Perhaps she was meeting someone, but if she was, I do not think she was having an assignation with a lover, or gathering wood or food," Adelar noted.

"That is a serious charge, Adelar. I thought you did not distrust the Danes now."

"I do not distrust Bayard's wife. That is why I said nothing to Bayard. But I think the serving woman should be watched."

"I agree, although I'm sure it is nothing to concern us."

Ranulf and Ordella came into the hall, and Godwin grinned. "St. Swithins in a swamp, aren't they the happy ones? Look at her face—like she drank the juice of lemons."

"I think Ranulf has enjoyed Gleda's charms."

"Ranulf, too?" Godwin guffawed. "No wonder Ordella looks like that!"

"I should warn you, Godwin, that Gleda's got her eye on you. She wants a husband."

"I do not think Gleda wishes a gleeman for a husband. She would set her sights higher." He looked pointedly at Adelar.

"She is a generous and kind-hearted wench—which means I would not suit her," he remarked.

"*That* I cannot argue with. She likes a man who can make her laugh."

"She may be right, then, to look at you as she does." He nodded slightly toward Gleda, who was indeed eyeing Godwin much as a woman might eye a piece of cloth she was of a mind to buy.

"I have no wish to marry a soiled dove," Godwin said, his tone so contemptuous that Adelar looked at him in surprise.

Godwin grinned at once and said with mock humility, "A gleeman I may be, but I have *some* pride, my lord." He nodded toward Ylla. "What do you intend to do about Ylla?"

"Do about her?"

"Yes. Are you finished with her?"

"I have never started."

Godwin's eyes gleamed eagerly. "Truly, Adelar?"

"Truly, Godwin."

Ylla glanced their way, and Adelar gestured for her to join them. "But I intend to."

As she made her way to the bench, Adelar looked curiously at Godwin. "Are you interested in her?"

"It would not matter if I was," the gleeman replied with a grin and a shrug. "How can I compete with a handsome, noble warrior like you?"

Ylla waited nearby, obviously unsure what was wanted of her, until Adelar patted the bench beside him. "Join me."

"Do you not intend to sit higher at the table?" she asked, her gaze shifting from Adelar to Godwin uncertainly.

"I intend to sit with Godwin, and with you."

Ylla smiled with such genuine, unabashed pleasure that Adelar was ashamed of himself. What tangled web was he helping to weave, and who would be caught in it?

"I have my duties to attend to, my lord."

He took hold of her hand and leaned closer. "Perhaps your duties might take you to the weaving shed tonight when the evening meal is finished."

Her eyes widened, and then—oh, how much he hated even this lesser treachery—she smiled, her face lighting as if a candle had been kindled within. "I shall be there, my lord," she whispered intently, withdrawing her hand ever so slowly from his before moving away.

"And you wonder why I do not try," Godwin muttered sarcastically.

* * *

Adelar and Bayard met in the shadowy stable when the moon was halfway through its course, and quickly exchanged cloaks and tunics. "When you hear me call like an owl, you must go," Bayard said, pulling up the hood of the light cloak.

Adelar nodded his agreement. "Or if you hear me."

"Where is Ylla?"

"She is waiting for you in the weaving shed. Where is Helmi?"

"In the hall, as she will be every night. She was not pleased, but she will not disobey me."

"How much do you trust her?"

"Helmi? Not a great deal, but she seems to have great affection for Endredi, and I doubt she would want to see her mistress disgraced. Nevertheless, I thought it wise to send her from the bower."

"I fear she may be a spy."

"Helmi?" Bayard asked doubtfully. "She has never once been from the *burh.*"

"Can you be certain? I saw a strange woman in the woods while I was hunting, more than once. I think it might be wise to set a watch on her."

"I have always had a watch on her. Although I believe I can trust Endredi, I have never had any confidence in Helmi's loyalty. Indeed, I would rather send her back to Dagfinn, but Endredi fears the woman would be punished. It must have been another woman, probably gathering firewood." He went to the door, then hesitated and turned on the threshold. "Adelar, you do understand that I do not enjoy deceiving Endredi this way."

"Yes, Bayard. I do. And Ylla is a fine young woman."

Bayard sighed. "Adelar, perhaps we should end all this."

"The harm has already been done."

"Once. One sin. To continue, however..."

"Bayard, you wanted this. You asked me. I agreed and now I have no wish to end it."

"What are you saying?"

"I am saying that I want Endredi more than the breath in my body."

"Adelar, she is my wife!"

"Do you think my heart is made of stone, Bayard? I care for her very much, and not merely as the potential mother of a son."

"How dare you speak so to me!"

"I dare because it is the truth!"

"I care for Endredi, too."

"So much you would let another man sleep with her? So much you yourself would take a wench pretending to be another to throw off suspicion? Look at us, Bayard," he said coldly, gesturing at their exchanged clothing. "What kind of demons have we become?"

Bayard slumped down on a nearby pile of straw. "You are right, Adelar. I never should have asked you this. I thought I had everything planned, but I forgot that hearts cannot be made to obey. I do care for Endredi, and it fills me with pain every time I think of you with her.'' He looked at Adelar, his expression full of anguish and sorrow. ''I began this because I need a son and I cannot provide one. I still want a son more than anything, even more than Endredi. All you want is Endredi herself. When I am dead, I hope you will marry her. For the present, I leave it to you, Adelar, to continue or end this deception tonight.''

Adelar knew there was only one answer he could give, only one his heart would allow. ''We have embarked on this course, Bayard, and I cannot turn from it now, come what may.''

Chapter Twelve

The hoot of an owl interrupted the silence of the autumn night. Entwined in Endredi's arms, Adelar raised his head. "The hour grows late," he whispered, stroking her silky cheek with his fingertips.

She bent her head to kiss his callused palm. "I wish you could remain with me," she said softly.

"I, too." But even as he spoke, he got out of the bed.

She reached out and caressed his naked back. "You are shivering."

"It's cold," he said, reaching for his breeches. He twisted and gave her a roguish smile. "Without the benefit of your body to give me warmth."

"Is that all I am to you, my bold Saxon? A body to keep you warm?"

He turned toward her, his face solemn. "Oh, no. You are much more than that, Endredi." The intense, passionate expression in his eyes thrilled her beyond the power to answer, either seriously or in jest.

The owl hooted again, and Adelar once more began to dress.

She allowed herself the enjoyment of watching him. How muscular he was, slim and lithe in his movements. Graceful, like a cat.

He pulled on his tunic, one she had never known him to wear before, a black garment rather like the one Bayard had worn that evening. In it, he resembled his cousin even more. He picked up his cloak and put it on.

"That is Bayard's cloak," Endredi said, recognizing it at once.

"I must have taken the wrong one from the hall."

"You had better be sure to put it back," she answered, a measure of concern in her voice. For a moment, she had forgotten the forbidden nature of their love. "It is a good thing Bayard chose to stay there, or he would be searching for it."

"Yes."

"Why did he remain in the hall?"

"Godwin was telling the story of Beowulf again, and Bayard stayed to hear it."

"I am grateful to Godwin, then, for spinning so long a tale."

"Me, too, Endredi, me, too. But Godwin must be nearly finished by now, and so I dare not stay."

"Forgive this intrusion, my lord," one of the watchmen said as he peered into the darkened bower. "I have news of the woman we were told to look out for."

Endredi tugged the covers up to her chin and glanced at Adelar, who had turned swiftly away from the door and reached for the vessel filled with wine on the small table, as if he was pouring himself a drink.

"Woman?" she asked, wondering what woman was so important that the watchman would come to Bayard's bower at this late hour.

"Have you seen her?" Adelar asked, his voice little more than a mumble. He sounded enough like Bayard to fool this fellow, who was only a foot soldier.

"I saw someone creeping through the woods and went at once to the commander of the watch. He sent me and Matthew to follow her, but I regret to say, my lord, that we could not find her."

"She moved quickly, then?"

"She was bent like an old woman, but moved very fast for a crone."

"I see. Next time, take Baldric and the best hounds."

"Aye, my lord."

"You may go."

"Aye, my lord."

Endredi waited until the watchman had gone, then rose from the bed and pulled on her fur-lined robe. "What woman is this that you spoke of? Bayard has said nothing to me of her."

"It may be nothing. I have seen a strange old woman in the woods more than once. I simply want to know who she is."

"You fear a spy?"

Adelar gazed at her steadily and nodded. "I do not like mysterious strangers, even if they are only old women."

"Nor do I." Endredi glanced at the door nervously. "I think you should leave, Adelar, before another watchman comes."

He saw the tension in her face, and cursed the watchman for coming to the bower. She was as nervous as she had been the first time they had been together.

And yet, perhaps she was wise to be leery. It would be a mistake to let his guard down. Although Bayard was a willing participant, it would be disastrous if Ranulf or Ordella discovered this liaison.

He pulled Endredi into his arms. "Very well, I will go."

"Take care, Adelar."

"Always."

Godwin shoved the bundle beneath the weaving shed into the hiding place he had prepared. Then he straightened, trying to slow his rasping breaths as he hid in the shadows.

That had been too close, he thought as he scanned the walls in the distance, the sentries visible in the moonlight. He had been seen and nearly caught this time.

And for what? He had had little enough to tell Dagfinn, other than the fact that Ranulf had dallied again with a serving wench and enraged his wife. The fellow seemed less and less capable of acting even slightly wise, for any fool could see that Ranulf's wife was the clever schemer. Nor did he expect Dagfinn to use the information he gleaned. Dagfinn would relay it to the Danes close to Aethelwold, though.

Godwin peered around the building. No one in sight, and the nearest sentry was speaking to another guard. Godwin slipped around the side of the building and hurried toward the gate. Once there, he began to whistle a jaunty tune.

"Who's there?" the watchman called out.

"Godwin," he answered. He waited for the gate to open.

"What are you doing about so late?" the soldier asked suspiciously.

"Visiting a friend," the gleeman replied with a wink.

"These are dangerous times, my friend," the soldier said warily. "You had best keep your weapon sheathed."

"What good is a weapon in a sheath?" Godwin asked with a grin. "I would rather keep in practice." He moved his hips suggestively, which made the soldier smile.

"Still, I would suggest you do not linger quite so long," the sentry remarked.

"Why? Are you expecting trouble?"

"Perhaps."

"Well then, I shall do as you say," Godwin answered before proceeding on his way.

Too close indeed, he thought. He might have already overstayed the time for safety. And yet it galled him to leave with Bayard and his people so secure. This was an important *burh* in the defense of Wessex; if only he could leave its leadership a shambles, so that it could be easily conquered. He did not want the *burh* destroyed, though. It would be a fine jewel in the crown of a king. A Mercian king.

A slight movement caught his attention. Instinctively he moved into the shadow of a building, every sense alert.

It was the door to Bayard's bower opening—so late? He thought Bayard would have retired long since.

The figure of a man in the doorway was illuminated by the light inside for a brief instant, then he walked stealthily away. By the way his head moved from side to side, he was watching the sentries as carefully as Godwin had.

What was Bayard doing sneaking out of his own bower at this time of night? Was he meeting someone? A lover, perhaps? Or was it something else?

No. He was merely going to the hall. Except...as Godwin watched the man continue cautiously toward the hall, he noted something familiar about the lithe ease of the man's movements. His gait was *like* Bayard's, but different...and the man's height was not quite right. Indeed, the fellow was more like...*Adelar!*

Godwin stared, straining to see in the dark. No, he could not be mistaken. He had spent more time than anyone in Adelar's company.

For a heady moment the import of what he had seen swamped Godwin. Here was the thing he needed, the dagger that would rip the fabric of this *burh* to ribbons! Adelar, spending part of the night in Bayard's bower, surely with Bayard's wife!

For a proud man like Bayard, this double betrayal of a wife and trusted cousin would wound nearly to the death. It would certainly be the death of Adelar, and possibly the Viking woman.

If that happened—or if it merely seemed a possibility—it would be the perfect moment for Dagfinn or a more ambitious Dane to strike. They could claim Bayard's punishment of his wife was an insult to her people, for the Danes believed in divorce, whereas the Christians did not. Godwin was certain one of them would welcome the opportunity to avenge an insult, real or imagined, if it meant a chance to loot Bayard's *burh*.

The question now was exactly how to proceed with the accusation. He should not be the one to tell Bayard, for here he was considered little better than a servant.

Ranulf. He should be the one.

There were some here who would support a bid by Ranulf for power, if this came to light, for Ranulf was rich and would surely pay those who gave him their allegiance.

Godwin also knew it was imperative that he be gone when Ranulf made his accusation. The man was a fool you couldn't trust with such information for long. Should Bayard somehow manage to get through the upheaval, Godwin wanted to be far from Bayard's vengeance.

Therefore, Godwin decided to wait awhile to be completely certain of the adultery before telling Ranulf. Even then, he would say only that he suspected. In the meantime, he would go to Dagfinn and warn him that Ranulf was going to accuse Endredi of adultery and that he should be prepared to take advantage of the situation. Afterward, home to Mercia, where he would tell his *ealdorman* that the Danes were moving on Oakenbrook and the defense of Wessex would be that much weaker.

Godwin smiled. Adelar and Endredi had given him the very weapon he needed to see the end of Bayard, and quite possibly Wessex, as well.

Several days later, Helmi muttered to herself as she tidied up the bower. "Look at this stitching," she whined, examining the hem of one of Endredi's gowns. "Terrible. A blind woman could do better than Ylla. You don't need her. You should have left her a slave."

Endredi sighed wearily. She felt ill and tired and had little patience for either Helmi's complaints or her gossip. "Would you please get me some cool water?" she asked, anxious to have the woman gone.

Helmi nodded. "Very well, since who knows where that girl is? She should have been back with the fresh herbs long ago. I tell you, my lady, it is shameful the way she carries on! Proud she's getting, beyond her station! Just because she thinks sleeping with Adelar—"

"What?" Endredi demanded, suddenly alert. "What did you say?"

Helmi paused on her way to the door and turned to Endredi, her face the picture of surprise. "Didn't you know about the two of them?"

"What is there to know?" Endredi asked slowly and deliberately.

Helmi's expression changed from genuine surprise to sly triumph. "That little whore's been with him in the night—and then too tired to do a proper day's work afterward. Whenever I tell her she should rest more, the saucy creature has the gall to—"

"Get out."

"I thought you knew and didn't care. I knew you liked the girl, my lady, and didn't want you to think I was jealous or anything, as if I could be. Why, I can do twice the work she can—"

"*Get out!*"

Helmi stared at Endredi as if she had suddenly changed into an ogre, then she flushed deeply and hurried out of the bower.

Endredi sat on the nearest stool, so heartsick and nauseous she could barely think. Had Adelar been leaving her at night to go elsewhere, to be with another woman? He had said he would pay attention to Ylla to draw away suspicion. Just how much and what kind of attention did he mean?

Oh, what had she done?

She laid her hand on her stomach, fighting the feeling of queasiness, although she could no longer fight the knowledge that she was with child, a child who was not Bayard's. Who could not be Bayard's. He had not been with her since her last woman's time. Bayard had claimed he was unwell. She had seen some evidence of this and taken it as an explanation for why he preferred not to make love with her.

Fool! Blind, lovesick fool! She would surely pay for her folly now! Justly so, for she had betrayed her husband.

He deserved a loyal wife, and she had deceived him. Worse still, she wanted to keep on betraying him.

With a man who might be—no. She simply could not believe what Helmi said. It had to be a lie, or a mistake. Adelar cared for her too much. Nonetheless, despite her faith, a small remnant of doubt remained, for she would have said it impossible for her to commit adultery, too.

But what about the baby? In her heart, she knew that whatever punishment Bayard decreed, he would not seek her death. Banishment, perhaps. A life apart from Adelar seemed as bad as death.

Yet her child would live. Must live, so that she would have a part of Adelar to love for the rest of her life.

She rose and went to the small chest where she had put the broken pieces of her spice box. Her marriage—her life—was like the box, broken and with seemingly no way to be mended.

Soon she must tell Bayard.

Undoubtedly it would be better to keep the knowledge of the child's sire to herself. But what of Adelar?

He would guess it was his. Surely he would know that they must keep the secret. As for the child, the two men looked so alike, no one would question the identity of the babe's father.

Endredi fingered the broken pieces, then fitted them together. She, too, had been the product of an adulterous relationship and knew the stain that could color her child's life.

She had not been at fault for her birth, and neither would the child she bore, even if she had to lie to make certain he did not suffer any shame because of his parentage. That would mean Bayard could not have even the slightest suspicion—

As if in answer to her thoughts, Bayard came limping into the bower and sank onto a stool with a sigh.

Endredi hurried to him. "What is it? Are you injured?"

He smiled wanly. "No. It is nothing. A slight pain in my side. That is all."

Endredi knelt beside him. "Let me help."

He winced when she touched him and drew back. "It is not perilous. I have had it before."

She eyed him warily. "How many times before?"

"All my life."

"Oh."

"It will soon pass."

Endredi rose. She had heard of this, people who had a weakness in the bowel that flared into pain from time to time, then subsided. That would explain the drawn look on his face and the lines of strain. She examined his eyes. If the whites were yellowed, it would be a sign of a more potent illness. She saw nothing amiss, but she also knew the yellowing could come on so gradually it might be easily overlooked. And she had been so wrapped in her own concerns, it could be that she had missed the changes. "This pain, is it sharp or dull?" she asked anxiously.

"It has passed already." He grinned with his more usual good humor. "I thought it best not to tempt fate by hunting anymore. Besides, I was loath to have you sitting alone here."

He picked up the pieces of the box. "I will set someone to mending this."

"No," she said, "it was quite intricate. It would not be the same."

"I am sorry it was ruined."

"You are so kind to me, Bayard," she said softly as she faced him, determined to do what she must, for her child's sake. She placed her hands on his arm and knelt before him. "The servants are not here and I . . . I have missed you."

"I am glad I left the hunt, then."

She put a smile on her face. "I mean, you spend so much time in the hall."

"The men like it when their lord spends time in their company. Since it is very likely we shall have to do battle soon, it is important to breed a sense of brotherhood."

Her hand slid upwards toward his shoulder. "I understand. But sometimes I get lonely."

He smiled at her again, and this time, she knew he understood her purpose. "Not now, Endredi, please. As much as I would care to, I fear the pain would return. It would be better if I were to rest awhile."

Disappointed and relieved and hating herself for acting no better than Gleda, Endredi nodded her acquiescence.

"Are you feeling better today?" he asked.

"Yes."

"Good. People are beginning to remark upon your absence from the hall. It has been a long time since you have joined us there."

"I was too ill to be good company, my lord."

"I understand, of course. Your attendance at Mass, despite your illness, has been noticed. You have certainly won over Father Derrick. I, too, admire your devotion, but others wonder if you are truly sick, or simply seek to be alone—which they consider a slight."

"Especially Ordella and Ranulf, I suppose," she noted dryly.

"I see you know my nephew and his wife well. Yes, especially those two."

"I will go to the hall for the evening meal."

Bayard watched her as she put away the pieces of the box. His scrutiny disturbed her, and she could not look at him.

"You *are* better, are you not?" he asked kindly. "If you are ill, what those two think does not matter."

"I am much better."

Bayard hesitated a moment. "I had hoped it was the sickness that comes of being with child," he said wistfully. "I would give anything to have a child, Endredi."

If he had been with her recently, she would have told him of her condition then. But he had not, and so she knew she must say nothing, no matter how melancholy he seemed. To be sure, there would be some questions later, when the child was born. She would say the baby came earlier than its time.

Still, she must give Bayard reason to believe the child was his. She reached out and pulled him to her, kissing him gently. "Stay with me now, Bayard," she whispered, hating herself and this deception.

He drew back, a pleased yet unusual expression on his face. "Not now," he said.

She tried to smile. "Then is there anything I can do to make you more comfortable, Bayard?"

"Some of that strong wine Duff has hidden away in the kitchen stores always helps," he said. "Would you mind asking him to bring it?"

"Of course not," she replied. "Would you like Godwin to come to amuse you with a story? There may even be time for Beowulf before the evening meal."

"No. I am in no mood for jests," he answered truthfully. "And I hate Beowulf."

Endredi gave him a strange look as she went to the door. Perhaps he had sounded in more pain than he intended, Bayard thought. Nonetheless, she said nothing and hurried out of the bower.

When he was sure Endredi was gone, Bayard bent over and moaned in agony. The pains were worse and coming with increasing frequency. The wine would help some.

He went over to his own chest, beside the bed, and slowly lifted the lid. Hidden in a compartment was a small vial containing a very rare, very expensive mixture made in the East from poppies. He put the vial to his lips and drank a small amount. He had done so whenever the pain was bad, and every night before he went to the weaving shed, lest he have an attack when he was with Ylla.

He lay down on the bed and thought about Ylla and last night. She was so sweet and eager, so proud and happy to think herself chosen by Adelar.

Although Bayard liked and respected Endredi, he always felt there was a part of her she would never let him near, some deep core to her heart that she would not share with him.

Another pain assailed him, and with a groan, Bayard put his hand on the tender spot and hoped that God would forgive him all his treachery when he died.

Chapter Thirteen

"What do *you* want, gleeman?" Ordella demanded as she glared at Godwin on the threshold of her bower.

"I...I know not who else to trust with this," he said conspiratorially.

"With what?" As Ranulf waited for Godwin's answer, he tried to fill his empty goblet from the silver vessel that also stood on the small table. Unfortunately, his hand was not steady, and more ale spilled on the table than landed in his goblet.

Ordella gave her drunken husband a disgusted look and gestured for Godwin to enter. "This had best be important," she muttered.

Godwin forced his dislike from his face and made himself look properly concerned. "I believe this is not something for servants' ears," he said pointedly, looking at the woman who waited upon Ordella.

She waved impatiently at the middle-aged female, who hurriedly left. "Now, what is this that is so important and so secret, eh?"

"It is about Adelar and Bayard's wife."

That got their complete attention. Ranulf straightened like one of Bayard's hounds on the trail of a wounded animal. Ordella's reaction was slightly more subtle. Slightly. "What about them?" she asked.

"I . . . that is, the other night— Oh, perhaps it is nothing after all." He turned to leave.

"Stop!" Ranulf almost shouted. He lurched to his feet and grabbed Godwin's arm, dragging him back inside the bower. The stench of ale was almost overpowering, but Godwin let himself be led. "Si'down," Ranulf slurred, pushing the gleeman onto a stool.

Ordella hovered over Godwin like a carrion crow. "What about the other night? Which night?"

"It was a few days ago," Godwin answered with seeming reluctance. "I was late returning from an . . . assignation."

"We don't care what *you* were doing," Ordella said.

"Well, it was late. Very late. I was on my way back to the hall when I saw someone come out of Bayard's bower."

"Someone?" Ordella and Ranulf leaned so close to hear, he feared they were going to fall on top of him.

He stood up, unable to bear their proximity, and began to pace as if agitated. "It was *not* Bayard. I am quite certain it was Adelar."

"Are you sure?" both demanded at once.

"As sure as I can be," he replied. "I thought of going to Bayard, but I simply could not tell him of this . . . this *base* treachery! He trusts Adelar like a brother."

"I always knew that was a mistake!" Ordella cried triumphantly. "I knew those two would make mischief." She gave Ranulf a significant look. "Now *Godwin*, Adelar's greatest friend, has seen it."

Ranulf staggered to the door. "I mush revi... revel...tell Bayard," he mumbled.

"No!" Ordella and Godwin cried in unison. Ranulf halted so abruptly he fell over.

As Ranulf climbed to his feet, Godwin looked at Ordella, instantly suspicious. What was she up to? "I'm not sure that would be wise," he began uncertainly, hesitating until he saw the way the wind was filling Ordella's sails.

"No, it would not. Not now, when his wife has been ill. And it must not be a mere gleeman who accuses him. It must be *you*, Ranulf."

Her husband grinned like a simpleton.

"But we must wait until one of *us* has seen this for ourselves, to give our words credence." She looked pointedly at Godwin, and he knew exactly who she wanted that to be.

"Very well. But we must wait a little yet. I...I may be mistaken, but I believe Adelar may have seen me. He might be watchful, in case someone is spying on him."

"How could you be so stupid?" Ordella demanded.

Godwin shrugged.

"Very well," she said peevishly. "We will wait a few more days, but then I will see this treachery myself."

"Endredi?" Adelar whispered as he entered her bower. He removed the cloak and moved closer to the bed surrounded by closed drapery. "Endredi?" He reached out and pulled back the curtains.

She lay on her side with her back to the opening. "Why are you here, Adelar?" she asked in a sorrowful whisper.

"Because I cannot stay away."

"If you are lonely, perhaps Ylla will be happy to keep company with you," she replied, getting out of the bed and drawing her fur robe over her shoulders.

He came around the bed toward her. "Endredi!"

"Are you such a marvel, Adelar? First me, then Ylla, all on the same night?"

He frowned. "You know otherwise. I thought that if anyone suspected there was more between us than there should be, their suspicions would waver if I seemed occupied with Ylla."

"What do you mean, occupied?" She walked away from him, and the action made him suffer.

"Endredi, I desire no one but you. You know that. You cannot doubt it, after what we have shared."

"What we shared was a sin, Adelar. A terrible sin."

He went to her and took her in his arms, holding her gently. "No, we were destined for each other, Endredi," he said firmly, believing it. "Why else would God send you back to me?"

She embraced him tightly and sighed softly. "I am sorry to doubt you, Adelar. But Helmi said—"

"Never mind what Helmi said. All that matters now is us."

"No. There is Bayard, too, who deserves better."

When Adelar did not respond, she took a deep breath and went on. "I...I am with child, Adelar. Your child."

A host of emotions flooded through Adelar. Joy that he and Endredi had created a child. Fear for Endredi's health. Relief for Bayard, that his goal had been achieved. But under everything, he felt an overwhelming sorrow that this child could never be rightfully acknowledged as his.

She pulled back and stepped away. Her stern eyes were so relentless, it was as if all the strength of her Viking blood was there for the world to see. "Bayard must believe the child is his. You should leave, Adelar. If I have to continue to be Bayard's wife and the mother of the child everyone thinks is his, then you must not come to me again."

"Endredi, would you kill me?" Adelar pleaded softly, stepping toward her with outstretched hands. He drew her once more into his arms. "I cannot live simply watching you, not being able to do this—" he kissed her cheek "—or this—" he pressed his lips to her eyes "—or this..." His mouth touched hers.

Strong she was, and resolute, yet she was not strong enough or resolute enough to resist the man she had always desired. Who was a part of her, and would be forever.

She took a deep breath. "Then we must run away together."

"We will be dishonored." *And Bayard's dream will be destroyed. Ranulf will win.*

"I know. But I want to be with you, Adelar. We cannot live here, with such deceit and lies. How long will it be before someone discovers our crime?"

Adelar took her face gently in his hands. "Endredi, the die was cast when you came back into my life, but it is not only ourselves we must consider. Bayard, too, would be dishonored. And there is something more." He hesitated, then went on. "He is not well, Endredi."

"What?"

"Surely you have noticed?"

"He told me he was merely tired."

"I believe it to be worse." There was no need for her to know the full extent of Bayard's condition. Not yet. It would only add to her anxiety, and she was troubled enough. "If we were to run off, he might worsen. Then Ranulf would be like a vulture over his sickbed."

"Yes. Ranulf," Endredi said softly, moving away from him. "I was forgetting Ranulf."

"Have you told Bayard about the child?"

She shook her head.

"Then you should, and soon. It will cheer him."

"Yes." She gazed into Adelar's eyes, which were as dark as a moonless night. "Adelar, you will never be able to acknowledge this child. It must always be considered Bayard's."

"I know that. It would be better for the child's sake, too."

"Yes."

"But in my heart, I will always know that it is *our* child, Endredi. The offspring of our love."

"Yes," she whispered, lifting her face for his kiss.

Then she thought no more of Bayard or betrayal or deception. All she knew was that Adelar was here with her, wanting her, needing her as she needed him.

Passion flared, heat licking along their veins. With swift, eager hands and hushed commands, they disrobed each other and sank onto the pile of their clothing.

His body covered hers, strong and hot. Eagerly, she raised herself to meet the thrust of his loins, delighting in the feel of him as he joined with her. Swiftly, surely, he possessed her. And she possessed him.

"I drink to your continued health!" Dunstan bellowed a few days later, raising his drinking horn in a salute in Bayard's general direction. Around the hall, others followed suit, including Endredi. The smell of the smoke was making her feel ill, so she leaned as far away from the hearth as possible and tried to listen to the conversation—and not watch Adelar, seated some distance away with several of Dunstan's soldiers.

Dunstan had arrived that afternoon with more orders from his father. The young man obviously appreciated the food Duff prepared and the wine Bayard offered, for he had been sampling both most liberally.

"My father was very concerned for your health," Dunstan reiterated, leaning so close to Bayard that he came perilously close to tumbling from the bench. "He heard you were unwell."

"I am quite recovered," Bayard replied.

"You know, Bayard, my father would have never forgiven any of his other thanes for marrying a Dane without consulting him. But he thinks most highly of you. I, too, of course, would not want anything to befall you before we deal with that miscreant Aethelwold."

"I knew he would approve." Bayard glanced at Endredi, a grin hovering at the corner of his lips. "Is there any news of the traitor?" he asked, suddenly serious. Endredi forced herself to pay attention.

"None. Aethelwold is probably sitting sulking in some hall, getting drunk and bedding wenches, now that he's left that nun behind." Obviously Dunstan drew no parallel between his conduct and that of Aethelwold. Although a man of lascivious and insatiable appetites, Dunstan would never risk the censure of his men by kidnapping a nun, as Aethelwold had.

"May God have pity on his foul, damned soul," Father Derrick intoned with no mercy in his voice.

"My father thinks, though, that Aethelwold and the Danes may yet surprise us."

"How so?"

"If he leads the Danes against Mercia and leaves the Saxons alone, the Mercians will not be pleased. The alliance between us could be destroyed."

"Does Cynath really believe he will do that?" Ranulf asked.

"He doubts that Aethelwold is clever enough to think of it, but he knows someone else might. The Danes are not stupid, if Aethelwold is." Dunstan nudged Ranulf, seated beside him. "That wench grows more comely with every passing day," he noted, nodding at Ylla, who walked slowly along the benches filling drinking horns.

Dunstan caught Endredi's disapproving eye.

"I believe I shall have to resign myself to living like a priest," he muttered by way of apology.

Father Derrick heard Dunstan's remark and gave the man a severe look. "You speak as if that is something distasteful, Dunstan. I assure you, should you have the perseverance, you will find yourself closer to God."

"Or mad," Dunstan whispered with a broad grin at Bayard.

Endredi noticed Godwin hovering behind Bayard and Dunstan. She pushed her platter of food away and addressed him. "What is it, Godwin?"

Godwin grinned. "Excuse me for interrupting, my lords and ladies. I was about to begin a song and I hoped to find out what our noble guest might prefer. I can assure you, my lord Dunstan, that I am no ordinary gleeman."

Dunstan belched and eyed the man skeptically.

"He speaks the truth," Bayard said with a laugh. "Doesn't he, Endredi?"

She nodded. "Indeed, my lord, he is most talented."

Dunstan's brow furrowed with thought. "I think . . . Beowulf."

Bayard turned aside to Endredi and sighed heavily. She rose at once. "My lords, if you will excuse me," she said, "I am rather weary. I shall retire for the evening. I bid you sleep well."

Bayard rose, too, his expression concerned but his eyes smiling. "My dear, please allow me to escort you to the bower. You will excuse me, too, won't you, Dunstan? I shall return . . . sometime."

Bayard took Endredi by the arm and accompanied her outside. She looked at no one as they left. Not Ranulf. Not Ordella. Not Adelar.

Once out of the hall, she took a deep breath of the cooler air.

"I thank you for providing me with an opportunity to escape," her husband said as they entered their bower. Helmi waited inside, and he nodded toward the door. "You may leave us."

When she was gone, he reached for a goblet of ale Helmi had prepared. "The notion of sitting beside that lout Dunstan through that whole poem is enough to make one truly sick."

When she did not answer at once, he looked at her quizzically. "Are you ill, Endredi? You look very pale."

"I am well." She knew she had hesitated long enough and began to disrobe. "I am happy you are fit again, Bayard."

He watched her for a long moment, until she was clad only in her linen shift, and she went toward him. She took the goblet from his hand and set it on the table. "Take me," she whispered, wrapping her arms about his neck.

She had to do this. She had to give herself to this man she did not desire. She must . . .

He returned her kiss tenderly.

Adulteress! The ugly word burst into her brain, yet still she kissed him.

Liar! She fought to ignore the protests of her heart. She had to do this. Had to...

Bayard held her so gently.

He deserves better than you! Oh, dear God, gentle Freya, what had she become?

Bayard suddenly drew back. "Endredi, what is it?" he demanded quietly. "You are crying."

She put her hands over her face as her shoulders began to shake with her sobs. "Oh, Bayard! Do not even look at me!"

He removed her hands from her face. "What is it, Endredi?" he asked, the words as much a command as an entreaty. "Tell me!"

She choked back a sob and twisted away from him. "Forgive me, Bayard. I am with child!"

He gasped and took hold of her shoulders, forcing her to face him. "Are you certain?"

She nodded, speechless with misery, waiting for him to denounce her.

Instead, Bayard smiled. "This is wonderful news, Endredi! You have given me such joy. A child—think of it! A child." He hugged her fiercely. "I must go to the hall and announce this great news!"

"Bayard!" she cried with so much urgency that he stopped smiling at once. How could she continue to deceive him when he was so good and kind? She could not repay him with a base falsehood. "Bayard, you must know the truth," she began, determined to do what was right. "The child—"

"Makes me the happiest man in the kingdom."

"Bayard, please let me explain. Every night you lingered in the hall—"

"You grew drowsy. When I joined you, many times you were half asleep."

Endredi stared at him, confused by his responses. There was a smile still on his face, but his eyes—in his eyes she saw a flicker not of anger or even confusion, but contrition.

Why should Bayard look contrite?

Adelar appeared on the threshold. "Forgive this intrusion, Bayard. The sentries wish to know—"

He paused, looking at the two of them with sudden uncertainty.

"Enter, Adelar, and hear my good news," Bayard said jovially. He put his arm around his cousin and drew him inside. "Endredi is with child."

A look passed between the two men, standing so close, so alike. Both pleased, yet not pleased.

Endredi's hands covered her stomach instinctively, protectively. It was as if they were enjoined in some kind of conspiracy, Bayard not suspicious, Adelar not guilty....

Stunned as a possible explanation washed over her, she staggered backward toward a stool and sat down heavily, staring at them. They both looked at her then, the two. The man who wanted a child above all things. The man who had made the child. Her husband. Her lover.

Conspirators.

"I want the truth," she announced, determined to know it. Determined to hear it from their own lips.

"I do not understand you," Bayard said.

But Adelar did. She saw it in his eyes, which looked guilty now. "Endredi," he murmured.

"I will not speak with you yet, Adelar. I want to hear from my husband."

"Again, I do not understand you," Bayard replied.

"That Adelar has been my lover has been no secret to you, has it? You knew about Adelar and me all along, didn't you? You willingly looked the other way. I want to know why."

"Endredi, you must be more ill than I guessed. This accusation makes no sense—"

"How much of a fool do you take me for, Bayard?" she demanded, anger welling inside her. "Tell him, Adelar. Tell him I knew from the first that it was not my husband in my bed."

Bayard's face grew pale, and he turned to face Adelar. "She knew it was you all the time?" he asked softly, disbelief mingling with contrition in his voice.

"Yes," Adelar admitted. "Yes, she did."

Endredi rose majestically. "I willingly committed adultery."

Bayard looked away, but when he spoke, he glanced at Adelar. "Why did you not tell me?"

"I thought there was no reason."

"It was to save what pride I had left, was it not?"

"Pride? Who dares to speak of pride here?" Endredi cried. "We are all shameful creatures. You, Bayard, for your approval. Me, for taking a lover because I . . . because I wanted him and I thought he wanted me.''

"I only did what Bayard asked because I wanted you so much, Endredi,'' Adelar said firmly. "I couldn't be with you any other way. I would have done anything to be with you.''

"Endredi, hear me,'' Bayard said, his voice soft and sorrowful. "If there is blame in this, it is mine. All this was my plan, my scheme.''

"Bayard *asked?* There was a *plan?*'' she queried with surprise and disbelief. "Why?''

"I cannot father a child,'' Bayard replied quietly.

"You asked Adelar to get me with child? But you are not impotent.''

"Nor can I make children, and so I sought to change the fate God had given me by asking Adelar to . . . help me.''

"And you agreed to act the stallion's part?'' she said scornfully to Adelar, hating him for agreeing and herself for giving in to his honeyed words. "What if Adelar had refused? Who would you have asked then?''

"Endredi, please, no one,'' Bayard answered. "It had to be Adelar, because he looks so like me, no one would question the child's parentage.'' Bayard's voice grew stronger. "Please understand. I need a child, Endredi, for I will not leave what I have built to Ranulf, and so I did what I thought must be done. I am sorry for deceiving you.''

"I *understand* that I am simply a vessel for your plans and desires. Did you think of me—*me*, Endredi—at all? Did you give no thought to my fears, my worries, my shame?''

"I regret the lies," Bayard said immediately. "I regret the pain I have caused. I do care for you, Endredi, as a wise and good friend." He paused and looked at Adelar. "I will not lie and say I enjoyed what I planned, but Adelar cares for you more than I ever could. And I am pleased about the babe. I had hoped you need never know the truth of this."

Endredi rose and went toward Adelar. "I understand why Bayard did what he did, although I do not condone it, and that I cared for you beyond the bounds of law and honor. But what of you, my fine Saxon warrior? Why did you do this? Out of compassion for Bayard?''

Adelar gazed at her with dark-eyed intensity. "Endredi, I meant every word I said to you about wanting and needing you. You must believe me," he said fervently, taking her hands tightly in his own. "I have wanted you since we were children together. I have never desired any woman as much as you."

Before Endredi could speak, Bayard said, "You knew her then? Why did you say nothing of this before?''

"When would have been the right time?" Adelar responded with a touch of anger, twisting to face him. "I was not sure it was the same Endredi until your wedding day. Even then, it had been years. She was a widow—I thought she no longer cared for me."

"Indeed, it would have been better if I did not," Endredi said bitterly, moving away.

"Why did you resist my suggestion, then?" Bayard asked.

"Because it seemed dishonorable. Because it was."

"You lost that scruple soon enough," Bayard observed coldly.

"Do not chide me now. It was your suggestion, and all to do Ranulf out of some money and power."

"What can you really know of *my* reasons, Adelar?" Bayard demanded. "You will never take command, so you will never know the joy and the pain of it. *You* will never see your work nearly completed and then know that some fool may destroy it! And how can you speak of scruples to me, you who would bed any woman who looked willing enough!"

"Are you some holy man, to tell me to leave women alone? At least I do not offer my wife to another like a brood mare!"

"Stop!" Endredi cried. "Stop!" She looked at the two men, her anger diminished by anguish and sorrow. "We are all guilty here. Of many things. But the time for recriminations is past." She tried to sound strong. "All that matters is my child. None of this must ever be known."

"My child," Adelar declared.

"Yes, your child," Bayard admitted reluctantly. "You are right, Endredi."

"That is why you must go," Endredi said to Adelar, fighting to ignore the pain in her heart as she looked at him. "Leave this place. Leave *us*."

"Endredi," he pleaded. "I had no wish to hurt you. You must see that."

Bayard went to his wife and stood beside her, facing him. "I believe she is right in this, as well, Adelar. It would be better if you were to leave, at least until the child is born."

Adelar glared at his cousin. "What am I now, Bayard? A churl piece to be used and discarded? You need me yet. What of your illness?" His eyes narrowed. "Or was that a lie?"

"No, it was no lie. I *am* dying."

"*What?*" Endredi cried, turning to Bayard and grabbing his shoulders, staring into his face. "You said the illness was not serious. You have had it all your life. You cannot be dying."

Bayard tried to smile, but his eyes—oh, the agony in his eyes! "The illness is mortal, my wife. Another lie I must beg forgiveness for. I do not know how long I have. That is why I asked Adelar to do what he did. I must have a son before I die."

"Bayard, Bayard!" she whispered, shaking her head. "You should have told me of this! I can help!"

"No, you cannot."

Adelar watched them, the husband and his wife. Oh, dear God, he had no place here, after all. For the child's sake, he should go, for he would not be able to stay away from her. So far, they were safe from suspicion, but he dare not risk the exposure of their secret.

Bayard had other warriors, many of them fine, loyal men. Surely there would be one who could replace a cousin. One to be relied upon to share the burden of command.

"I will go as you ask," he said reluctantly. "Today. But know that this is the last thing I will do for you, Bayard."

"You have my thanks, Adelar," his cousin replied, "but you cannot go just yet. What will Ranulf say if you leave so suddenly?"

Adelar went toward him slowly. "I do not *care* what Ranulf will say. You have a golden tongue, Bayard. You will think of some explanation. Just as my father would."

He looked once more at Endredi, at her pale face surrounded by her red-gold hair that glowed in the firelight. That he would never touch again. That he would never even see again. "You and I both feared that I would be like Kendric, yet I think you have married the one who resembles him most, after all."

"Do not go until I make the announcement to the others in my hall," Bayard said, stepping away from his wife. "I beg of you, Adelar."

"Begging does not become you, Bayard. For the child's sake, I will wait until the day after the Sabbath."

Bayard nodded his approval. "Endredi," he said. "You must come to the hall, too."

She looked at the two of them, her anger gone. There was only a deep and painful sadness, for despite what they had done, she could not find it in her heart to hate them. "As you wish, Bayard."

Chapter Fourteen

Godwin set down his harp when Bayard rose from the settle. Endredi, looking pale and somewhat ill, watched her husband as he held up his hand for silence.

"I have great news, which I wish to share with you all," Bayard declared.

Godwin frowned slightly.

"My wife is with child!"

The hall erupted into a cacophony of cheers and good wishes. Godwin smiled, but inwardly he was trying to calculate what this might mean in the future.

Then Ranulf stepped into the center of the hall. "My lords!" he shouted, drawing everyone's attention. "This child may not be Bayard's!"

Gasps of surprise were replaced by shocked whispers. Startled as much as anyone, Godwin half rose in his seat, staring at Ranulf. The *fool!* This was not the time. He was supposed to be well away. Nor was it wise to make this accusation when Bayard was so obviously pleased about the child.

The people looked at Endredi. The woman turned pale as a washed lamb's fleece, but she did not faint.

While Endredi held everyone's attention, Godwin stood up and sidled toward the door.

Bayard slowly approached Ranulf, who had not moved. "What was that you said, Nephew?" he asked calmly, yet his gaze made the younger man tremble, which was not helped by the sight of an enraged Adelar rising from his place at the table like an avenging angel.

Ranulf glanced nervously at his wife, whose attention did not leave Bayard. *She* was not pleased by Ranulf's outburst, either, to judge by her grim lips, but what was she doing, looking at Bayard that way?

"I—I . . ." Ranulf stuttered, looking around wildly until he spotted Godwin. "Gleeman!" he called out. "Stop the gleeman!"

Godwin knew he dare not flee. To do so would only arouse suspicion. The Mercian silently cursed himself for ever taking Ranulf into his confidence.

Then Godwin realized that Cynath's son was watching like the simplest peasant at a gleeman's easiest trick. He seemed willing to believe Ranulf's hasty words. Perhaps there were others wavering, too.

"This is none of a lowly gleeman's business," Godwin said, sounding astonished.

"It was Godwin who first accused Adelar and Endredi," Ranulf cried.

Godwin stared wide-eyed at Ranulf, who obviously expected him to act as witness. He immediately decided to remain silent as Bayard motioned him forward. He would not speak until he was more certain of Bayard's feelings in the matter, as it appeared Ordella was doing. Adelar was watching him closely, but he did not look in the Saxon's direction.

"What exactly did Godwin accuse them of?" Bayard inquired coldly.

Ranulf, alone in the center of the hall, looked like a frightened child.

"What do you accuse my cousin and my wife of?"

"I accuse them of nothing, my lord, but Godwin—"

"What crime does *Godwin* say they have been guilty of, then?"

"Adultery," Ranulf replied softly, with another nervous glance at Adelar.

"I did not hear you, Nephew."

"Adultery!" Ranulf squeaked.

Adelar jumped over the table and had his hands on Ranulf's throat before anyone had time to blink.

"Stop!" Bayard shouted, hurrying forward.

Adelar did not.

"I said stop!" Bayard grabbed Adelar and dragged him away from the spluttering, gasping Ranulf. "I will deal with this, Adelar!"

The two men faced each other, and for a moment Godwin thought Adelar meant to disobey. But then he gave a brief nod and stepped back.

"Thou shalt not commit adultery!" Father Derrick said sternly, rising to his feet as if he was the embodiment of the Church and all its laws.

"No one has formally accused anyone of such a heinous crime," Bayard said pointedly. "Or are you?" he asked Ranulf.

"Godwin said it first, my lord," Ranulf rasped. "I myself saw nothing and make no accusation."

Disgust filled Godwin. Ranulf was a coward, a base, stupid coward. Adelar should have killed him.

"Well, Godwin, what say you?" Bayard asked, as calmly if they were discussing a poem or a song.

What was wrong with Bayard? Godwin wondered. He had barely blinked when Ranulf interrupted the celebration. Even now, he looked far from disturbed. Adelar, too, looked more angry than fearful, yet he would have to know no nobleman would forgive adultery.

The only one of them who seemed truly upset was the woman, standing pale and motionless.

But Bayard should be angry. By God, Bayard should be murderous—unless he thought this a lie told by Ranulf. The truth must be known now, then, if his plan of disruption was to work.

Godwin slumped sorrowfully and spoke with seeming reluctance. "I saw Adelar leave your bower in the middle of the night."

As Bayard walked thoughtfully to his place, Godwin scanned the others in the hall. Father Derrick had his eyes closed, as if in prayer. Ranulf was pale and had beads of sweat on his brow. Adelar's gaze was fastened on his cousin. For the rest, they were also looking at Bayard, and those who were not would not meet Godwin's eyes. As if *he* was the guilty one.

This accusation was supposed to cause dissension among Bayard's warriors and a crisis of faith in Bayard as a leader. Yet many of his men seemed as calm and unperturbed as Bayard, the stupid, blind fools.

Godwin straightened his shoulders defiantly. "Bayard, it was my regard for you that held my tongue, but now I must speak. I am *certain* it was Adelar leaving your bower in the night. Not once, but many times."

"Adelar and I look much alike, Godwin," Bayard said, taking his seat. "I ask you again, do you accuse Adelar of committing adultery with my wife? Think carefully, gleeman." It was a warning, without question.

"I have no doubt of it, Bayard," Godwin said more firmly. Then he raised his arm and pointed at Ordella. "*She* saw him, too."

Bayard's cold, dark eyes sought out Ordella. "Do you also accuse Adelar and Endredi?"

There was a long moment of silence before Ordella spoke. "No, my lord, I do not."

"*What?*" Godwin shrieked. She had as much to gain by accusing Adelar and Endredi of adultery as he did.

"Godwin came to us with this tale, my lord, it is true," Ordella said, ignoring Godwin's outburst. "But like you, we were loath to believe him. I mean, he is merely a Mercian gleeman. Still, we were most concerned for your happiness and the safety of the *burh*, so we did not wish to dismiss his words completely. He asked me to accompany him, to spy upon your wife. I did, but I assure you, Bayard, I saw nothing."

"You lying *bitch!*" Godwin snarled, lunging at her. "I'll make you tell the truth! You saw him with your own eyes!"

Before he got to Ordella, Adelar tackled him and brought him crashing down on top of one of the oak tables. Godwin struggled in his grasp, but Adelar was holding him with all his considerable strength.

Panting, Godwin shoved Adelar away and faced Bayard, glaring at the thane. The man was a cuckold, and he let every measure of his scorn show on his face.

"Ylla!" Bayard called.

"Here, my lord," came the girl's timid voice.

"Can you tell us where Adelar has been in the middle of the night?"

The girl nodded timidly. "With me, my lord."

"Every night?"

"No... but most nights."

"Helmi!" Bayard shouted.

The serving woman stepped forth, her face full of contempt as she looked at Godwin and then a cowering Ranulf. Without waiting to be asked anything, she said in halting Saxon, "The man is a lying dog, my lord. Adelar cannot have been in your bower, or I would have known."

"She spent her nights in the hall," Godwin protested.

Helmi curled her lip eloquently. "I would have known if a stranger had been there, either by sight or smell. Men have their own scent."

Baldric, who had been unnoticed at the back, suddenly spoke. "She's right, my lord. The dogs can always tell men apart!"

"Am I to be contradicted by an old Danish servant and a dog keeper?" Godwin demanded. He glared at Adelar, who had a slightly scornful smile on his face. Then at Bayard, whose expression was nearly identical.

Nearly identical.

Yet Godwin did not doubt it had been Adelar coming out of Bayard's bower. Where had Bayard been?

With a woman who thought she was with Adelar? It didn't seem possible, but how else to explain Bayard's complacency, unless he had known?

More than known? Conspired to let his cousin share his wife's bed? Why?

Did Bayard prefer a servant's embrace?

And then Godwin got a look at Bayard's hard, dark eyes and knew that it did not matter why, for he would never know. He had already lost.

But he would not be defeated. Not yet. "I know what you've done," he said through clenched teeth. "You are not worthy to be a thane."

"Watch your words, gleeman," Bayard warned.

"I am no peasant gleeman who must sing for his supper!" he cried. "I tell you, I *know!* Can't you see what he's done?" He faced the other warriors and gestured toward the cousins. "He and Adelar have taken each other's places."

There was a sudden hush. An incredible, incredulous silence.

Until Endredi strode around the table to face her accuser. The moment she had been dreading had arrived, and she knew what she had to do to save her child's reputation, as well as her own and that of those she cared for.

She halted in front of Godwin. "Do you—or any man here—think I would not know if it was not my husband in my bed?" she asked scornfully. Slowly she pivoted and surveyed everyone in the hall, stopping when she encountered her husband's deep brown eyes. "And if I did, I assure you all, my screams would have reached the highest heavens. I value my honor as much as Bayard or Adelar. I say again, is there *any* person here who can believe I would not realize it was another man in my bed?"

The men around her shook their heads, including Father Derrick and Ranulf. Even Ordella looked as if she had to admit such a fraud was not possible.

She faced Godwin. "Why are you saying this, Godwin?"

"Because it is true!"

Adelar stepped forward, but Bayard held up his hand. "No, it is not true. The child Endredi bears is mine, and only mine," Bayard said firmly.

Endredi went to sit beside her husband, avoiding Adelar's eyes. "Why should anyone believe you about anything, Godwin," she said slowly, "if you are not a gleeman, as you have just said? And if you are not a gleeman, Godwin, who or what *are* you?"

Godwin drew himself up and said, "I do not have to answer a Dane."

The change in his posture struck Adelar. Suddenly he remembered the day Godwin had surprised him when he stood with Endredi near the meadow, and the cloak he had carried, although the day was warm. Before Godwin straightened, he was nearly the same height as the mysterious woman. If he stooped even more, as if he was an old hag... and he often disappeared into the woods.

"Answer my wife!" Bayard ordered. "Who are you?"

"I do not have to answer you, either, but I will say this. My family have been kings and princes in Mercia for years upon years."

"You are a spy!" Adelar accused loudly. "Bayard, I am sure he is the one I saw, in the woods, coming from the direction of the Danelaw!"

"Judas!" Father Derrick bellowed.

Godwin whirled to face Adelar. "The Saxons are fools! Soon you will all be peasants, as you deserve!"

The warriors would have set upon him then, had not Bayard once again held up his hand. Such was the force of his authority that they all fell back as one.

"I do not need your pity!" Godwin cried wildly. He pulled out a *scramasax* he had hidden in his tunic and waved it frantically. "Kill me if you can—but I will kill some of you first! And then the Danes will come!" Godwin looked at Endredi and grinned, a demonic version of his former common expression. "Dagfinn paid well for what I had to tell him."

"My wife has already warned me of Dagfinn's questionable trustworthiness," Bayard said to the

Saxons. "We are prepared for any treachery from Dagfinn."

He looked at Godwin with a mixture of loathing and regret. "You were a fine gleeman, Godwin." He raised his voice so that all in the hall would hear. "Godwin has condemned himself with his own tongue as a spy and a traitor, and slandered my wife and my cousin." He gestured for one of his soldiers to step forward. "The sentence should be death, but he does not want my pity, so I will not give him a quick and merciful death. Take Godwin to the barracks and find out what he has told Dagfinn, however you can. When he has told you, cut out his tongue, blind him and cast him out of my *burh*."

"My lord!" Adelar called out above the tumult in the hall after Godwin was taken away.

Endredi watched Adelar come forward, his face haggard and drawn. She felt as if a lifetime had passed in this one evening, and wondered if he did, too.

"What is it, Cousin?" Bayard asked, taking his seat wearily. His face, too, was careworn and pale, the strain of the confrontation clearly visible.

"I cannot remain where I have been so blatantly insulted."

"Cousin," Bayard said, his tone sincere, "do not allow Ranulf's hasty words to upset you." The *burh-ware* glared at his subdued nephew.

"Indeed," Ranulf said quickly, "you have my abject apologies."

Adelar scowled darkly at the lean, anxious man. "This is not the first insult, Ranulf, but it will be the last you offer me. Bayard, I will leave in the morning, lest I be tempted to do murder."

Endredi knew in her heart that Adelar was clever to use this excuse to go in this manner, so that no suspicion would attach to either Bayard or herself. But to lose the last precious few days with him, even though they would not have been able to be alone, was more hardship to bear. "Where will you go?" she asked softly, telling herself there was no reason she should not.

"I do not know."

How cold, how hard his voice! Maybe he was glad of the excuse to go at once. He had been so angry. Yet she had been wronged just as much, and perhaps more.

Oh, she did not want to part this way!

"Should I have need of you, will you return?" Bayard inquired.

"I do not know what my obligations may be, my lord," he replied. "I may owe my duty to another lord by then." A flicker of sorrow passed over his face, and Endredi's heart was torn again.

He did not want to go. She did not want him to go. But he must. He must.

"I hope you will return to us when my child is born," Bayard said. Endredi heard the urgency and the forgiveness and the regret in his voice, and hoped Adelar heard it, too.

"Perhaps," was all Adelar said before striding down the hall and out the door.

Chapter Fifteen

Adelar's hood dripped with the steady spring rain that had been falling for three days. He strained to see ahead along the muddy road. There. He could see his destination now.

Bitter, angry and with a heart full of pain, he had left Oakenbrook with no clear plan of where he would go. Indeed, he had had none for most of the winter, except that he would stay far away from them.

For the whole season he had ridden aimlessly though the countryside, going from one *burh* to another as he had when he had first left his home. Because of his fighting skills, he was well-remembered, so he had no trouble finding welcome.

Yet never was he content to stay at any one place. Always there was something to send him on his way, whether it was a table poorly stocked, belligerent companions or a homely daughter with lust in her eyes.

And always there was a constant, vast loneliness for Endredi. She was all he could think about. It had been nearly the length of time it would be until the birth of

his child, yet he still dreamed of her in his arms, safe
and happy, and wondered about the child that would
be born soon. How much he wanted Endredi and the
child to be well and how much he wanted to be with
them.

Naturally, he thought of Bayard, too. Despite what
had happened between them, he hoped that his cousin's illness would not become grave until another
burhware could be found. Ranulf the fool intruded on
his mind, too, as well as the waspish Ordella, and
Godwin the traitor.

Many times he had almost gone back, prepared to
swallow his pride to find out how the people of Oakenbrook fared.

Too many. But if Endredi was so firm in her resolve
to see him gone, could he not stay away?

Yesterday he had realized just where he was, and
how close to his old home. It was mere coincidence, he
had told himself. He had not taken proper notice of the
land and trees.

But now, as he drew closer, when he could see the
very timbers of the wall, he knew that he had been
heading here slowly and steadily since the day he had
left Oakenbrook. On the verge of becoming a father
himself, he had come to see his own again.

To discover, once and for all, how alike they were.

Very little had changed at his father's *burh* in the
years Adelar had been gone, he realized, as he rode toward the fortress that dominated the area.

He peered at the gate through the driving rain. The
wood was worn and gray with age, but the walls still

looked stout and strong, although he could make out no watchmen on them.

This *burh* was much farther south than Oakenbrook, so perhaps watchmen were not so necessary. It was a fine, strong *burh*. Still, a band of Vikings had once made its way up the river, so surely another could, too.

It was too fine a fortress for a man like Kendric, he had thought at one time, but who was he to cast stones at his father, he who had fathered a child on another man's wife? Who had let his desire for a woman sweep away all the bonds of loyalty, and all the oaths of kin and friendship.

He had had plenty of time to think about what had happened, and to realize that if he had any regret, it was that he had not stopped the marriage last spring. If he had, then all this pain and sorrow might have been prevented.

But he had not, so now he had no choice except to stay away from Oakenbrook.

"Who's there?" a quavering voice called out, the wind and the heavy rain making the man's words hard to hear.

"Adelar!" he replied loudly.

"Eh?" An old man looked out, his head shrouded in a soaking hood. A hooked nose was the only visible feature Adelar could see.

The Saxon dismounted and took hold of his horse's bridle. He approached the gate. "It is I, Adelar."

The old man opened the gate a little wider. He pulled back his hood and tilted his gray-haired head to look

up at the taller man. Adelar recognized him now. It was
Ern, who had once been a warrior, now bent and
toothless with age. Ern gave no smile or any sign of
welcome. He simply gestured for Adelar to lead his
horse inside and then closed the gate behind them.

Well, he had not expected any warm greetings here.

Adelar looked around. While from the outside the
burh looked unchanged, inside was a different matter.
What had once been a fine fortress was now a collection of buildings in various states of disrepair. Some of
the bowers had fallen down completely, others were
obviously about to do so. The weapons store and the
food stores looked in somewhat better condition. Indeed, the *burh* appeared deserted, and Adelar wondered if a sickness had come upon the inhabitants. Or
perhaps they had only taken shelter from the rain.

In the middle of the *burh* stood the huge hall his father had built after Endredi's father had destroyed the
other village. It was still an imposing structure, little
changed from the night Kendric had taken Endredi
there. She would have no trouble recognizing it.

Adelar's lip curled with disgust. Of all the buildings
here, it was the one he would gladly see demolished.
Yet it had ever been his father's way to take care of his
own goods first and foremost.

Adelar led his horse to the stables and looked around
for someone to feed and water the animal. The old man
tottered in. "Nobody here but me," he mumbled. "I'll
take care of your horse, my lord. Then you'd best see
the thane. He don't like bein' ignored."

Adelar fished a coin from his purse and gave it to the old man before he hurried across the pitted and puddled yard and entered the hall.

This was his father's hall, which had once been the most luxurious for miles? The walls were bare of tapestries of any kind. Nor were any of his weapons displayed there, either. One table still stood on the dais at the far end. The other pieces of furniture were either missing or, judging by the remnants in the hearth, gone for firewood. Scattered about lay several drinking vessels and casks for ale and wine, most obviously empty. The rushes were so soiled, Adelar could believe they had not been swept for a year. Two bony hounds rose from the mess, growling softly.

For a moment Adelar thought this building deserted, too, except for the dogs, until he saw a man and a woman sleeping on a pile of straw. He cautiously moved closer.

The woman lay on top of the man, snoring softly. Her skirt was pulled up nearly to her waist, revealing filthy, heavy legs. Her tangled hair covered the man's face and straggled over her tattered gown, which had once been very fine.

That had once been his mother's gown, Adelar realized with a jolt. With a sudden burst of suspicion, he kicked the man savagely. "Get up!" he snarled, determined to know just what had happened here and why this dirty wench was wearing his mother's gown.

His father sat up drunkenly. His face was flushed and choleric, his eyes red, and he had grown very stout.

"By Saint Peter, who the—" He stopped, his eyes widening as he encountered Adelar's hostile glare.

"Greetings, *Father*."

Kendric rose as quickly as he could, sending the wench rolling in the straw. The drunken woman simply mumbled something and continued to sleep while Kendric straightened his stained tunic and smiled. He had lost several teeth. "I knew you'd come back," he cried excitedly. He nudged the woman with his foot. "You see! I told you he'd come back."

The woman didn't respond, but Kendric did not seem to notice. He took hold of Adelar's arm and pulled him closer to the cold hearth. "I knew you'd come back, Adelar. After all, family's family, eh? Let's have some wine. Or ale."

"What has happened here?" Adelar asked, his voice as cold as the hearth.

Kendric paused in his search of all the nearby drinking vessels. "That scoundrel Cerdric."

Adelar crossed his arms. Cerdric was Kendric's oldest illegitimate son, the one Kendric had shouted would have all of Kendric's possessions on the day Adelar had gone away, vowing never to return. "What has he done?"

Kendric took a swig of the dregs in one of the drinking vessels and wiped his mouth with the back of his hand. "Can't you see? He's robbed me, that's what."

"How?"

"Took nearly everything, the ungrateful bastard. I treated him well, too. He had whatever he wanted. Money. Weapons. Women. And then one day, he tells me he wants the *burh*. Of course I refused. He got angry, the impudent pup! Angry! At me!''

Adelar believed his father. He had met Cerdric, who could give even Ranulf lessons in greed.

''So he left and took everything he could carry. Most of the warriors went with him. Leeches! Wait till his money's gone. They'll walk away from him fast enough then!

''I told him you'd come back. I told him I would see to it that he never got command of this *burh* or any other! And do you know what he said? He told me he didn't need me! After I gave him everything! He had nothing before.''

Adelar watched dispassionately as his father began to search for something to drink again. ''The ungrateful wretch! He'll see! One day the money will be gone and he'll come crawling back to me, eh, Adelar? He'll come back. They all do. Try to make their way in the world without me and fail. I know he'll come back, too, and beg my forgiveness.''

''Is that why you think I have come, to ask your forgiveness?''

Kendric wavered as he straightened. ''No...no! Of course not, my son.'' He smiled at Adelar, the hypocrite still. ''You've come back just as a dutiful son should, eh? To help me in my old age. I knew you would not forget your duty. We've both made mistakes, eh, my son, but that was in the past. We'll show that bastard. This place will be as great as it was before, now that you're back. Cerdric will see. We'll show him.''

Adelar did not doubt that his father was pleased to see him, but only because he believed Adelar could help him restore his *burh* to the status it had enjoyed before.

Kendric had no love in his heart for anyone save himself. He never had and he never would, and now he was left with nothing.

As Adelar looked at the wreck of the man who had sired him, all the hatred he had borne for so long withered and disappeared. Kendric could have been a great man once, and now he *was* nothing. Not even worthy of hate.

He had sinned because he loved Endredi and would have done anything to be with her. Even now, he was staying away from her because it was what she wanted, although it went against every dictate of his heart.

Adelar reached into his tunic and took out the pouch containing the last of his money. He handed it to his father. "Here. You will need this."

"Why? Aren't you staying? This *burh*—I will see that you command it."

"I have no wish to take it."

"Ah! I see what you're doing! You came to get what you could out of me before Bayard dies. Then you think to have *my* money and *his* command!" his father shouted, growing even redder.

"What is this you say?"

Kendric grinned malevolently. "Do you think you can fool me with that innocent look? Everyone knows Bayard is dying. Has been since the Yuletide. You won't get anything from him, either!"

Adelar stared at Kendric. Since he had left Bayard's *burh,* he had never asked about Bayard, thinking the less said about his past the better. Nor had anyone said anything to him. If there had been talk, he had not heard it.

He spun on his heel and marched toward the door.

"Adelar! Adelar, come back!" Kendric ran after his son. "I spoke without thinking! Adelar, come back! I need you! We have to show Cerdric!"

But by the time he got to the door, Adelar's horse was galloping out of the gate.

"What do you mean, do not let them enter?" Ranulf demanded, his eyes full of fear as he stared at Endredi, sitting beside the bed where Bayard lay. Helmi hovered nearby and made no secret of her disgust for Ranulf's cowardly demeanor.

Endredi turned to her husband's nephew wearily. Ever since the Yuletide, when Bayard had suddenly worsened and they could no longer keep his illness a secret, Ranulf had been trying to assume command. Because of the trouble with Godwin, he—and his wife—were being very subtle. Nonetheless, not a day passed that Endredi did not fear they would try to seize command of the *burh*. Or that Dagfinn would attack.

And not a day passed that she did not yearn for Adelar with her whole heart.

"What does Dagfinn want?" she asked, wondering if Ranulf was exaggerating. Although she did not credit Dagfinn with generous feelings, it could be that he had come not to attack, but to visit an ally.

Of course, he had probably already heard of Bayard's illness, so a visit might just as easily become an attack if Dagfinn felt the *burh* vulnerable enough.

"Don't you understand?" Ranulf cried anxiously. "There are at least two hundred Danes out there, waiting at the gate. Every one of them is armed and ready for battle. I cannot simply tell Dagfinn to go away!"

Bayard had spent all the time he could trying to teach Ranulf how to defend the *burh,* explaining strategy, trying to educate the man in the ways of leadership.

But obviously to no avail. Ranulf was a coward who could never command.

"I have no wish to speak to Dagfinn," Endredi replied, wiping Bayard's sweaty brow. She felt very ill herself this morning, with little strength to face Ranulf or Dagfinn or anyone else. The sun had been up only a short while, and she had had no sleep. A series of cramping pains had kept her from what little rest she got after nursing Bayard. It was nearly time for her child to be born, and she feared the pains were due to that. Nevertheless, sometimes—especially it if was a first child—the pains would simply cease.

"He won't believe I am being truthful with him," Ranulf whined.

"Explain to him that Bayard is occupied with other business, and I am ill and cannot see him."

"Could you not speak with him yourself?"

Helmi stepped forward, her lips a thin, determined line. "I will tell that troll Dagfinn to go away and leave us in peace, if you will not."

Bayard's weak voice interrupted them. The *burh-ware* heaved himself to a sitting position, his once powerful body wasted, his eyes bright with the fever that never left him now. "I am not dead *yet*, Ranulf. Tell Dagfinn that, too, and that I can guess why he has come. He would never dare to attack while I was healthy and had Adelar at my side. He comes now like a crow, thinking it an easy matter to defeat me. Tell him to go or we will send him from here with force. Then order my men to arm themselves. I will lead them myself, lest Dagfinn not believe my words, either. Now, Ranulf!"

His nephew nodded jerkily and withdrew. Bayard put his feet upon the ground.

"Bayard, you must not stand!" Endredi entreated.

He smiled at her, the expression a pain-racked version of his former joviality. "Helmi, fetch me my leather tunic and *byrnie*. Endredi, stay here."

When Helmi brought the waist-length coat of mail and the undercoat of padded leather, Bayard rose slowly. He looked at the maidservant. "Find Ylla and Gleda and bring them here. I will send an armed guard to protect this bower. Whatever happens, once you return with the women, you are not to leave my wife. Do you understand?"

"Yes, my lord." Helmi bowed and hurried away.

"Bayard!"

Bayard took Endredi's hands in his. "While I have strength left in my body, I will fight to protect you and the child. You and I both know why Dagfinn has come. The wonder of it is that it has taken him this long." He caressed her cheek. "If it comes to battle, and the battle is lost, you must flee from here. Go to Cynath."

"It will not come to battle," Endredi said fervently. "It must not."

Bayard dropped her hands and sighed. "I hope Dagfinn will leave. All the same, I wish Adelar was here."

"He may return," she whispered.

"If you were in his place, after all that has happened, would you?" Bayard asked.

"I . . . I do not know. But I am not Adelar. If he has heard of your illness . . ."

"Adelar is a proud man. I myself cannot be certain of what he will do. However, should Adelar not come back, Cynath will aid you. He will also see that the child inherits. Father Derrick has my will safely hidden in the chapel. Even a fire would not touch it, and the Danes would never find it."

His words were so like last instructions that Endredi's eyes filled with tears. "Bayard, do not speak like this!"

He struggled into his padded tunic. While she helped him to fasten it, he said, "If Adelar returns after I am dead and asks you to be his wife, will you agree?"

She paused at her task.

"I think you should, Endredi. He cares for you more than I have ever seen a man care for a woman. And I know, in your heart, you want him still."

"Bayard, please! This is not the time—"

"Yes, it is." He took her cheeks in his hands, the gesture so reminiscent of Adelar's that she could scarcely tolerate it. "Endredi," her husband said softly, "I care for Adelar very much, in my own way. And I could never give my heart to any woman. I would die happy knowing that you will be together. You and Adelar and the child." Bayard stepped away and slowly lifted the coat of mail. "I think he will come back. For your sake, if nothing else, Endredi."

"I hope so, for all our sakes. He did not abandon me before, although it seemed he had. Surely he will not abandon us when we have the greatest need for him."

Bayard, dressed for battle, picked up his sword. "Remember, this should go to Cynath, with my respect and thanks." His hand clutched it tightly, but his fingers trembled.

"You do not intend to go into battle yourself, do you? You are too weak."

"I am the *burhware*, Endredi. It is my duty." He gave her the ghost of his smile. "However, let us hope that Dagfinn will leave us in peace if he believes he must fight *me* for what he wants. Still, if a battle is what must be, we both know there are worse ways to die." He placed his hand gently on her swollen stomach. "Take care of the babe, Endredi."

She nodded, proud to be his wife. "I will protect this child with my life."

Ranulf came rushing into the bower, his eyes wide with fright. "They won't listen! They said I am lying. They asked if Bayard was already dead. They have moved back a little, but I believe they mean to fight!"

"Then you had better arm yourself, Ranulf," Bayard remarked calmly, "for Dagfinn will not get my *burh* as long as I draw breath."

His nephew went pale. "You are too sick to fight!" he cried. "You cannot lead us to battle!"

"Do you wish to take command?" Bayard asked.

"No! No, my lord! It . . . it is not my place," Ranulf sputtered.

"I thought that was what you would say." Bayard turned to Endredi. "Farewell, Endredi."

She lifted his thin hand and pressed it to her cheek. "Farewell, Bayard," she whispered.

Ranulf turned and ran out ahead of Bayard.

Suddenly, Endredi felt a sharp cramp, and as she doubled over, her water broke.

Bayard stared at her helplessly. "Endredi!"

She made her way to the table, another pain gripping her womb. "It is the child, Bayard. I am going to have the baby. I thought . . . hoped the pains were false."

"What should I do?"

"Helmi and the others will be here soon. I have been teaching Ylla." She leaned with her hands on the table and closed her eyes. "It may be some time yet. Go. All will be well."

Bayard looked at her pale, pain-racked face. "While you fight your battle, Endredi, I will fight mine. And I promise you, I will win."

Adelar dismounted in the cover of the woods. From his position on the ridge, he could see the line of Danes drawn up on the open space before Bayard's *burh*. The men stood restlessly in the bright sunlight, their weapons in their hands, helmets glinting on their heads.

The gate of the *burh* opened and the first group of Saxon warriors ran out holding their spears and round shields. They began to form the shield wall, a defensive line in front of the commander. Behind them came the churls bearing spears and swords, shields and clubs. On the walls, archers took their places.

The Danes had come to do battle, and Bayard's men were answering their challenge. There could be no doubt of it.

Swiftly Adelar tore his *byrnie* from his pack and drew it on. In the next instant he had his broadsword in one hand, his *scramasax* in the other, his shield over his back and was hurrying down the dew-slippery slope. The Danes were shouting insults to the Saxons as they took position, and the Saxons were responding in kind, so there was no need for Adelar to keep silent.

He crashed to a halt in some holly bushes near the bottom of the ridge as a helmeted figure came slowly through the gate of Oakenbrook to take a position in the center of the men.

Bayard. It had to be Bayard, surrounded by his warriors, ready to signal them to battle. And behind him came Father Derrick, armed for battle and calling upon God to bless the Saxons and curse the Danes to the everlasting flames of hell.

How slowly Bayard moved, as if in pain.

Where was a second-in-command? Or even Ranulf?

How soon could he go to the aid of the Saxons? He was behind the Danes' line. Could he get around it and join Bayard's men?

Suddenly, with a blood-curdling cry, Bayard lifted his arm and gave the signal to attack. At once, a hail of arrows fell upon the Danes as they rushed forward.

Before he could move, Adelar heard a sound nearby, of hastily spoken words and running feet. He turned and spotted two people hurrying through the woods.

Ranulf and Ordella. Ranulf carried not arms and mail, but a chest that weighed heavily, to judge by how he carried it. Full of coins or other booty, surely. Ordella, too, was similarly burdened.

At once Adelar moved to intercept them. "Ranulf!" he called out. "The battlefield is behind you, *nithing*."

They both halted, staring at him.

"What are you doing here?" Ordella demanded with bravado, although her gaze shifted nervously as the sounds of battle grew louder. "I know what you are, Adelar, despite my words to Bayard to the contrary. If you are wise, you will leave us to go our own way."

"Yes," Ranulf answered nervously. "I . . . I am going to Cynath. I am a messenger, sent to warn the overlord—"

"You are a coward, Ranulf."

"Do not try to stop us!" Ordella warned as he came closer. She put down the heavy cask she carried. "What have you got in that chest?" Adelar demanded, halting in front of Ranulf. Around them they could hear the dull thud of errant arrows striking the trees and the ground.

"I must be on my way to tell Cynath about the Danes," Ranulf insisted.

And then Adelar felt a sharp, stabbing pain in his side. He twisted as Ordella jumped away, grabbing the hilt of the small dagger she had thrust into him. He yanked it out, realizing that although the wound was more than a scratch, his *byrnie* had saved him from a mortal injury.

He lifted his sword, ready to strike, when Ordella's eyes suddenly widened. She pitched forward, an arrow in her back.

Ranulf dropped the chest he carried and darted away. But before he got far, Adelar dropped his sword and threw his *scramasax* toward the fleeing man. Ranulf stopped, his arms thrown wide, then he fell to the earth like a dead bird.

Panting from the pain and the effort, Adelar picked up his broadsword and staggered toward Ordella. Yes, she was dead, her expression frozen into a wide-eyed grimace.

He knelt and closed her eyes. Then he ripped off a piece of her gown and stuffed it beneath his *byrnie* to staunch his wound.

As quickly as he could he went to the battlefield, pausing for a moment to search out Bayard.

There, in the center, stood his cousin. With a fierce battle cry, Adelar ran at the Danes, slashing his way toward Bayard.

The Danes, startled and confused by what they thought an attack from the rear, moved aside—until they realized it was only one lone Saxon. But by then, Adelar was near to Bayard.

"Adelar!" the *burhware* cried. "Do you come to fight for me, or against me?"

"I come to protect Endredi," he said, taking his position to guard his cousin's back.

"I am glad of it," Bayard shouted above the din.

Then, with another battle cry, Adelar made toward Dagfinn.

Endredi pressed her lips together to keep from screaming as the pain assailed her again. Perspiration blinded her as she strained to bring her child into the world.

Something was wrong. She had no idea what, couldn't think beyond the pain that seemed to be tearing her apart.

"Get out!" she heard Helmi say through her agony. "We don't want you here!"

Baldric's growling voice answered the servant. "I helped more bitches whelp than you've hairs on your head, woman. Stand aside!"

Endredi struggled to sit up. "Baldric?"

"Yes," he replied bluntly. He ran his hand expertly over her stomach. "On your feet, my lady."

She nodded. The time must be near. "Something is...wrong," she moaned, twisting to set her feet on the ground.

"Not a bit," Bayard replied. "Always hard the first time."

He was but a dog keeper, yet his words made her relieved as she stood, holding on to the bed for support. She groaned softly when another pain came.

"My lady!" Ylla interrupted, her words piercing the mist of agony.

"What?" Endredi panted as the pain lessened. She looked up at the serving maid standing nearby. She had sent Ylla to the walls to find out what she could of the battle.

"The Danes are falling back."

Endredi nodded, then ground her teeth when the pain came again.

"My lady!"

"Save your chatter for afterward," Helmi said sharply.

"Let her speak!" Endredi said.

"Adelar has come, but..."

Endredi opened her eyes, then, with no warning and no conscious thought, burst into tears.

"But?" Baldric grunted.

"I do not know for whom he fights," Ylla said. "He came from the line of the Danes."

"He will not fight against Bayard," Endredi said, choking back her sobs, believing it to the very core of her soul. No matter what harsh words had been exchanged, no matter what his father had been, Adelar had not abandoned her. He had come back when he was needed most, as she had said he would.

Then she cried out, the pain overpowering.

"Move away, girl!" Baldric cried impatiently to Ylla. "This baby is in a hurry to be born. Now is the time to push, my lady."

The battle lasted a very long time. All Adelar was aware of after he had killed Dagfinn was the need to protect himself and strike at whatever Danes he could, driving them farther and father away from the *burh*. He did not think of the men he had killed as men like himself. They were animals, trying to attack the people he cared about.

So he took no notice of the dead, or the wounded, or the bodies he trod upon, or the limbs he bloodied. He paid no heed to his own exhaustion, or the wound in his side. At times, he thought he heard Father Derrick shouting admonitions, or the groans of wounded men, but they were mere noises.

Until the moment he realized there was no one left for him to fight. The few Danes he could see were running off through the trees, leaving behind the dead and the near dead.

Adelar bent over and put his hands on his knees, his bloodied sword still in his hand. He heard someone panting heavily, and after a short time came to know that it was himself. Then slowly, he lifted his head and looked around.

Father Derrick was not far off, kneeling beside someone. Adelar strained to see who. Bayard. Bayard, on the ground.

Adelar forgot his pain and his fatigue to rush to his cousin. A broken spear protruded from Bayard's side, and the ground around him was red with blood.

Father Derrick finished his blessing, then moved away when Bayard weakly waved his hand. "I would be alone with Adelar," he whispered, his chest rising and falling rapidly as he struggled to breathe. "So, you have come back to me," he said, valiantly trying to smile.

"I would have come sooner, had I heard."

"Truly, Cousin?"

"Truly. Forgive my words to you before, Bayard. I was angry and hurt and—"

"It is you who must forgive me, Cousin. You and Endredi."

"I forgive you, Bayard, for giving me what I most desired."

Ylla came running toward them, staring about her with wide-eyed fright, then down at Bayard with terror and pity.

"What is it?" Adelar asked.

Ylla did not look at him, but knelt beside Bayard, too. "My lord, you have a son. A fine, healthy son!"

Adelar rose to his feet. "Endredi?" he demanded. "How is Endredi?"

"She is well, too."

Bayard smiled fully then, and looked at Adelar with tears in his eyes. "Do you hear? A son!"

Adelar was beside him instantly. "Bayard, do not speak! Save your strength."

"I am ready to die," Bayard whispered. "Do not pity me, Adelar. I am getting a better death than I had hoped. Better, perhaps, than I deserve."

"Take him to his bower," Adelar ordered as a group of churls arrived carrying a bier. "He must see the child."

Chapter Sixteen

Endredi lifted herself on her elbows to see who entered the bower. In a cradle beside the bed her child, her son, slept peacefully, swaddled tightly, his downy head just barely visible.

It was Adelar, his *byrnie* damp with blood and mud, his face streaked with dirt and sweat. He had never looked more wonderful to her. Despite her exhaustion and her fears about the battle, overwhelming joy filled her. "Adelar," she cried softly as he hurried to her side. He took her hand and pressed a kiss to her palm.

She blinked away tears of happiness and peered past him. "Bayard...?"

"Is wounded," Adelar said quietly, anguish in his dark eyes. "Mortally, I fear."

Before she could fully take in his words, a group of men carrying a bier entered. She struggled to her feet, ignoring Helmi's protests.

Father Derrick came, too, muttering prayers as Endredi made her way to Bayard, seeing at once the gray face, the drawn lips, the mark of death upon his brow.

Her husband's eyes opened and looked about searchingly. "The baby?"

Endredi quickly picked up her slumbering child and, with a glance at Adelar, laid him in Bayard's arms. "This child is to have all my worldly goods," Bayard whispered hoarsely. "And this land, when he is of an age. It is all in my will."

"Yes, my lord," Father Derrick said quietly. "I shall see that it is as God—and you—have intended."

"Endredi?" Bayard held out the babe and she took him, cradling him tenderly as she knelt beside the bier. He turned to look at her and she knew he had but moments left. "Thank you, Endredi, for this child. Adelar?"

His cousin knelt on the other side.

"Give me your hand, Adelar." He did, and Bayard lifted it across his chest. "You, too, Endredi." He joined their hands beneath his own weak one. "This is how it should be. How it should always have been," he whispered. "Forgive me."

And then he died.

Some days later, Cynath sat in Bayard's hall and sighed deeply. "It is a pity Bayard died so young," Cynath said softly. "A measure of peace in our land at last, since that fool Aethelwold is dead, although I was ready to curse the Kentish men for hanging back."

"Yes. If they had not, Aethelwold might yet be alive," Adelar replied.

By now all knew that the attack on Oakenbrook had been but the first of a series of attacks on the borderlands by the Danes, the men of Essex and Aethelwold. While Adelar held Oakenbrook, Edward had retaliated with an invasion deep into that part of Mercia taken by the Danes. He had ordered a retreat, but the Kentish men, for reasons of their own, had lingered, only to be met by Aethelwold and the Danish army. After a fierce battle, Aethelwold was dead, as well as the Danish king, Eohric.

"Edward will not be content with this, though," Cynath ruminated. "His father would have been, but Edward is made of different stuff. I believe he will not rest content until the Saxons have control of the Danelaw once more."

"He will never get rid of the Danes," Adelar observed. "They are too settled now."

"Then let them stay, as long as they obey the English king and English law."

"I think they might, if we do not interfere with trade."

"You are so sure they are more interested in trade than war, Adelar."

"I lived among the Vikings, my lord. Most of them want peace as much as any man."

"Well, I shall have to rely on your superior knowledge, as Bayard did, eh?"

They sat in companionable silence. Adelar hoped there would finally indeed be peace. He was tired of war and talk of war. He wanted only to seek contentment, provided that could be in Endredi's arms.

Since Bayard's death, she had wisely treated him with the proper deference due to a *burhware*. There seemed no question in anyone's mind that Adelar was the commander in truth, if not in name. Nonetheless, he often saw in her eyes that she cared for him still. He was only waiting for the appropriate time to declare his undying passion for her.

Cynath picked up a long piece of wood and stirred the fire so that the flames leaped into the darkness. "Your father is dead, Adelar."

"When?"

"A fortnight ago."

"How?"

"Cerdric returned, and as Kendric upbraided the fellow, he had a sudden fit and fell down dead."

Adelar's eyes welled with sudden tears he blinked away, surprised that he should feel anything at all at this news.

And yet, when Cynath spoke, he remembered his father in better days, teaching him to ride and to hunt. Those had been good times. He must see to it that *his* son had such happy memories, and no taint of shame to cloud his days.

"Cerdric is laying claim to his *burh*. It *is* in your father's will."

When Adelar did not respond, Cynath eyed him shrewdly. "Will you return there? You are his son, in law."

"No. I owe my loyalty to Bayard's widow. He was better to me than my father was."

"Despite the will, the king may not grant his *burh* to Cerdric. That lout is nothing but a drunkard and a fool. The land may pass into other hands."

"So be it, then, my lord."

"I must ask you this, Adelar. Do you believe the stories about your father?"

Adelar faced Cynath. "They were all true, Cynath. He was a traitor."

"You are not your father, Adelar," Cynath said quietly. "Bayard believed you to be worthy, and I do, too. I was simply curious."

Cynath gave Adelar a piercing look. "I have heard other rumors. Of you and Bayard's wife."

"They are only rumors," Adelar said, prepared to lie for Bayard's sake. Indeed, he would never tell the truth of things as long as he lived, to preserve Bayard's reputation and that of his son.

"Whatever the truth is," Cynath said slowly, "Bayard deserves nothing but honor, alive or dead."

"Yes, my lord." Adelar stared into the flames. He would miss his cousin's easy banter, his jokes, his wisdom.

"At least my decision is an easy one."

"What decision is that, my lord?"

"I know who I will make *burhware* in Bayard's place."

"Oh?"

Cynath chuckled. "Do not play the coy maiden with me, Adelar. You are the obvious choice. Bayard favored you, and that fool Ranulf is dead. A shameful way to die, running from battle. But we will not speak of him. What say you, Adelar? Will you be *burhware* of Oakenbrook?"

Adelar opened his mouth, intending to say that he had no interest in command, as he had said to Bayard so many times. He was even about to suggest that Dunstan, who had fought valiantly, be made *burh-ware*.

But he did not, because suddenly he knew that he wanted the command. He was ready, as he had never been before, to take the responsibility. "Thank you, my lord," he said. "I would be honored."

"I think the king will not hesitate to approve my choice, especially if you marry Bayard's widow."

"My lord?"

"She is a good woman. Not as attractive as some, I grant you, but I believe she is worthy to be the wife of a *burhware,* especially if, as you say, the Danes are here to stay. Also, I think you would do well by Bayard's child, and that is important to me. I cared a great deal for your cousin."

"I know, my lord. I give you my word that I will treat him as my own son."

"Good. Has Endredi named the child?"

"She has chosen to call him Bayard, after his father."

"Let us hope he is worthy of his name."

"With such a mother, he will be."

"You sound as if you admire her."

"I do."

"Then I see no reason to delay the marriage. Who knows how long this peace will last?"

Adelar stared at Cynath, who grinned broadly. "Would you rather wait?"

"Not at all, my lord," the Saxon answered truthfully. "Not at all. But perhaps Father Derrick and the others will think we act with unseemly haste."

"Father Derrick and the other thanes will not dare to speak against my decision," Cynath said confidently. He gave Adelar another of his searching gazes. "Do you not want the woman?"

"I do, my lord."

"Then there is no more to be said. I will tell her of my decision in the morning."

A man's hand crept slowly up Endredi's bare back while she lay sleeping in bed. She awakened at once, and a gasp escaped her lips as she twisted to strike the intruder beside her.

The man grasped her hand. Then Adelar's mouth covered hers in a warm, sensual kiss. With a low moan, she wrapped her arms about him and drew him toward her. "You should not be here," she murmured, delighted that he was. She had missed him so much and yearned to have him with her again. Nonetheless, he should not be in her bed.

"I am not leaving you." His naked body covered hers. "Not ever again. Endredi, will you be my wife?"

"Adelar, we have made so many mistakes—"

He stopped her by placing his finger against her lips. "The past is finished," he said softly. "Our lives begin now. Here. The two of us."

She felt the tension in his body, and realized he was not completely sure of her feelings. "You are all I have ever wanted, Adelar," she whispered. She reached up and pulled him to her for a long, deep kiss.

Although they were not wed in law, they both knew it was but a small particular. Free at last to love each other, they began a slow, delightful dance of reacquaintance.

"Is it too soon after the birth?" Adelar muttered as his hands caressed her tenderly.

"I do not believe so," Endredi replied, stroking his muscular shoulders. "I will tell you if it is."

It was not.

Later, as they lay together in each other's arms, satisfied and complete, the whimpers of the baby reached Endredi's ears. "He is hungry," she said apologetically, getting up and putting on her robe.

"Will you not spoil him if you go each time he makes a sound?" Adelar asked lazily, taking her hand as if to hold her there.

"And will I not spoil you if I listen to your advice? How many children have you nursed, my lord?"

He smiled broadly. "None."

"That is obvious, my lord," Helmi said, striking a light. "Or you would know that if the baby cries, there is no point not to feed him."

Endredi halted in her tracks. "Helmi! Where did you come from?"

The serving woman lifted the infant from his cradle and brought him toward her. "From my place outside the door. It is well Adelar was gone through the winter or my joints would be stiff yet. Order me to sleep in the hall, indeed, with all those Saxon barbarians? I should think not! Besides, I know where my duty is. I made a snug place for myself in the alley between the hall and the bower. I suppose you two were too enamored of each other to notice? Warm enough in the spring and autumn, but I might have perished of the cold in the winter. Well, it does not matter, since all this sneaking about must end."

The baby started to wail in earnest. Endredi took her son, sat on a stool and began to feed him. With fearful eyes she looked at Adelar, who still sat in the bed.

Helmi put her hands on her thin hips and frowned. "Did you think I did not know? You have no secrets from me, either one of you. Which is as it should be. And have I once given you cause to doubt me?"

"What secrets?" Adelar demanded.

Helmi gave him a sardonic look. "This will not be the first time you come to this bed, my lord."

"What do you mean?" Endredi asked sternly, glancing uneasily at Adelar.

"Am I a dolt? A fool? As blind as a bat? No. Of course I knew all along that Adelar was your lover. And I also know that Cynath wants you two to marry. A wise man, for a Saxon. Ylla knew it, too. Just as she knew who she was really spending her nights with."

Endredi and Adelar were too surprised to answer.

"Did you think we are both stupid?"

"No...no, that is, you never said...when Godwin accused us and Bayard *asked* you—" Endredi stuttered.

"Is that why Ylla has said nothing to me at all since I returned?" Adelar asked. "I wondered."

"But of course you said nothing to her, either. Do not worry, my lord. She is not pining for you. She shed many tears for Bayard's sake, though."

"Why did you both answer as you did when Ranulf and Godwin spoke of adultery?" Endredi asked.

"Do you think I would ever agree with anything Ranulf said?" Helmi countered. "If he said the sky was blue, I would have said it was black. And you know I have no wish to go back to any village Bera inhabits. As for Ylla, did you expect her to contradict Bayard, or Adelar, or even Ranulf, a thane?"

"What are you going to do?"

"Do? Help you prepare for bed."

"That will not be necessary," Endredi said, relieved and certain Helmi would not betray their secret. "You may leave."

"'Helmi, leave us. Helmi, you may go,'" the old woman muttered sarcastically. "Everybody's always sending me away as if I cannot be trusted. *You* had better leave, my lord, before your absence is noted."

"I know you will say nothing of this to anyone," Adelar remarked when he got out of the bed and put on his breeches and tunic.

"Of course not. I liked Bayard, but he did not understand the Danes. You do. I think you two were destined for each other by the gods."

"And Ylla?"

Helmi grinned broadly. "Have you seen Baldric lately?"

"Yes," Endredi said, trying to remember anything unusual about Baldric, but she really had not paid much attention.

"Noticed anything?"

"He's cleaner," Adelar said at once.

"Aye. He wants Ylla, and she's making him dance to her tune, I can tell you."

"Ylla and Baldric?" Adelar said.

"What's wrong with that? And you'd best watch out for Merilda's temper these days. Gleda and Duff are getting married, but who knows when because he's getting her wares for free anyway—"

Endredi cast a baleful look at Adelar. She had the distinct impression that Helmi meant to stay and gossip all night.

Adelar winked and cleared his throat. "Helmi, go to the hall and do not come back until the morning."

The woman halted in mid-sentence and stared. "After all I said?"

"Yes. As the *burhware,* I command it."

Helmi sniffed indignantly. "This is my lady's bower for the present and—"

"Helmi, leave us," Endredi ordered.

"But—"

"Leave us, please."

Her face a picture of displeasure, Helmi finally obeyed.

Endredi smiled warmly at Adelar. "You give orders well, for a man who did not want such responsibilities."

Adelar came to her and looked down at the woman he loved and the child she held. "Should I give you some orders?"

"About what?"

He glanced slyly at the bed.

"Perhaps later. For the present our son requires my attention."

"Very well. He is a fine boy, is he not?"

"Perfect." She looked at him with sadness in her eyes. "You can never claim him for your own."

"We will have other children, Endredi. And in my heart, I will always know he is my true son."

Endredi put the nearly slumbering infant to her shoulder and patted his back before she returned him to his cradle. He settled down at once to sleep.

She sighed softly and stroked his small head. "You must go now, Adelar."

"One last time I will creep away like a thief," he said, coming to her and taking her in his arms. "Cynath would have us wed at once. I believe I shall tell him tomorrow is a good day."

"Cynath proposed our marriage?"

Adelar smiled mischievously. "Yes, although he admits it might be a hardship for me. I did not tell him otherwise."

She eyed him warily. "Do you marry me to please Cynath?"

"What do you think, Endredi?"

The Saxon pulled her close and kissed her, and there was no need for her to wonder anymore.

* * * * *

Harlequin® Historical

What do A.E. Maxwell, Miranda Jarrett, Merline Lovelace and Cassandra Austin have in common?

They are all part of Harlequin Historical's efforts to bring you longer books by some of your favorite authors. Pick up one of these upcoming titles today and see what a difference an historical from Harlequin can make!

REDWOOD EMPIRE—A.E. Maxwell Don't miss the reissue of this exciting saga from award-winning authors Ann and Evan Maxwell, coming in May 1995.

SPARHAWK'S LADY—Miranda Jarrett From this popular author comes another sweeping Sparhawk adventure full of passion and emotion in June 1995.

HIS LADY'S RANSOM—Merline Lovelace A gripping Medieval tale from the talented author of the Destiny's Women series that is sure to delight, coming in July 1995.

TRUSTING SARAH—Cassandra Austin And in August 1995, the long-awaited new Western by the author whose *Wait for the Sunrise* touched readers' hearts.

Watch for them this spring and summer wherever Harlequin Historicals are sold.

ANNOUNCING THE

FLYAWAY VACATION SWEEPSTAKES!

This month's destination:

Beautiful SAN FRANCISCO!

This month, as a special surprise, we're offering an exciting FREE VACATION!

Think how much fun it would be to visit San Francisco "on us"! You could ride cable cars, visit Chinatown, see the Golden Gate Bridge and dine in some of the finest restaurants in America!

The facing page contains two Entry Coupons (as does every book you received this shipment). Complete and return *all* the entry coupons; **the more times you enter, the better your chances of winning!**

Then keep your fingers crossed, because you'll find out by June 15, 1995 if you're the winner! If you are, here's what you'll get:

- Round-trip airfare for two to beautiful San Francisco!
- 4 days/3 nights at a first-class hotel!
- $500.00 pocket money for meals and sightseeing!

Remember: The more times you enter, the better your chances of winning!*

*NO PURCHASE OR OBLIGATION TO CONTINUE BEING A SUBSCRIBER NECESSARY TO ENTER. SEE REVERSE SIDE OR ANY ENTRY COUPON FOR ALTERNATIVE MEANS OF ENTRY.

VSF KAL

FLYAWAY VACATION
SWEEPSTAKES

OFFICIAL ENTRY COUPON

This entry must be received by: MAY 30, 1995
This month's winner will be notified by: JUNE 15, 1995
Trip must be taken between: JULY 30, 1995-JULY 30, 1996

YES, I want to win the San Francisco vacation for two. I understand the prize includes round-trip airfare, first-class hotel and $500.00 spending money. Please let me know if I'm the winner!

Name_____

Address _____ Apt. _____

City   State/Prov.   Zip/Postal Code

Account #_____

Return entry with invoice in reply envelope.

© 1995 HARLEQUIN ENTERPRISES LTD.   CSF KAL

OFFICIAL RULES
FLYAWAY VACATION SWEEPSTAKES 3449
NO PURCHASE OR OBLIGATION NECESSARY

Three Harlequin Reader Service 1995 shipments will contain respectively, coupons for entry into three different prize drawings, one for a trip for two to San Francisco, another for a trip for two to Las Vegas and the third for a trip for two to Orlando, Florida. To enter any drawing using an Entry Coupon, simply complete and mail according to directions.

There is no obligation to continue using the Reader Service to enter and be eligible for any prize drawing. You may also enter any drawing by hand printing the words "Flyaway Vacation," your name and address on a 3"x5" card and the destination of the prize you wish that entry to be considered for (i.e., San Francisco trip, Las Vegas trip or Orlando trip). Send your 3"x5" entries via first-class mail (limit: one entry per envelope) to: Flyaway Vacation Sweepstakes 3449, c/o Prize Destination you wish that entry to be considered for, P.O. Box 1315, Buffalo, NY 14269-1315, USA or P.O. Box 610, Fort Erie, Ontario L2A 5X3, Canada.

To be eligible for the San Francisco trip, entries must be received by 5/30/95; for the Las Vegas trip, 7/30/95; and for the Orlando trip, 9/30/95.

Winners will be determined in random drawings conducted under the supervision of D.L. Blair, Inc., an independent judging organization whose decisions are final, from among all eligible entries received for that drawing. San Francisco trip prize includes round-trip airfare for two, 4-day/3-night weekend accommodations at a first-class hotel, and $500 in cash (trip must be taken between 7/30/95—7/30/96, approximate prize value—$3,500); Las Vegas trip includes round-trip airfare for two, 4-day/3-night weekend accommodations at a first-class hotel, and $500 in cash (trip must be taken between 9/30/95—9/30/96, approximate prize value—$3,500); Orlando trip includes round-trip airfare for two, 4-day/3-night weekend accommodations at a first-class hotel, and $500 in cash (trip must be taken between 11/30/95—11/30/96, approximate prize value—$3,500). All travelers must sign and return a Release of Liability prior to travel. Hotel accommodations and flights are subject to accommodation and schedule availability. Sweepstakes open to residents of the U.S. (except Puerto Rico) and Canada, 18 years of age or older. Employees and immediate family members of Harlequin Enterprises, Ltd., D.L. Blair, Inc., their affiliates, subsidiaries and all other agencies, entities and persons connected with the use, marketing or conduct of this sweepstakes are not eligible. Odds of winning a prize are dependent upon the number of eligible entries received for that drawing. Prize drawing and winner notification for each drawing will occur no later than 15 days after deadline for entry eligibility for that drawing. Limit: one prize to an individual, family or organization. All applicable laws and regulations apply. Sweepstakes offer void wherever prohibited by law. Any litigation within the province of Quebec respecting the conduct and awarding of the prizes in this sweepstakes must be submitted to the Regies des loteries et Courses du Quebec. In order to win a prize, residents of Canada will be required to correctly answer a time-limited arithmetical skill-testing question. Value of prizes are in U.S. currency.

Winners will be obligated to sign and return an Affidavit of Eligibility within 30 days of notification. In the event of noncompliance within this time period, prize may not be awarded. If any prize or prize notification is returned as undeliverable, that prize will not be awarded. By acceptance of a prize, winner consents to use of his/her name, photograph or other likeness for purposes of advertising, trade and promotion on behalf of Harlequin Enterprises, Ltd., without further compensation, unless prohibited by law.

For the names of prizewinners (available after 12/31/95), send a self-addressed, stamped envelope to: Flyaway Vacation Sweepstakes 3449 Winners, P.O. Box 4200, Blair, NE 68009.

RVC KAL